PANDORA

NEW TALES
OF THE VAMPIRES

Anne Rice

ARROW

Published in the United Kingdom in 1999 by
Arrow Books

9 10

Copyright © Anne O'Brien Rice, 1998

The right of Anne Rice to be identified as the author of this
work has been asserted by her in accordance with the
Copyright, Designs and Patents Act, 1988

First published in the United Kingdom in 1998 by Chatto & Windus

Arrow Books Limited
Random House UK Ltd
20 Vauxhall Bridge Road, London, SW1V 2SA

Random House Australia (Pty) Limited
20 Alfred Street, Milsons Point, Sydney,
New South Wales 2061, Australia

Random House New Zealand Limited
18 Poland Road, Glenfield, Auckland 10, New Zealand

Random House South Africa (Pty) Limited
Endulini, 5a Jubilee Road, Parktown, 2193, South Africa

Random House UK Limited Reg. No. 954009

A CIP catalogue record for this book is available
from the British Library

Papers used by Random House UK Limited are natural,
recyclable products made from wood grown in sustainable
forests. The manufacturing processes conform to the
environmental regulations of the country of origin

Typeset by SX Composing DTP, Rayleigh, Essex
Printed and bound in Great Britain by
Cox & Wyman Ltd, Reading, Berkshire.

ISBN 0 09 927108 7

DEDICATED

TO

STAN, CHRISTOPHER AND MICHELE RICE

TO

SUZANNE SCOTT QUIROZ

AND

VICTORIA WILSON

TO THE MEMORY OF

JOHN PRESTON

TO

THE IRISH OF NEW ORLEANS

WHO, IN THE 1850S,

BUILT ON CONSTANCE STREET

THE GREAT CHURCH OF ST. ALPHONSUS,

WHILE PASSING ON TO US

THROUGH FAITH, ARCHITECTURE AND ART

A SPLENDID MONUMENT

TO

'THE GLORY THAT WAS GREECE

AND

THE GRANDEUR THAT WAS ROME'

Of Mrs. Moore and the echo
in the Marabar Caves:
. . . but the echo began in some indescrib-
able way to undermine her hold on life.
Coming at a moment when she chanced to
be fatigued, it had managed to murmur
'Pathos, piety courage – they exist, but
are identical, and so is filth. Everything
exists, nothing has value.'

E. M. FORSTER
A Passage to India

Thou believest that there is
one God; thou doest well: the devils
also believe, and tremble.

The General Epistle of James
2:19

How ridiculous and what a stranger he is
who is surprised at anything which happens in life.

MARCUS AURELIUS
Meditations

Another part of our same belief is that many creatures will be damned; for example the angels who fell from heaven through pride, and are now fiends; and those men on earth who die apart from the Faith of Holy Church, namely, the heathen; and those, too, who are christened but live unchristian lives, and so die out of love – all these shall be condemned to hell everlastingly as Holy Church teaches me to believe. This being so I thought it quite impossible that everything should turn out well, as our Lord was now showing me. But I had no answer to this revelation save this: 'What is impossible to you is not impossible to me. I shall honour my word in every respect, and I will make everything turn out for the best.' Thus was I taught by God's grace. . . .

JULIAN OF NORWICH
Revelations of Divine Love

PANDORA

1

Not twenty minutes has passed since you left me here in the café, since I said No to your request, that I would never write out for you the story of my mortal life, how I became a vampire – how I came upon Marius only years after he had lost his human life.

Now here I am with your notebook open, using one of the sharp pointed eternal ink pens you left me, delighted at the sensuous press of the black ink into the expensive and flawless white paper.

Naturally, David, you would leave me something elegant, an inviting page. This notebook bound in dark varnished leather, is it not, tooled with a design of rich roses, thornless, yet leafy, a design that means only Design in the final analysis but bespeaks an authority. What is written beneath this heavy and handsome book cover will count, sayeth this cover.

The thick pages are ruled in light blue – you are practical, so thoughtful, and you probably know I almost never put pen to paper to write anything at all.

Even the sound of the pen has its allure, the sharp scratch rather like the finest quills in ancient Rome when I would put them to parchment to write my letters to my Father, when I would write in a diary my own laments . . . ah, that sound. The only thing missing here is the smell of ink, but we have the fine plastic pen which will not run out for volumes, making as fine and deep a black mark as I choose to make.

I am thinking about your request in writing. You see you will get something from me. I find myself yielding to it, almost as one of our human victims yields to us, discovering perhaps as the rain continues to fall outside, as the café continues with its noisy chatter, to think that this might not be the agony I presumed – reaching back over the two thousand years – but almost a pleasure, like the act of drinking blood itself.

I reach now for a victim who is not easy for me to overcome: my own past. Perhaps this victim will flee from me with a speed that equals my own. Whatever, I seek now a victim that I have never faced. And there is the thrill of the hunt in it, what the modern world calls investigation.

Why else would I see those times so vividly now? You had no magic potion to give me to loosen my thoughts. There is but one potion for us and it is blood.

You said at one point as we walked towards the café, 'You will remember everything.'

You, who are so young amongst us yet were so old as a mortal, and such a scholar as a mortal. Perhaps it is natural that you so boldly attempt to collect our stories.

But why seek to explain here such curiosity as yours, such bravery in face of blood-drenched truth?

How could you have kindled in me this longing to go back, two thousand years, almost exactly – to tell of my mortal days on Earth in Rome, and how I joined Marius, and what little chance he had against Fate.

How could origins so deeply buried and so long denied suddenly beckon to me. A door snaps open. A light shines. Come in.

I sit back now in the café.

I write, but I pause and look around me at the people of this Paris café. I see the drab unisex fabrics of this age, the fresh American girl in her olive green military clothes, all of her possessions slung over her shoulder in a back-pack; I see the old Frenchman who has come here for decades merely to look at the bare legs and arms of the young, to feed on the gestures as if he were a vampire, to wait for some exotic jewel of a moment when a woman sits back laughing, cigarette in hand, and the cloth of her synthetic blouse becomes tight over her breasts and there the nipples are visible.

Ah, old man. He is gray-haired and wears an expensive coat. He is no menace to anyone. He lives entirely in vision. Tonight he will go back to a modest but elegant apartment which he has maintained since the last Great World War, and he will watch films of the young beauty Brigitte Bardot. He lives in his eyes. He has not touched a woman in ten years.

I don't drift, David. I drop anchor here. For I will not have my story pour forth as from a drunken oracle.

I see these mortals in a more attentive light. They are so fresh, so exotic and yet so luscious to me, these mortals; they look like tropical birds must have looked when I was a child; so full of fluttering, rebellious life, I wanted to clutch them to have it, to make their wings flap in my hands, to capture flight and own it and partake of it. Ah, that terrible moment in childhood when one accidentally crushes the life from a bright-red bird.

Yet they are sinister in their darker vestments, some of these mortals: the inevitable cocaine dealer – and they are everywhere, our finest prey – who waits for his contact in the far corner, his long leather coat styled by a noted Italian designer, his hair shaved close on the side and left bushy on the top to make him look distinctive, which it does, though there is no need when one considers his huge black eyes, and the hardness of what nature intended to be a generous mouth. He makes those quick impatient gestures with his cigarette lighter on the small marble table, the mark of the addicted; he twists, he turns, he cannot be comfortable. He doesn't know that he will never be comfortable in life again. He wants to leave to snort the cocaine for which he burns and yet he must wait for the contact. His shoes are too shiny and his long thin hands will never grow old.

I think he will die tonight, this man. I feel a slow gathering desire to kill him myself. He has fed so much poison to so many. Tracking him, wrapping him in my arms, I would not even have to wreathe him with visions. I would let him know that death has come in the form of a woman too white to be human, too smoothed by

5

the centuries to be anything but a statue come to life. But those for whom he waits plot to kill him. And why should I intervene?

What do I look like to these people? A woman with long wavy clean brown hair that covers me much like a nun's mantle, a face so white it appears cosmetically created, and eyes, abnormally brilliant, even from behind golden glasses.

Ah, we have a lot to be grateful for in the many styles of eyeglasses in this age – for if I were to take these off, I should have to keep my head bowed, not to startle people with the mere play of yellow and brown and gold in my eyes, that have grown ever more jewel-like over the centuries, so that I seem a blind woman set with topaz for her pupils, or rather carefully formed orbs of topaz, sapphire, even aquamarine.

Look, I have filled so many pages, and all I am saying is Yes, I will tell you how it began for me.

Yes, I will tell you the story of my mortal life in ancient Rome, how I came to love Marius and how we came to be together and then to part.

What a transformation in me, this resolution.

How powerful I feel as I hold this pen, and how eager to put us in sharp and clear perspective before I begin fulfilling your request.

This is Paris, in a time of peace. There is rain. High regal gray buildings with their double windows and iron balconies line this boulevard. Loud, tiny, dangerous automobiles race in the streets. Cafés, such as this, are overflowing with international tourists. Ancient churches are crowded here by tenements, palaces turned to museums, in whose rooms I linger for hours gazing at objects from Egypt or Sumer which are even older than me. Roman architecture is everywhere, absolute replicas of Temples of my time now serve as banks. The words of my native Latin suffuse the English language. Ovid, my beloved Ovid, the poet who predicted his poetry would outlast the Roman Empire, has been proved true.

Walk into any bookstore and you find him in neat, small paperbacks, designed to appeal to students.

Roman influence seeds itself, sprouting mighty oaks right through the modern forest of computers, digital disks, microviruses and space satellites.

It is easy here – as always – to find an embraceable evil, a despair worth tender fulfillment.

And with me there must always be some love

of the victim, some mercy, some self-delusion that the death I bring does not mar the great shroud of inevitability, woven of trees and earth and stars, and human events, which hovers forever around us ready to close on all that is created, all that we know.

Last night, when you found me, how did it seem to you? I was alone on the bridge over the Seine, walking in the last dangerous darkness before dawn.

You saw me before I knew you were there. My hood was down and I let my eyes in the dim light of the bridge have their little moment of glory. My victim stood at the railing, no more than a child, but bruised and robbed by a hundred men. She wanted to die in the water. I don't know if the Seine is deep enough for one to drown there. So near the Ile St.-Louis. So near Notre Dame. Perhaps it is, if one can resist a last struggle for life.

But I felt this victim's soul like ashes, as though her spirit had been cremated and only the body remained, a worn, disease-ridden shell. I put my arm around her, and when I saw the fear in her small black eyes, when I saw the question coming, I wreathed her with images. The soot that covered my skin was not enough to keep me from looking like the Virgin Mary, and she sank into hymns and devotion, she even saw my veils in the colors she had known in churches of childhood, as she yielded to me, and I – knowing that I needn't drink, but thirsting for her, thirsting for the anguish she could give forth in her final moment, thirsting for the tasty red blood that would fill my mouth and make me feel human for one instant in my very monstrosity – I gave in to her visions, bent her neck, ran my fingers over her sore tender skin, and then it was, when I sank my teeth into her, when I drank from her – it was then that I knew you were there. You watched.

I knew it, and I felt it, and I saw the image of us in your eye, distractingly, as the pleasure nevertheless flushed through me, making me believe I was alive, somehow connected to fields of clover or trees with roots deeper in the earth than the branches they raise to the welkin above.

At first I hated you. You saw me as I feasted. You saw me as I gave in. You knew nothing of my months of starvation, restraint, wandering. You saw only the sudden release of my unclean desire to suck her very soul from her, to make her heart rise in the flesh inside her, to drag from her veins every precious particle of her that still wanted to survive.

And she did want to survive. Wrapped in

saints, and dreaming suddenly of the breasts that nursed her, her young body fought, pumping and pumping against me, she so soft, and my own form hard as a statue, my milkless nipples enshrined in marble, no comfort. Let her see her mother, dead, gone and now waiting. Let me glimpse through her dying eyes the light through which she sped towards this certain salvation.

Then I forgot about you. I would not be robbed. I slowed the drinking, I let her sigh, I let her lungs fill with the cold river air, her mother drawing closer and closer so that death now was as safe for her as the womb. I took every drop from her that she could give.

She hung dead against me, as one I'd rescued, one I would help from the bridge, some weakened, sickened, drunken girl. I slid my hand into her body, breaking the flesh so easily even with these delicate fingers, and I closed my fingers around her heart and brought it to my lips and sucked it, my head tucked down by her face, sucked the heart like fruit, until no blood was left in any fiber or chamber, and then slowly – perhaps for your benefit –I lifted her and let her fall down into the water she had so desired.

Now there would be no struggle as her lungs filled with the river. Now there would be no last desperate thrashing. I fed from the heart one last time, to take even the color of blood out of it, and then sent it after her – crushed grapes – poor child, child of a hundred men.

Then I faced you, let you know that I knew you watched from the quay. I think I tried to frighten you. In rage I let you know how weak you were, that all the blood given to you by Lestat would make you no match should I choose to dismember you, pitch a fatal heat into you and immolate you, or only punish you with penetrating scar – simply for having spied upon me.

Actually I have never done such a thing to a younger one. I feel sorry for them when they see us, the ancient ones, and quake in terror. But I should, by all the knowledge of myself I possess, have retreated so quickly that you could not follow me in the night.

Something in your demeanor charmed me, the manner in which you approached me on the bridge, your young Anglo-Indian brown-skinned body gifted by your true mortal age with such seductive grace. Your very posture seemed to ask of me, without humiliation:

'Pandora, may we speak?'

My mind wandered. Perhaps you knew it. I don't remember whether I shut you out of my

11

thoughts, and I know that your telepathic abilities are not really very strong. My mind wandered suddenly, perhaps of itself, perhaps at your prodding. I thought of all the things I could tell you, which were so different from the tales of Lestat, and those of Marius through Lestat, and I wanted to warn you, warn you of the ancient vampires of the Far East who would kill you if you went into their territory, simply because you were there.

I wanted to make certain you understood what we all had to accept – the Fount of our immortal vampiric hunger did reside in two beings – Mekare and Maharet – so ancient they are now both horrible to look upon, more than beautiful. And if they destroy themselves we will all die with them.

I wanted to tell you of others who have never known us as a tribe or known our history, who survived the terrible fire brought down on her children by our Mother Akasha. I wanted to tell you that there were things walking the Earth that look like us but are not of our breed any more than they are human. And I wanted suddenly to take you under my wing.

It must have been your prodding. You stood there, the English gentleman, wearing your decorum more lightly and naturally than any man I'd ever seen. I marveled at your fine clothes, that you'd indulged yourself in a light black cloak of worsted wool, that you had even given yourself the luxury of a gleaming red silk scarf – so unlike you when you were newly made.

Understand, I was not aware the night that Lestat transformed you into a vampire. I didn't feel that moment.

All the preternatural world shimmered weeks earlier, however, with the knowledge that a mortal had jumped into the body of another mortal; we know these things, as if the stars tell us. One preternatural mind picks up the ripples of this sharp cut in the fabric of the ordinary, then another mind receives the image, and on and on it goes.

David Talbot, the name we all knew from the venerable order of psychic detectives, the Talamasca, had managed to move his entire soul and etheric body – into that of another man. That body itself was in the possession of a body thief whom you forced from it. And once anchored in the young body, you, with all your scruples and values, all your knowledge of seventy-four years, remained anchored in the young cells.

And so it was David the Reborn, David with

the high-gloss India beauty and raw well-nourished strength of British lineage, that Lestat had made into a vampire, bringing over both body and soul, compounding miracle with the Dark Trick, achieving once more a sin that should stun his contemporaries and his elders.

And this, this was done to you by your best friend!

Welcome to the darkness, David. Welcome to the domain of Shakespeare's 'inconstant moon.'

Bravely you came up the bridge towards me. 'Forgive me, Pandora,' you said so quietly. Flawless British upper-class accent, and the usual beguiling British rhythm that is so seductive it seems to say that 'we will all save the world.'

You kept a polite distance between us, as if I were a virgin girl of the last century and you didn't want to alarm me and my tender sensibilities. I smiled.

I indulged myself then. I took your full measure, this fledgling that Lestat – against Marius's injunction – had dared to make. I saw the components of you as a man: an immense human soul, fearless, yet half in love with despair, and a body which Lestat had almost injured himself to render powerful. He had given you more blood than he could easily give in your transformation. He had tried to give you his courage, his cleverness, his cunning; he had tried to transport an armory for you through the blood.

He had done well. Your strength was complex and obvious. Our Queen Mother Akasha's blood was mixed with that of Lestat. Marius, my ancient lover, had given him blood as well. Lestat, ah, now what do they say, they say that he may even have drunk the blood of the Christ.

It was this first issue I took up with you, my curiosity overwhelming me, for to scan the world for knowledge is often to rake in such tragedy that I abhor it.

'Tell me the truth of it,' I said. 'This story *Memnoch the Devil*. Lestat claimed he went to Heaven and to Hell. He brought back a veil from St. Veronica. The face of Christ was on it! It converted thousands to Christianity, it cured alienation and succored bitterness. It drove other Children of Darkness to throw up their arms to the deadly morning light, as if the sun were in fact the fire of God.'

'Yes, it's all happened, as I described it,' you said, lowering your head with a polite but unexaggerated modesty. 'And you know a few . . . of *us* perished in this fervor, whilst newspapers and scientists collected our ashes for examination.'

I marveled at your calm attitude. A Twentieth-Century sensibility A mind dominated by an incalculable wealth of information, and quick of tongue with an intellect devoted to swiftness, synthesis, probabilities, and all this against the backdrop of horrid experiences, wars, massacres, the worst perhaps the world has ever seen.

'It all happened,' you said. 'And I did meet with Mekare and Maharet, the ancient ones, and you needn't fear for me that I don't know how fragile is the root. It was kind of you to think so protectively of me.'

I was quietly charmed.

'What did you think of this Holy Veil yourself?' I asked.

'Our Lady of Fatima,' you said softly. 'The Shroud of Turin, a cripple rising from the Miraculous Waters of Lourdes! What a consolation it must be to accept such a thing so easily.'

'And you did not?'

You shook your head. 'And neither did Lestat, really. It was the mortal girl, Dora, snatching the Veil from him, who took it out into the world. But it was a most singular and meticulously made thing, I'll tell you that, more worthy of the word 'relic' perhaps than any other I've ever seen.'

You sounded dejected suddenly.

'Some immense intent went into its making,' you said.

'And the vampire Armand, the delicate boy-like Armand, he believed it?' I asked. 'Armand looked at it and saw the face of Christ,' I said, seeking your confirmation.

'Enough to die for it,' you said solemnly. 'Enough to open his arms to the morning sun.'

You looked away, and you closed your eyes. This was a simple unadorned plea to me not to make you speak of Armand and how he had gone into the morning fire.

I gave a sigh – surprised and gently fascinated to find you so articulate, skeptical, yet so sharply and frankly connected to the others.

You said in a shaken voice, 'Armand.' And still looking away from me. 'What a Requiem. And does he know now if Memnoch was real, if God Incarnate who tempted Lestat was in fact the Son of the God Almighty? Does anyone?'

I was taken with your earnestness, your passion. You were not jaded or cynical. There was an immediacy to your feelings for these happenings, these creatures, these questions you posed.

'They locked up the Veil, you know,' you

said. 'It's in the Vatican. There were two weeks of frenzy on Fifth Avenue in St. Patrick's Cathedral in which people came to look into the eyes of The Lord, and then they had it, gone, taken to their vaults. I doubt there is a nation on the Earth with the power to gain even a glimpse of it now.'

'And Lestat,' I said. 'Where is he now?'

'Paralyzed, silent,' you said. 'Lestat lies on the floor of a chapel in New Orleans. He doesn't move. He says nothing. His Mother has come to him. You knew her, Gabrielle, he made a vampire of her.'

'Yes, I remember her.'

'Even she draws no response from him. Whatever he saw, in his journey to Heaven and Hell, he doesn't know the truth of it one way or the other – he tried to tell this to Dora! And eventually, after I'd written down the whole story for him, he passed within a few nights into this state.

'His eyes are fixed and his body pliant. They made a curious Pietà, he and Gabrielle, in this abandoned convent and its chapel. His mind is closed, or worse – it's empty'

I found I liked very much your manner of speaking. In fact, I was taken off guard.

'I left Lestat because he was beyond my help

18

and my reach,' you said. 'And I must know if there are old ones who want to put an end to me; I must make my pilgrimages and my progresses to know the dangers of this world to which I've been admitted.'

'You're so forthright. You have no cunning.'

'On the contrary. I conceal my keenest assets from you.' You gave me a slow, polite smile. 'Your beauty rather confuses me. Are you used to this?'

'Quite,' I said. 'And weary of it. Come beyond it. Let me just warn, there are old ones, ones no one knows or can explain. It's rumored you've been with Maharet and Mekare, who are now the Eldest and the Fount from which we all spring. Obviously they've drawn back from us, from all the world, into some secret place, and have no taste for authority.'

'You're so very correct,' you said, 'and my audience with them was beautiful but brief. They don't want to rule over anyone, nor will Maharet, as long as the history of the world and her own physical descendants are in it – her own thousands of human descendants from a time so ancient there is no date for it – Maharet will never destroy herself and her sister, thereby destroying all of us.'

'Yes,' I said, 'in that she believes, the Great

Family, the generations she has traced for thousands of years. I saw her when we all gathered. She doesn't see us as evil – you, or me, or Lestat – she thinks that we're natural, rather like volcanoes or fires that rage through forests, or bolts of lightning that strike a man dead.'

'Precisely' you said. 'There is no Queen of the Damned now. I fear only one other immortal, and that's your lover, Marius. Because it was Marius who laid down the strict rule before he left the others that no more blood drinkers could be made. I'm base-born in the mind of Marius. That is, were he an Englishman, those would be his words.'

I shook my head. 'I can't believe he would harm you. Hasn't he come to Lestat? Did he not come to see the Veil with his own eyes?'

You said No to both questions.

'Heed this advice: whenever you sense his presence, talk to him. Talk to him as you have to me. Begin a conversation which he won't have the confidence to bring to a close.'

You smiled again. 'That's such a clever way of putting it,' you said.

'But I don't think you have to fear him. If he wanted you gone off the Earth, you'd be gone. What we have to fear is the same things humans fear – that there are others of our same species, of varying power and belief, and we are never entirely sure where they are or what they do. That's my advice to you.'

'You are so kind to take your time with me,' you said.

I could have wept. 'On the contrary. You don't know the silence and solitude in which I wander, and pray, you never know it, and here you've given me heat without death, you've given me nourishment without blood. I'm glad you've come.'

I saw you look up at the sky, the habit of the young ones.

'I know, we have to part now.'

You turned to me suddenly 'Meet me tomorrow night,' you said imploringly. 'Let this exchange continue! I'll come to you in the café where you sit every night musing. I'll find you. Let us talk to each other.'

'So you've seen me there.'

'Oh, often,' you said. 'Yes.' You looked away again. I saw it was to conceal feeling. Then your dark eyes turned back to me.

'Pandora, we have the world, don't we?' you whispered.

'I don't know, David. But I'll meet you tomorrow night. Why haven't you come to me there? Where it was warm and lighted?'

'It seemed a far more outrageous intrusion, to move in on you in the sanctified privacy of a crowded café. People go to such places to be alone, don't they? This seemed somehow more proper. And I did not mean to be the voyeur. Like many fledglings, I have to feed every night. It was an accident that we saw each other at that moment.'

'That is charming, David,' I said. 'It is a long time since anyone has charmed me. I'll meet you there . . . tomorrow night.'

And then a wickedness possessed me. I came towards you and embraced you, knowing that the hardness and coldness of my ancient body would strike the deepest chord of terror in you, newborn as you were, passing so easily for mortal.

But you didn't draw back. And when I kissed your cheek, you kissed mine.

I wonder now, as I sit here in the café, writing . . . trying to give you more with these words perhaps than you ask for . . . what I would have done had you not kissed me, had you shrunk back with the fear that is so common in the young.

David, you are indeed a puzzle.

You see that I have begun to chronicle not my life here, but what has passed these two nights between you and me.

Allow this, David. Allow that I speak of you and me, and then perhaps I can retrieve my lost life.

When you came into the café tonight, I thought nothing much about the notebooks. You had two. They were thick.

The leather of the notebooks smelled good and old, and when you set them down on the table, only then did I detect a glimmer from your disciplined and restrained mind that they had to do with me.

I had chosen this table in the crowded center of the room, as though I wanted to be in the middle of the whirlpool of mortal scent and activity. You seemed pleased, unafraid, utterly at home.

You wore another stunning suit of modern cut with a full cape of worsted wool, very taste-ful, yet Old World, and with your golden skin and radiant eyes, you turned the head of every woman in the place and you turned the heads of some of the men.

You smiled. I must have seemed a snail to you beneath my cloak and hood, gold glasses covering well over half my face, and a trace of commercial lipstick on my lips, a soft purple pink that had made me think of bruises. It had seemed very enticing in the mirror at the store, and I liked that my mouth was something I didn't have to hide. My lips are now almost colorless. With this lipstick I could smile.

I wore these gloves of mine, black lace, with their sheared-off tips so that my fingers can feel, and I had sooted my nails so they would not sparkle like crystal in the café. And I reached out my hand to you and you kissed it.

There was your same boldness and decorum. And then the warmest smile from you, a smile in which I think your former physiology must have dominated because you looked far too wise for one so young and strong of build. I marveled at the perfect picture you had made of yourself.

'You don't know what a joy it is to me,' you said, 'that you've come, that you've let me join you here at this table.'

'You have made me want this,' I said, raising my hands, and seeing that your eyes were dazzled by my crystalline fingernails, in spite of the soot.

I reached towards you, expecting you to pull back, but you entrusted to my cold white fingers your warm dark hand.

'You find in me a living being?' I asked you.

'Oh, yes, most definitely, most radiantly and perfectly a living being.'

We ordered our coffee, as mortals expect us to do, deriving more pleasure from the heat and aroma than they could ever imagine, even stirring our little cups with our spoons. I had before me a red dessert. The dessert is still here of course. I ordered it simply because it was red – strawberries covered in syrup – with a strong sweet smell that bees would like.

I smiled at your blandishments. I liked them.

Playfully, I mocked them. I let my hood slip down and I shook out my hair so that its fullness and dark brown color could shimmer in the light.

Of course it's no signal to mortals, as is Marius's blond hair or that of Lestat. But I love my own hair, I love the veil of it when it is down over my shoulders, and I loved what I saw in your eyes.

'Somehere deep inside me there is a woman,' I said.

To write it now – in this notebook as I sit here alone – it gives architecture to a trivial moment, and seems so dire a confession.

David, the more I write, the more the concept of narrative excites me, the more I believe in the weight of a coherence which is possible on the page though not in life.

But again, I didn't know I meant to pick up

this pen of yours at all. We were talking:

'Pandora, if anyone does not know you're a woman, then he is a fool,' you said.

'How angry Marius would be with me for being pleased by that,' I said. 'Oh, no. Rather he would seize it as a strong point in favor of his position. I left him, left him without a word, the last time we were together – that was before Lestat went on his little escapade of running around in a human body, and long before he encountered Memnoch the Devil – I left Marius, and suddenly I wish I could reach him! I wish I could talk with him as you and I are talking now.'

You looked so troubled for me, and with reason. On some level, you must have known that I had not evinced this much enthusiasm over anything in many a dreary year.

'Would you write your story for me, Pandora?' you asked suddenly.

I was totally surprised.

'Write it in these notebooks?' you pressed.

'Write about the time when you were alive, the time when you and Marius came together, write what you will of Marius. But it's your story that I most want.'

I was stunned.

'Why in the world would you want this of me?'

You didn't answer.

'David, surely you've not returned to that order of human beings, the Talamasca, they know too much –'

You put up your hand.

'No, and I will never; and if there was ever any doubt of it, I learnt it once and for all in the archives kept by Maharet.'

'She allowed you to see her archives, the books she's saved over the course of time?'

'Yes, it was remarkable, you know . . . a storehouse of tablets, scrolls, parchments – books and poems from cultures of which the world knows nothing, I think. Books lost from time. Of course she forbade me to reveal anything I found or speak in detail of our meeting. She said it was too rash tampering with things, and she confirmed your fear that I might go to the Talamasca – my old mortal psychic friends. I have not. I will not. But it is a very easy vow to keep.'

'Why so?'

'Pandora, when I saw all those old writings – I knew I was no longer human. I knew that the history lying there to be collected was no longer mine! I am not one of these!' Your eyes swept the room. 'Of course you must have heard this a thousand times from fledgling vampires! But you see, I had a fervent faith that philosophy and reason would make a bridge for me by which I could go and come in both worlds. Well, there is no bridge. It's gone.'

Your sadness shimmered about you, flashing in your young eyes and in the softness of your new flesh.

'So you know that,' I said. I didn't plan the words. But out they came. 'You know.' I gave a soft bitter laugh.

'Indeed I do. I knew when I held documents from your time, so many from your time, Imperial Rome, and other crumbling bits of inscribed rock I couldn't even hope to place. I knew. I didn't care about them, Pandora! I care about what we are, what we are now.'

'How remarkable,' I said. 'You don't know how much I admire you, or how attractive is your disposition to me.'

'I am happy to hear this,' you said. Then you leaned forward towards me: 'I don't say we do not carry our human souls with us, our history; of course we do.

'I remember once a long time ago, Armand told me that he asked Lestat, 'How will I ever understand the human race?' Lestat said, 'Read or see all the plays of Shakespeare and you will know all you ever need to know about the human race.' Armand did it. He devoured the poems, he sat through the plays, he watched the brilliant new films with Laurence Fishburne and Kenneth Branagh and Leonardo DiCaprio. And when Armand and I last spoke together, this is what he said of his education:

'"Lestat was right. He gave me not books but a passage into understanding. This man Shakespeare writes," – and I quote both Armand and Shakespeare now as Armand spoke it, as I will to you – as if it came from my heart:

Tomorrow, and tomorrow, and tomorrow,
Creeps in this petty pace from day to day,
To the last syllable of recorded time;
And all our yesterdays have lighted fools
The way to dusty death. Out, out brief candle.
Life's but a walking shadow; a poor player,
That struts and frets his hour upon the stage,
And then is heard no more; it is a tale
Told by an idiot, full of sound and fury,
Signifying nothing.

'"This man writes this," said Armand to me, "and we all know that it is absolutely the truth and every revelation has sooner or later fallen before it, and yet we want to love the way he has said it, we want to hear it again! We want to

29

remember it! We want to never forget a single word." '

We were both silent for a moment. You looked down, you rested your chin on your knuckles. I knew the whole weight of Armand's going into the sun was on you, and I had so loved your recitation of the words, and the words themselves.

Finally, I said, 'And this gives me pleasure. Think of it, pleasure. That you recite these words to me now.'

You smiled.

'I want to know now what we can learn,' you said. 'I want to know what we can see! So I come to you, a Child of the Millennia, a vampire who drank from the Queen Akasha herself, one who has survived two thousand years. And I ask you, Pandora, please will you write for me, write your story, write what you will.'

For a long moment I gave you no answer.

Then I said sharply that I could not. But something had stirred in me. I saw and heard arguments and tirades of centuries ago, I saw the poet's lifted light shine on eras I had known intimately out of love. Other eras I had never known, wandering, ignorant, a wraith.

Yes, there was a tale to be written. There was. But at the moment I could not admit it.

You were in misery, having thought of Armand, having remembered his walking into the morning sun. You mourned for Armand.

'Was there any bond between you?' you asked. 'Forgive me my boldness, but I mean was there any bond between you and Armand when you met, because Marius had given you both the Dark Gift? I know no jealousy exists, that I can feel. I wouldn't bring up the very name Armand if I detected a hurt in you, but all else is an absence, a silence. Was there no bond?'

'The bond is only grief. He went into the sun. And grief is absolutely the easiest and safest of bonds.'

You laughed under your breath.

'What can I do to make you consider my request? Have pity on me, Gracious Lady, entrust to me your song.'

I smiled indulgently, but it was impossible, I thought.

'It's far too dissonant, my dear,' I said. 'It's far too —'

I shut my eyes.

I had wanted to say that my song was far too painful to sing.

Suddenly your eyes moved upwards. Your expression changed. It was almost as if you were deliberately trying to appear to enter a trance. Slowly you turned your head. You pointed, with your hand close to the table, then let your hand go lax.

'What is it, David?' I said. 'What are you seeing?'

'Spirits, Pandora, ghosts.'

You shuddered as if to clear your head.

'But that's unheard of,' I said. Yet I knew that he was telling the truth. 'The Dark Gift takes away that power. Even the ancient witches, Maharet and Mekare, told us this, that once Akasha's blood entered them, and they became vampires, they never heard or saw the spirits again. You've recently been with them. Did you tell them of this power?'

He nodded. Obviously some loyalty bound him not to say that they did not have it. But I knew they did not. I saw it in his mind, and I had known it myself when I had encountered the ancient twins, the twins who had struck down the Queen of the Damned.

'I can see spirits, Pandora,' you said with the most troubled expression. 'I can see them anywhere if I try, and in some very specific places when they choose. Lestat saw the ghost of Roger, his victim in *Memnoch the Devil*.'

'But that was an exception, a surge of love in

the man's soul that somehow defied death, or delayed the soul's termination – something we can't understand.'

'I see spirits, but I haven't come to burden you with this or frighten you.'

'You must tell me more about this,' I said. 'What did you see right now?'

'A weak spirit. It couldn't harm anyone. It's one of those sad sad humans who does not know he's dead. They *are* an atmosphere around the planet. The "earthbound" is the name for them. But Pandora, I have more than that in myself to explore.'

You continued:

'Apparently each century yields a new kind of vampire, or let us say that our course of growth was not set in the beginning any more than the course of human beings. Some night perhaps I will tell you everything I see – these spirits who were never clear to me when I was mortal – I'll tell you about something Armand confided to me, about the colors he saw when he took life, how the soul left body in waves of radiating color!'

'I've never heard of such a thing!'

'I too see this,' you said.

I could see it hurt you almost too much to speak of Armand.

'But whatever possessed Armand to believe in the Veil?' I asked, suddenly amazed at my own passion. 'Why did he go into the sun? How could such a thing kill Lestat's reason and will? Veronica. Did they know the very name means *Vera Ikon,* that there was never any such person, that she could not be found by one drawn back to ancient Jerusalem on the day Christ carried his cross; she was a concoction of Priests. Didn't they know?'

I think I had taken the two notebooks in hand, for I looked down and I saw that I did indeed hold them. In fact, I clutched both of them to my breast and examined one of the pens.

'Reason,' I whispered. 'Oh, precious reason! And consciousness within a void.' I shook my head, smiling kindly at you. 'And vampires who speak now with spirits! Humans who can travel from body to body.'

I went on with a wholly unfamiliar energy.

'A lively fashionable modern cult of angels, devotion thriving everywhere. And people rising from operating tables to speak of life after death, a tunnel, an embracing love! Oh, you have been created perhaps in an auspicious time! I don't know what to make of it.'

You were obviously quite impressed by these words, or rather the way that my perspective

34

had been drawn from me. So was I.

'I've only started,' you said, 'and will keep company alike with brilliant Children of the Millennia and street-corner fortune tellers who deal out the cards of the Tarot. I'm eager to gaze into crystal balls and darkened mirrors. I'll search now among those whom others dismiss as mad, or among *us* – among those like you, who have looked on something that they do not believe they should share! That's it, isn't it? But I ask you to share it. I'm finished with the ordinary human soul. I am finished with science and psychology, with microscopes and perhaps even with the telescopes aimed at the stars.'

I was quite enthralled. How strongly you meant it. I could feel my face so warm with feeling for you as I looked at you. I think my mouth was slack with wonder.

'I am a miracle unto myself,' you said. 'I am immortal, and I want to learn about us! You have a tale to tell, you are ancient, and deeply broken. I feel love for you and cherish that it is what it is and nothing more.'

'What a strange thing to say!'

'Love.' You shrugged your shoulders. You looked up and then back at me for emphasis. 'And it rained and it rained for millions of years, and the volcanoes boiled and the oceans

35

cooled, and then there was love?' You shrugged to make a mock of the absurdity.

I couldn't help but laugh at your little gest. Too perfect, I thought. But I was suddenly so torn.

'This is very unexpected,' I said. 'Because if I do have a story, a very small story –'

'Yes?'

'Well, my story – if I have one – is very much to the point. It's linked to the very points you've made.'

Suddenly something came over me. I laughed again softly.

'I understand you!' I said. 'Oh, not that you can see spirits, for that is a great subject unto itself.

'But I see now the source of your strength. You have lived an entire human life. Unlike Marius, unlike me, you weren't taken in your prime. You were taken near the moment of your natural death, and you will not settle for the adventures and faults of the earthbound! You are determined to forge ahead with the courage of one who has died of old age and then finds himself risen from the grave. You've kicked aside the funeral wreaths. You are ready for Mount Olympus, aren't you?'

'Or for Osiris in the depths of the darkness,'

you said. 'Or for the shades in Hades. Certainly I am ready for the spirits, for the vampires, for those who see the future and claim to know past lives, for you who have a stunning intellect encased beautifully, to endure for so many years, an intellect which has perhaps all but destroyed your heart.'

I gasped.

'Forgive me. That was not proper of me,' you said.

'No, explain your meaning.'

'You always take the hearts from the victims, isn't it so? You want the heart.'

'Perhaps. Don't expect wisdom from me as it might come from Marius, or the ancient twins.'

'You draw me to you,' you said.

'Why?'

'Because you do have a story inside you; it lies articulate and waiting to be written – behind your silence and your suffering.'

'You are too romantic, friend,' I said.

You waited patiently. I think you could feel the tumult in me, the shivering of my soul in the face of so much new emotion.

'It's such a small story,' I said. I saw images, memories, moments, the stuff that can incite souls to action and creation. I saw the very faintest possibility of faith.

I think you already knew the answer.

You knew what I would do when I did not.

You smiled discreetly, but you were eager and waiting.

I looked at you and thought of trying to write it, write it all out . . .

'You want me to leave now, don't you?' you said. You rose, collected your rain-spattered coat and bent over gracefully to kiss my hand.

My hands were clutching the notebooks.

'No,' I said, 'I can't do it.'

You made no immediate judgment.

'Come back in two nights,' I said. 'I promise you I will have your two notebooks for you, even if they are completely empty or only contain a better explanation of why I can't retrieve my lost life. I won't disappoint you. But expect nothing, except that I will come and I will put these books in your hands.'

'Two nights,' you said, 'and we meet here again.'

In silence I watched you leave the café.

And now you see it has begun, David.

And now you see, David, I have made our meeting the introduction to the story you asked me to tell.

2

PANDORA'S STORY

I was born in Rome, during the reign of Augustus Caesar, in the year that you now reckon to have been 15 B.C., or fifteen years 'before Christ.'

All the Roman history and Roman names I give here are accurate; I have not falsified them or made up stories or created false political events. Everything bears upon my ultimate fate and the fate of Marius. Nothing is included for love of the past.

I have omitted my family name. I did this because my family has a history, and I cannot bring myself to connect their ancient reputations, deeds, epitaphs to this tale. Also Marius, when he confided in Lestat, did not give the full name of his Roman family. And I respect this and that also is not revealed.

Augustus had been Emperor for over ten

years, and it was a marvelous time to be an educated woman in Rome, women had immense freedom, and I had a rich Senator for a father, five prosperous brothers, and grew up Motherless but cherished by teams of Greek tutors and nurses who gave me everything I wanted.

Now, if I really wanted to make this difficult for you, David, I'd write it in classical Latin. But I won't. And I must tell you that, unlike you, I came by my education in English haphazardly, and certainly I never learnt it from Shakespeare's plays.

Indeed I have passed through many stages of the English language in my wanderings and in my reading, but the great majority of my true acquaintance with it has been in this century and I am writing for you in colloquial English.

There's another reason for this, which I'm sure you'll understand if you've read the modern translation of Petronius's *Satyricon* or Juvenal's satires. Very modern English is a really true equivalent to the Latin of my time.

The formal letters of Imperial Rome won't tell you this. But the graffiti scratched on the walls of Pompeii will make it obvious. We had a sophisticated tongue, countless clever verbal shortcuts and common expressions.

I'm going to write, therefore, in the English

which feels equivalent and natural to me.

Let me say here quickly – while the action is at a halt – that I was never, as Marius said, a Greek Courtesan. I was living with such a pretense when Marius gave me the Dark Gift, and perhaps out of consideration for old mortal secrets he so described me. Or maybe it was contemptuous of him to style me this way. I don't know.

But Marius knew all about my Roman family, that it was a Senatorial family, as purely aristocratic and privileged as his own mortal family, and that my people dated back to the time of Romulus and Remus, the same as Marius's mortal line. Marius did not succumb to me because I had 'beautiful arms', as he indicated to Lestat. This trivialization was perhaps provocative.

I don't hold anything against either of them, Marius or Lestat. I don't know who got what wrong.

My feeling for my Father is so great to this very night, as I sit in the café, writing for you, David, that I am astonished at the power of writing – of putting words to paper and bringing back so vividly to myself my Father's loving face.

My Father was to meet a terrible end. He did

not deserve what happened to him. But some of our kinsmen survived and re-established our family in later times.

My Father was rich, one of the true millionaires of that age, and his capital was invested widely. He was a soldier more often than required of him, a Senator, a thoughtful and quiet man by disposition. And after the terrors of the Civil War, he was a great supporter of Caesar Augustus and very much in the Emperor's good graces.

Of course he dreamed that the Roman Republic would come back; we all did. But Augustus had brought unity and peace to the Empire.

I met Augustus many times in my youth, and it was always at some crowded social function and of no consequence. He looked like his portraits; a lean man with a long thin nose, short hair, average face; he was rather rational and pragmatic by nature and not invested with any abnormal cruelty. He had no personal vanity.

The poor man was really blessed that he couldn't see into the future – that he had no inkling of all the horrors and madness that would begin with Tiberius, his successor, and go on for so long under other members of his family.

Only in later times did I understand the full singularity and accomplishment of Augustus's long reign. Was it forty-four years of peace throughout the cities of the Empire?

Alas, to be born during this time was to be born during a time of creativity and prosperity, when Rome was *caput mundi,* or capital of the world. And when I look back on it, I realize what a powerful combination it was to have both tradition and vast sums of money; to have old values and new power.

Our family life was conservative, strict, even a little dusty. And yet we had every luxury. My Father grew more quiet and conservative over the years. He enjoyed his grandchildren, who were born while he was still vigorous and active.

Though he had fought principally in the Northern campaigns along the Rhine, he had been stationed in Syria for a while. He had studied in Athens. He had served so much and so well that he was being allowed an early retirement in the years during which I grew up, an early withdrawal from the social life that whirled around the Imperial Palace, though I did not realize this at the time.

My five brothers came before me. So there was no 'ritual Roman mourning' when I was born, as you hear tell of in Roman families when a girl comes into the world. Far from it.

Five times my Father had stood in the atrium – the main enclosed courtyard, or peristyle, of our house with its pillars and stairs and grand marble-work – five times he had stood there before the assembled family and held in his hands a newborn son, inspected it and then pronounced it perfect and fit to be reared as his own, as was his prerogative. Now, you know he had the power of life and death over his sons from that moment on.

If my Father hadn't wanted these boys for any reason, he would have 'exposed' them to die of starvation. It was against the law to steal such a child and make it a slave.

Having five boys already, my Father was expected by some to get rid of me immediately. Who needs a girl? But my Father never exposed or rejected any of my Mother's children.

And by the time I arrived, I'm told, he cried for joy

'Thank the gods! A little darling.' I heard the story ad nauseam from my brothers, who, every time I acted up – did something unseemly, frisky, and wild – said sneeringly, 'Thank the gods, a little darling!' It became a charming goad.

My Mother died when I was two, and all I recall of her are gentleness and sweetness. She'd lost as many children as she had birthed, and early death was typical enough. Her Epitaph was beautifully written by my Father, and her memory honored throughout my life. My Father never took another woman into the house. He slept with a few of the female slaves, but this was nothing unusual. My brothers did the same thing. This was common in a Roman household. My Father brought no new woman from another family to rule over me.

There is no grief in me for my Mother because I was simply too young for it, and if I cried when my Mother did not come back, I don't remember it.

What I remember is having the run of a big old rectangular palatial Roman house, with many rectangular rooms built onto the main rectangle, one off another, the whole nestled in a huge garden high on the Palatine Hill. It was a house of marble floors and richly painted walls, the garden meandering and surrounding every room of it.

I was the true jewel of my Father's eye, and I remember having a marvelous time watching my brothers practice outside with their short broadswords, or listening as their tutors instructed them, and then having fine teachers of my own who taught me how to read the entire *Aeneid* of Virgil before I was five years old.

I loved words. I love to sing them and speak them and even now, I must admit, I have fallen into the joy of writing them. I couldn't have told you that nights ago, David. You've brought back something to me and I must make the admission. And I must not write too fast in this mortal café, lest human beings notice!

Ah, so we continue.

My Father thought it was hysterical that I could recite verses from Virgil at so young an age and he liked nothing better than to show me off at banquets at which he entertained his conservative and somewhat old-fashioned Senatorial friends, and sometimes Caesar Augustus himself. Caesar Augustus was an agreeable man. I don't think my Father ever really wanted him at our house, however. But now and then, I suppose, the Emperor had to be wined and dined.

I'd rush in with my nurse, give a rousing recital and then be whisked away to where I could not see the proud Senators of Rome glutting themselves on peacock brains and *garum* — surely you know what *garum* is. It's the horrible sauce the Romans put on everything, rather like today's ketchup. Definitely it defeated the purpose of having eels and squids on your plate, or ostrich brains or unborn lamb or whatever other absurd delicacies were being brought by the platterful.

The point is, as you know, the Romans seemed to have a special place in their hearts for genuine gluttony, and the banquets inevitably became a disgrace. The guests would go off to the vomitorium of the house to heave up the first five courses of the meal so that they could then swallow the others. And I would lie upstairs, giggling in my bed, listening to all this laughter and vomiting.

Then the rape of the entire catering staff of slaves would follow, whether they were boys or girls or a mixture of both.

Family meals were an entirely different affair. Then we were old Romans. Everyone sat at the table; my Father was undisputed Master of his house, and would tolerate no criticism of Caesar Augustus, who, as you know, was Julius Caesar's nephew, and did not really rule as Emperor by law.

'When the time is right, he will step down,' said my Father. 'He knows he can't do it now. He is more weary and wise than ever he was ambitious. Who wants another Civil War?'

The times were actually too prosperous for men of stature to make a revolt.

Augustus kept the peace. He had profound respect for the Roman Senate. He rebuilt old Temples because he thought people needed the piety they had known under the Republic.

He gave free corn from Egypt to the poor. Nobody starved in Rome. He maintained a dizzying amount of old festivals, games and spectacles – enough to sicken one actually. But often as patriotic Romans we had to be there.

Of course there was great cruelty in the arena. There were cruel executions. There was the ever present cruelty of slavery.

But what is not understood by those today is that there coexisted with all this a sense of individual freedom on the part of even the poorest man.

The courts took time over their decisions. They consulted the past laws. They followed logic and code. People could speak their minds fairly openly.

I note this because it is key to this story: that Marius and I both were born in a time when Roman law was, as Marius would say, based on reason, as opposed to divine revelation.

We are totally unlike those blood drinkers

brought to Darkness in lands of Magic and Mystery.

Not only did we trust Augustus when we were alive, we also believed in the tangible power of the Roman Senate. We believed in public virtue and character; we held to a way of life which did not involve rituals, prayers, magic, except superficially. Virtue was embedded in character. That was the inheritance of the Roman Republic, which Marius and I shared.

Of course, our house was overcrowded with slaves. There were brilliant Greeks and grunting laborers and a fleet of women to rush about polishing busts and vases, and the city itself was choked with manumitted slaves – freedmen – some of whom were very rich.

They were all our people, our slaves.

My Father and I sat up all night when my old Greek teacher was dying. We held his hands until the body was cold. Nobody was flogged on our estate in Rome unless my Father himself gave the order. Our country slaves loafed under the fruit trees. Our stewards were rich, and showed off their wealth in their clothes.

I remember a time when there were so many old Greek slaves in the garden that I could sit day after day and listen to them argue. They had nothing else to do. I learned much from this.

I grew up more than happy. If you think I exaggerate the extent of my education, consult the letters of Pliny or other actual memoirs and correspondence of the times. Highborn young girls were well educated; modern Roman women went about unhampered for the most part by male interference. We partook of life as did men.

For example, I was scarcely eight years old when I was first taken to the arena with several of my brothers' wives, to have the dubious pleasure of seeing exotic creatures, such as giraffes, tear madly around before being shot to death with arrows, this display then followed by a small group of gladiators who would hack other gladiators to death, and then after that came the flock of criminals to be fed to the hungry lions.

David, I can hear the sound of those lions as if it were now. There's nothing between me and the moment that I sat in the wooden benches, perhaps two rows up – the premium seats – and I watched these beasts devour living beings, as I was supposed to do, with a pleasure meant to demonstrate a strength of heart, a fearlessness in the face of death, rather than simple and utter monstrousness.

The audience screamed and laughed as men and women ran from the beasts. Some victims would give the crowd no such satisfaction.

They merely stood there as the hungry lion attacked; those who were being devoured alive almost invariably lay in a stupor as though their souls had already taken flight, though the lion had not reached the throat.

I remember the smell of it. But more than anything, I remember the noise of the crowd.

I passed the test of character, I could look at all of it. I could watch the champion gladiator finally meet his end, lying there bloody in the sand, as the sword went through his chest.

But I can certainly remember my Father declaring under his breath that the whole affair was disgusting. In fact, everybody I knew thought it was all disgusting. My Father believed, as did others, that the common man needed all this blood. We, the highborn, had to preside over it for the common man. It had a religious quality to it, all this spectacular viciousness.

The making of these appalling spectacles was considered something of a social responsibility.

Also Roman life was a life of being outdoors, involved in things, attending ceremonies and spectacles, being seen, taking an interest, coming together with others.

You came together with all the other highborn and lowborn of the city and you joined in one mass to witness a triumphant procession, a great offering at the altar of Augustus, an ancient ceremony, a game, a chariot race.

Now in the Twentieth Century, when I watch the endless intrigue and slaughter in motion pictures and on television throughout our Western world, I wonder if people do not need it, do not need to see murder, slaughter, death in all forms. Television at times seems an unbroken series of gladiatorial fights or massacres. And look at the traffic now in video recordings of actual war.

Records of war have become art and entertainment.

The narrator speaks softly as the camera passes over the heap of bodies, or the skeletal children sobbing with their starving mothers. But it is gripping. One can wallow, shaking one's head, in all this death. Nights of television are devoted to old footage of men dying with guns in their hands.

I think we look because we are afraid. But in Rome, you had to look so that you would be hard, and that applied to women as well as men.

But the overall point is – I was not closeted away as a Greek woman might have been in some old Hellenistic household. I did not suffer under the earlier customs of the Roman Republic.

I vividly remember the absolute beauty of that time, and my Father's heartfelt avowal that Augustus was a god, and that Rome had never been more pleasing to her deities.

Now I want to give you one very important recollection. Let me set the scene. First, let's take up the question of Virgil, and the poem he wrote, the *Aeneid,* greatly amplifying and glorifying the adventures of the hero Aencas, a Trojan fleeing the horrors of defeat by the Greeks who came out of the famous Trojan horse to massacre Helen's city of Troy.

It's a charming story. I always loved it. Aeneas leaves dying Troy, valiantly journeys all the way to beautiful Italy and there founds our nation.

But the point is that Augustus loved and supported Virgil all of Virgil's life, and Virgil was a respected poet, a poet fine and decent to quote, an approved and patriotic poet. It was perfectly fine to like Virgil.

Virgil died before I was born. But by ten I'd read everything he'd written, and had read Horace as well, and Lucretius, much of Cicero, and all the Greek manuscripts we possessed, and there were plenty.

My Father didn't erect his library for show. It was a place where members of the family spent hours. It was also where he sat to write his letters – which he seemed endlessly to be doing – letters on behalf of the Senate, the Emperor, the courts, his friends, etc.

Back to Virgil. I had also read another Roman poet, who was alive still, and deeply and dangerously out of favor with Augustus, the god. This was the poet Ovid, the author of the *Metamorphoses,* and dozens of other earthy, hilarious and bawdy works.

Now, when I was too young to remember, Augustus turned on Ovid, whom Augustus had also loved, and Augustus banished Ovid to some horrible place on the Black Sea. Maybe it wasn't so horrible. But it was the sort of place cultured city Romans expect to be horrible – very far away from the capital and full of barbarians.

Ovid lived there a long time, and his books were banned all over Rome. You couldn't find them in the bookshops or the public libraries. Or at the book stands all over the marketplace.

You know this was a hot time for popular reading; books were everywhere – both in scroll form and in codex, that is, with bound pages – and many booksellers had teams of Greek slaves spending all day copying books for public consumption.

To continue, Ovid had fallen out of favor with Augustus, and he had been banned, but men like my Father were not about to burn their copies of the *Metamorphoses,* or any other of Ovid's work, and the only reason they didn't plead for Ovid's pardon was fear.

The whole scandal had something to do with Augustus's daughter, Julia, who was a notorious slut by anyone's standards. How Ovid became involved in Julia's love affairs I don't know. Perhaps his sensuous early poetry, the *Amores,* was considered to be a bad influence. There was also a lot of 'reform' in the air during the reign of Augustus, a lot of talk of old values.

I don't think anyone knows what really happened between Caesar Augustus and Ovid, but Ovid was banished for the rest of his life from Imperial Rome.

But I had read the *Amores* and the *Metamorphoses* in well-worn copies by the time of this incident which I want to recount. And many of my Father's friends were always worried about Ovid.

Now to the specific recollection. I was ten years old, I came in from playing, covered with dust from head to foot, my hair loose, my dress torn, and breezed into my Father's large receiving room – and I plopped down at the foot of his couch to listen to what was being said, as he lounged there with all appropriate Roman dignity, chatting with several other lounging men who had come to visit.

I knew all of the men but one, and this one was fair-haired and blue-eyed, and very tall, and he turned, during the conversation – which was all whispers and nods – and winked at me.

This was Marius, with skin slightly tanned from his travels and a flashing beauty in his eyes. He had three names like everyone else. But again, I will not disclose the name of his family. But I knew it. I knew he was sort of the 'bad boy' in an intellectual way, the 'poet' and the 'loafer.' What nobody had told me was that he was beautiful.

Now, on this day, this was Marius when he was alive, about fifteen years before he was to be made a vampire. I can calculate that he was only twenty-five. But I'm not certain.

To continue, the men paid no attention to me, and it became plain to my ever curious little mind that they were giving my Father news of Ovid, that the tall blond one with the remarkable blue eyes, the one called Marius, had just returned from the Baltic Coast, and he had given my Father several presents, which were in fact good copies of Ovid's work, both past and current.

The men assured my Father that it was still far too dangerous to go crying to Caesar Augustus over Ovid, and my Father accepted this. But if I'm not mistaken, he entrusted some money for Ovid to Marius, the blond one.

When the gentlemen were all leaving, I saw Marius in the atrium, got a measure of his full height, which was quite unusual for a Roman, and let out a girlish gasp and then a streak of laughter. He winked at me again.

Marius had his hair short then, clipped military-Roman-style with a few modest curls on his forehead; his hair was long when he was later made a vampire, and he wears it long now, but then it was the typical boring Roman military cut. But it was blond and full of sunlight in the atrium, and he seemed the brightest and most impressive man I'd ever laid eyes upon. He was full of kindness when he looked at me.

'Why are you so tall?' I asked him. My Father thought this was amusing, of course, and he did not care what anyone else thought of his dusty little daughter, hanging onto his arms and speaking to his honored company.

'My precious one,' Marius said, 'I'm tall because I'm a barbarian!' He laughed and was flirtatious when he laughed, with a deference to me as a little lady, which was rather rare.

Suddenly he made his hands into claws and ran at me like a bear.

I loved him instantly!

'No, truly!' I said. 'You can't be a barbarian. I know your Father and all your sisters; they live just down the hill. The family is always talking about you at the table, saying only nice things, of course.'

'Of that I'm sure,' he said, breaking into laughter.

I knew my Father was getting anxious.

What I didn't know was that a ten-year-old girl could be betrothed.

Marius drew himself up and said in his gentle very fine voice, trained for public rhetoric as well as words of love, 'I am descended through my mother from the Keltoi, little beauty, little muse. I come from the tall blond people of the North, the people of Gaul. My mother was a princess there, or so I am told. Do you know who they are?'

I said of course I knew and began to recite verbatim from Julius Caesar's account of conquering Gaul, or the land of the Keltoi: 'All

Gaul is made up of three parts . . .'

Marius was quite genuinely impressed. So was everybody. So I went on and on, 'The Keltoi are separated from the Aquitani by the river Garonne, and the tribe of the Belgae by the rivers Marne and Seine –'

My Father, being slightly embarrassed by this time, with his daughter glorying in attention, spoke up to gently assure everyone that I was his precious joy, and I was let to run wild, and please make nothing of it.

And I said, being bold, and a born troublemaker, 'Give my love to the great Ovid! Because I too wish he would come home to Rome.'

I then rattled off several steamy lines of the *Amores*:

She laughed and gave her best, whole hearted kisses,
They'd shake the three pronged bolt from Jove's hand.
Torture to think that fellow got such good ones!
I wish they hadn't been of the same brand!

All laughed, except my Father, and Marius went wild with delight, clapping his hands. That was all the encouragement I needed to rush at him now like a bear, as he had rushed at me, and to continue singing out Ovid's hot words:

What's more these kisses were better than I'd
*   taught her,*
She seemed possessed of knowledge that was
*   new.*
They pleased too well – bad sign! Her tongue
*   was in them,*
And my tongue was kissing too.

My Father grabbed me by the small of my upper arm, and said, 'That's it, Lydia, wrap it up!'

And the men laughed all the harder, commiserating with him, and embracing him, and then laughing again.

But I had to have one final victory over this team of adults.

'Pray Father,' I said, 'let me finish with some wise and patriotic words which Ovid said:

' "I congratulate myself on not having arrived into the world until the present time. This age suits my taste." '

This seemed to astonish Marius more than to amuse him. But my Father gathered me close and said very clearly:

'Lydia, Ovid wouldn't say that now, and now you, for being such a . . . a scholar and philosopher in one, should assure your Father's dearest friends that you know full well Ovid was banished from Rome by Augustus for good reason and that he can never return home.'

In other words, he was saying 'Shut up about Ovid.'

But Marius, undeterred, dropped on his knees before me, lean and handsome with mesmeric blue eyes, and he took my hand and kissed it and said, 'I will give Ovid your love, little Lydia. But your Father is right. We must all agree with the Emperor's censure. After all, we are Romans.' He then did the very strange thing of speaking to me purely as if I were an adult. 'Augustus Caesar has given far more to Rome, I think, than anyone ever hoped. And he too is a poet. He wrote a poem called "Ajax" and burnt it up himself because he said it wasn't good.'

I was having the time of my life. I would have run off with Marius then and there!

But all I could do was dance around him as he went out of the vestibule and out the gate.

I waved to him.

He lingered. 'Goodbye, little Lydia,' he said. He then spoke under his breath to my Father, and I heard my Father say:

61

'You are out of your mind!'

My Father turned his back on Marius, who gave me a sad smile and disappeared.

'What did he mean? What happened?' I asked my Father. 'What's the matter?'

'Listen, Lydia,' said my Father. 'Have you in all your readings come across the word "betrothed"?'

'Yes, Father, of course.'

'Well, that sort of wanderer and dreamer likes nothing better than to betroth himself to a young girl of ten because it means she is not old enough to marry and he has years of freedom, without the censure of the Emperor. They do it all the time.'

'No, no, Father,' I said. 'I shall never forget him.'

I think I forgot him the next day.

I didn't see Marius again for five years.

I remember because I was fifteen, and should have been married and didn't want to be married at all. I had wriggled out of it year after year, feigning illness, madness, total uncontrollable fits. But time was running out on me. In fact I'd been eligible for marriage since I was twelve.

At this time, we were all standing together at the foot of the Palatine Hill, watching a most sacrosanct ceremony – the Lupercalia – just one of so many festivals that were integral in Roman life.

Now the Lupercalia was very important to us, though there's no way to relate its significance to a Christian's concept of religion. It was pious to enjoy such a festival, to participate as a citizen and as a virtuous Roman.

And besides it was a great pleasure.

So I was there, not so far from the cave of the Lupercal, watching with other young women, as the two chosen men of that year were smeared with blood from a sacrifice of goats and then draped in the bleeding skins of the sacrificed animals. I couldn't see all of this very well, but I had seen it many times, and when years before two of my brothers had run in this festival, I had pushed to the front to get a good look at it.

On this occasion, I did have a fairly good view when each of the two young men took his own company and began his run around the base of the Palatine Hill. I moved forward because I was supposed to do it. The young men were hitting lightly on the arm of every young woman with a strip of goatskin, which was supposed to purify us. Render us fertile.

I stepped forward and received the

ceremonial blow, and then stepped back again, wishing I was a man and could run around the hill with the other men, not an unusual thought for me at any time in my mortal life.

I had some sarcastic inner thoughts about 'being purified,' but by this age I behaved in public and would not on any account have humiliated my Father or my brothers.

These strips of goatskin, as you know, David, are called *Februa,* and February comes from that word. So much for language and all the magic it unwittingly carries with it. Surely the Lupercalia had something to do with Romulus and Remus; perhaps it even echoed some ancient human sacrifice. After all, the young men's heads were smeared with goat blood. It gives me shivers, because in Etruscan times, long before I was born, this might have been a far more cruel ceremony.

Perhaps this was the occasion that Marius saw my arms. Because I was exposing them to this ceremonial lash, and was already, as you can see, much of a show-off in general, laughing with the others as the company of men continued their run.

In the crowd, I saw Marius. He looked at me, then back to his book. So strange. I saw him standing against a tree trunk and writing. No one did this – stand against a tree, hold a book in one hand and write with the other. The slave stood beside him with a bottle of ink.

Marius's hair was long and most beautiful. Quite wild.

I said to my Father, 'Look, there's our barbarian friend Marius, the tall one, and he's writing.'

My Father smiled and said, 'Marius is always writing. Marius is good for writing, if for nothing else. Turn around, Lydia. Be still.'

'But he looked at me, Father. I want to talk to him.'

'You will not, Lydia! You will not grace him with one small smile!'

On the way home, I asked my Father, 'If you're going to marry me to someone – if there's no way short of suicide that I can avoid this disgusting development – why don't you marry me to Marius? I don't understand it. I'm rich. He's rich. I know his Mother was a wild Keltoi princess, but his Father has adopted him.'

My Father said witheringly, 'Where have you learned all this?' He stopped in his tracks, always an ominous sign. The crowd broke and streamed around.

'I don't know; it's common knowledge.' I

turned. There was Marius hovering about, glancing at me. 'Father,' I said, 'please let me speak to him!'

My Father knelt down. Most of the crowd had gone on. 'Lydia, I know this is dreadful for you. I have caved to every objection you have raised to your suitors. But believe you me, the Emperor himself would not approve of you marrying such a mad wandering historian as Marius! He has never served in the military, he cannot enter the Senate, it is quite impossible. When you marry, you will marry well.'

As we walked away, I turned again, thinking only to pick Marius out from the others, but to my surprise he was stark still, looking at me. With his flowing hair, he much resembled the Vampire Lestat. He is taller than Lestat, but he has the same lithe build, the same very blue eyes and a muscular strength to him, and a squareness of face which is almost pretty.

I pulled away from my Father and ran up to him.

'Well, I wanted to marry you,' I said, 'but my Father has said no.'

I'll never forget the expression on his face. But before he could speak, my Father had gathered me up and gone into obliterating respectable conversation:

'How now, Marius, how goes it with your brother in the Army. And how is it with your history. I hear you have written thirteen volumes.'

My Father backed up, virtually carrying me away.

Marius did not move or answer. Soon we were with others hurrying up the hill.

All the course of our lives was changed at that moment. But there was no conceivable way Marius or I could have known it.

Twenty years would pass before we would meet again.

I was thirty-five, then. I can say that we met in a realm of darkness in more respects than one.

For now, let me fill up the gap.

I was married twice, due to pressure from the Imperial House. Augustus wanted us all to have children. I had none. My husbands seeded plenty, however, with slave girls. So I was legally divorced and freed twice over, and determined then to retire from social life, just so the Emperor Tiberius, who had come to the Imperial throne at the age of fifty, would not meddle with me, for he was more a public puritan and domestic dictator than Augustus. If I kept to the house, if I didn't go abroad to banquets and parties and hang around with the Empress Livia, Augustus's wife and mother of Tiberius, perhaps I wouldn't be pushed into becoming a stepmother! I'd stay home. I had to care for my Father. He deserved it. Even though he was perfectly healthy, he was still old!

With all due respect for the husbands I have mentioned, whose names are more than footnotes in common Roman histories, I was a wretched wife.

I had plenty of my own money from my Father, I listened to nothing, and yielded to the act of love only on my own terms, which I always obtained, being gifted with enough beauty to make men really suffer.

I became a member of the Cult of Isis just to spite these husbands and get away from them, so that I could hang around at the Temple of Isis, where I spent an enormous amount of time with other interesting women, some far more adventurous and unconventional than I dared to be. I was attracted to whores. I saw the brilliant, loose women as having conquered a barrier which I, the loving daughter of my Father, would never conquer.

I became a regular at the Temple. I was initiated at last in a secret ceremony, and I walked in every procession of Isis in Rome.

My husbands loathed this. Maybe that's why after I came home to my Father I gave up the worship. Whatever, it was a good thing perhaps that I had. But fortune could not be so easily shaped by any decision of mine.

Now Isis was an imported goddess, from Egypt, of course, and the old Romans were as suspicious of her as they were of the terrible Cybele, the Great Mother from the Far East, who led her male devotees to castrate themselves. The whole city was filled with these 'Eastern cults,' and the conservative population thought them dreadful.

These cults weren't rational; they were ecstatic or euphoric. They offered a complete rebirth through understanding.

The typical conservative Roman was far too practical for that. If you didn't know by age five that the gods were made-up creatures and the myths invented stories, then you were a fool.

But Isis had a curious distinction – something that set her far apart from the cruel Cybele. Isis was a loving mother and goddess. Isis forgave her worshipers anything. Isis had come before all Creation. Isis was patient and wise.

That's why the most degraded woman could pray at the Temple. That's why none were ever turned away.

69

Like the Blessed Virgin Mary, who is so well known today throughout the East and West, the Queen Isis had conceived her divine child by divine means. From the dead and castrated Osiris, she had drawn the living seed by her own power. And many a time she was pictured or sculpted holding her divine son, Horus, on her knee. Her breast was bare in all innocence to feed the young god.

And Osiris ruled in the land of the dead, his phallus lost forever in the waters of the Nile, where an endless semen flowed from it, fertilizing the remarkable fields of Egypt every year when the River overflowed its banks.

The music of our Temple was divine. We used the sistrum, a small rigid metal lyre of sorts, and flutes and timbrels. We danced, and we sang together. The poetry of Isis's litanies was fine and rapturous.

Isis was the Queen of Navigation, much like the Blessed Virgin Mary would be called later, 'Our Lady Star of the Sea.'

When her statue was carried to the shore each year, the procession was so splendid that all Rome turned out to see the Egyptian gods with their animal heads, the huge abundance of flowers and the statue of the Queen Mother herself. The air rang with hymns. Her Priests and

Priestesses walked in white linen robes. She herself, made of marble, and carried high, holding her sacred sistrum, dressed regally in a Grecian gown with Grecian hair.

That was my Isis. I fell away from her after my last divorce. My Father didn't like the worship, and I myself had enjoyed it long enough. As a free woman, I wasn't infatuated with prostitutes. I had it infinitely better. I kept my Father's house and he was just old enough, in spite of his black hair and his remarkably sharp vision, that the Emperor left me alone.

I can't say I remembered or thought of Marius. No one had mentioned Marius for years. He had disappeared out of my mind after the Lupercalia. There was no force on Earth that could come between me and my Father.

My brothers all had good luck. They married well, had children and came home from the hard wars in which they fought, keeping the boundaries of the Empire.

My youngest brother, Lucius, I did not like much, but he was always a little anxious and given to drinking and apparently also to gambling, which very much annoyed his wife.

She I loved, as I did all my sisters-in-law and my nieces and nephews. I loved it when they descended upon the house, these flocks of

children, squealing and running rampant with
'Aunt Lydia's blessing,' as they were never
allowed to do at home.

The eldest of my brothers, Antony, was in
potential a great man. Fate robbed him of great-
ness. But he had been most ready for it, well
schooled, trained and most wise.

The only foolish thing I ever knew Antony to
do was say to me very distinctly once that Livia,
Augustus's wife, had poisoned him so that her
son, Tiberius, would rise. My Father, the only
other occupant of the room, told him sternly:

'Antony, never speak of that again! Not here,
not anywhere!' My Father stood up, and without planning it, put in perspective the style of
life which he and I lived. 'Stay away from the
Imperial Palace, stay away from the Imperial
families, be in the front ranks of the games and
always in the Senate, but don't get into their
quarrels and their intrigues!'

Antony was very angry but the anger had
nothing to do with my Father. 'I said it only to
those two to whom I can say it, you and Lydia.
I detest eating dinner with a woman who
poisoned her husband! Augustus should have
re-established the Republic. He knew when
death was coming.'

'Yes, and he knew that he could not restore

the Republic. It was simply impossible. The Empire had grown to Britannia in the North, beyond Parthia in the East; it covers Northern Africa. If you want to be a good Roman, Antony, then stand up and speak your conscience in the Senate. Tiberius invites this.'

'Oh, Father, you are much deceived,' said Antony.

My Father put an end to this argument.

But he and I did live exactly the life he had described.

Tiberius was immediately unpopular with the noisy Roman crowds. He was too old, too dry, too humorless, too puritanical and tyrannical at the same time.

But he had one saving grace. Other than his extensive love and knowledge of philosophy, he had been a very good soldier. And that was the most important characteristic the Emperor had to possess.

The troops honored him.

He strengthened the Praetorian Guard around the Palace, hired a man named Sejanus to run things for him. But he didn't bring legions into Rome, and he spoke a damned good line about personal rights and freedom, that is, if you could stay awake to listen. I thought him a brooder.

The Senate went mad with impatience when he refused to make decisions. They didn't want to make the decisions! But all this seemed relatively safe.

Then a horrible incident occurred which made me positively detest the Emperor whole-heartedly and lose all my faith in the man and his ability to govern.

This incident involved the Temple of Isis. Some clever evil man, claiming to be the Egyptian god Anubis, had enticed a highborn devotee of Isis to the Temple and gone to bed with her, fooling her completely, though how on Earth he did it I can't imagine.

I remember her to this day as the stupidest woman in Rome. But there's probably more to it.

Anyway, it had all happened at the Temple.

And then this man, this fake Anubis, went before the highborn virtuous woman and told her in the plainest terms that he had had her! She went screaming to her husband. It was a scandal of extraordinary flair.

It had been years since I had been at the Temple, and I was glad of it.

But what followed from the Emperor was more dreadful than I ever dreamed.

The entire Temple was razed to the very

ground. All the worshipers were banished from Rome, and some of them executed. And our Priests and Priestesses were crucified, their bodies hung on the tree, as the old Roman expression goes, to die slowly and to rot, for all to see.

My Father came into my bedroom. He went to the small shrine of Isis. He took the statue and smashed it on the marble floor. Then he picked up the larger pieces and smashed each of them. He made dust of her.

I nodded.

I expected him to condemn me for my old habits. I was overcome with sadness and shock at what had happened. Other Eastern cults were being persecuted. The Emperor was moving to take away the right of Sanctuary from various Temples throughout the Empire.

'The man doesn't want to be Emperor of Rome,' said my Father. 'He's been bent by cruelty and losses. He's stiff, boring and completely in terror for his life! A man who would not be Emperor cannot be Emperor. Not now.'

'Maybe he'll step down,' I said sadly. 'He has adopted the young General Germanicus Julius Caesar. This means Germanicus is to be his heir, does it not?'

'What good did it do to the earlier heirs of

Augustus when they were adopted?' my Father asked.

'What do you mean?' I asked.

'Use your head,' said my Father. 'We cannot continue pretending we are a Republic. We must define the office of this Emperor and the limits of his power! We must outline a form of succession other than murder!'

I tried to calm him.

'Father, let's leave Rome. Let's go to our house in Tuscany. It's always beautiful there, Father.'

'That's just it, we can't, Lydia,' he said. 'I have to remain here. I have to be loyal to my Emperor. I must do so for all my family. I must stand in the Senate.'

Within months, Tiberius sent off his young and handsome nephew Germanicus Julius Caesar to the East, just to get him away from the adulation of the Roman public. As I said, people spoke their minds.

Germanicus was supposed to be Tiberius's heir! But Tiberius was too jealous to listen to the crowds screaming praise of Germanicus for his victories in battle. He wanted the man far from Rome.

And so this rather charming and seductive young general went to the East, to Syria; he vanished from the loving eyes of the Roman people, from the core of the Empire where a city crowd could determine the fate of the world.

Sooner or later there would be another campaign in the North, we all figured. Germanicus had hit hard at the German tribes in his last campaign.

My brothers vividly described it to me over the dinner table.

They told how they had gone back to avenge the hideous massacre of General Varus and his troops in the Teutoburg Forest. They could finish the job, if called up again, and my brothers would go. They were exactly the kind of old-fashioned patricians who would go!

Meantime there were rumors that the *Delatores,* the notorious spies of the Praetorian Guard, pocketed one-third of the estate of those against whom they informed. I found it horrible. My Father shook his head, and said, 'That started under Augustus.'

'Yes, Father,' I said, 'but then treason was considered a matter of what one did, not what one said.'

'Which is all the more reason to say nothing.' He sat back wearily. 'Lydia, sing to me. Get your lyre. Make up one of your comic epics. It's been a long time.'

'I'm too old for that,' I said, thinking of the silly, bawdy satires on Homer which I used to make up so quickly and freely that everyone marveled. But I jumped at that idea. I remember that night so palpably that I cannot tear myself loose now from the writing of this story, even though I know what pain I must confess and explore.

What does it mean to write? David, you'll see this question repeated, because with each page I understand more and more – I see the patterns that have before eluded me, and driven me to dream rather than live.

That night I did make a very funny epic. My Father laughed. He fell asleep on his couch. And then, as if from a trance state, he spoke, 'Lydia, don't live out your life alone on account of me. Marry for love! You must not give up!'

By the time I turned around, he was breathing deeply again.

Two weeks later, or maybe it was a month, our life came abruptly to an end.

I came home one day, found the house completely empty except for two terrified old slave men – men who actually belonged to the household of my brother Antony – who let me in and bolted the door ferociously.

I walked through the huge vestibule and then

into the peristyle and into the dining room. I beheld an amazing sight.

My Father was in full battle dress, armed with sword and dagger, lacking only his shield. He even wore his red cloak. His breastplate was polished and gleaming.

He stared at the floor and with reason. It had been dug up. The old Hearth from generations ago had been dug up. This had been the first room of this house in the very ancient days of Rome, and it was around this Hearth that the family gathered, worshiped, dined.

I had never even seen it. We had our household Shrines, but this, this giant circle of burnt stones! There were actually ashes there, uncovered. How ominous and sacred it appeared.

'What in the name of the gods is going on?' I asked. 'Where is everybody?'

'They are gone,' he said. 'I have freed the slaves, sent them packing. I've been waiting for you. You have to leave here now!'

'Not without you!'

'You will not disobey me, Lydia!' I had never seen such an imploring yet dignified expression in his face. 'There's a wagon out back, ready to take you to the coast, and a Jewish merchant who is my most trusted friend who will take you by ship out of Italy! I want you to go! Your money's been loaded on board the ship. Your clothing. Everything. These are men I trust. Nevertheless take this dagger.'

He picked up a dagger from the nearby table and gave it to me. 'You've watched your brothers enough to know how to use it,' he said, 'and this.' He reached for a sack. 'This is gold, the currency that all the world accepts. Take it and go.'

I always carried a dagger, and it was in the sling on my forearm but I could not shock him with this just now, so I put the dagger in my girdle and took the purse.

'Father, I'm not afraid to stand by you! Who's turned on us? Father, you are Senator of Rome. Accused of any crime, you are entitled to a trial before the Senate.'

'Oh, my precious quick-witted daughter! You think that evil Sejanus and his *Delatores* bring charges out in the open? His *Speculatores* have already surprised your brothers and their wives and children. These are Antony's slaves. He sent them to warn me as he fought, as he died. He saw his son dashed against the wall. Lydia, go.'

Of course I knew this was a Roman custom – to murder the entire family, to wipe out the spouse and offspring of the condemned. It was even the law. And in matters such as this, when word got out that the Emperor had turned his back on a man, any of his enemies could precede the assassins.

'You come with me,' I said. 'Why do you stay here?'

'I will die a Roman in my house,' he said. 'Now go if you love me, my poet, my singer, my thinker. My Lydia. Go! I will not be disobeyed. I have spent the last hour of my life arranging for your salvation! Kiss me and obey me.'

I ran to him, kissed him on the lips and at once the slaves led me through the garden.

I knew my Father. I could not revolt against him in this final wish. I knew that, in old-fashioned Roman style, he would probably take his life before the *Speculatores* broke down the front door.

When I reached the gate, when I saw the Hebrew merchants and their wagon, I couldn't go.

This is what I saw.

My Father had cut both his wrists and was walking around the household hearth in a circle, letting the blood flow right down onto the floor. He had really given his wrists the slash. He was turning white as he walked. In his eyes there was an expression I would only come to understand later.

There came a loud crash. The front door was being bashed in. My Father stopped quite still. And two of the Praetorian Guard came at him, one making sneering remarks, 'Why don't you finish yourself off, Maximus, and save us the trouble. Go on.'

'Are you proud of yourselves!' my Father said. 'Cowards. You like killing whole families? How much money do you get? Did you ever fight in a true battle. Come on, die with me!'

Turning his back on them, he whipped around with sword and dagger, and brought down both of them, as they came at him, with unanticipated thrusts. He stabbed them repeatedly.

My Father wobbled as if he would faint. He was white. The blood flowed and flowed from his wrists. His eyes rolled up into his head.

Mad schemes came to me. We must get him into the wagon. But a Roman like my Father would never have cooperated.

Suddenly the Hebrews, one young and one elderly, had me by the arms and were carrying me out of the house.

'I vowed I would save you,' said the old man.

'And you will not make a liar of me to my old friend.'

'Let go of me!' I whispered. 'I will see him through it!'

Throwing them off in their polite timidity I turned and saw from a great distance my Father's body by the hearth. He had finished himself with his own dagger.

I was thrown into the wagon, my eyes closed, my hands over my mouth. I fell among soft pillows, bolts of fabric, tumbling as the wagon began to roll very slowly down the winding road of the Palatine Hill.

Soldiers shouted at us to get the hell out of the way.

The elderly Hebrew said, 'I am nearly deaf, sir, what did you say?'

It worked perfectly. They rode past us.

The Hebrew knew exactly what he was doing. As crowds rushed past us he kept to his slow pace.

The one young one came into the back of the wagon. 'My name is Jacob,' he said. 'Here, put on all these white mantles. You look now like an Eastern woman. If questioned at the gate, hold up your veil and pretend you do not understand.'

We went through the Gates of Rome with

amazing ease. It was 'Hail David and Jacob, has it been a good trip?'

I was helped aboard a large merchant vessel, with galley slaves and sails, nothing unusual at all, and then into a small barren wooden room.

'This is all we have for you,' said Jacob. 'But we are sailing now.' He had long wavy brown hair and a beard. He wore striped robes to the ground.

'In the dark?' I asked. 'Sailing in the dark?'

This was not usual.

But as we moved out, as the oars began to dip, and the ship found its proper distance and began to move South, I saw what we were doing.

All the beautiful Southwestern coast of Italy was well lighted by her hundreds and hundreds of palatial villas. Lighthouses stood on the rocks.

'We will never see the Republic again,' said Jacob wearily, as though he were a Roman citizen, which I think in fact he was. 'But your Father's last wish is fulfilled. We are safe now.'

The old man stepped up to me. He told me that his name was David.

The old man apologized profusely that there were no female attendants for me. I was the only woman on board.

'Oh, please, banish any such thoughts from your mind! Why have you taken these risks?'

'For years we have done business with your Father,' said David. 'Years ago, when pirates sank our ships, your Father carried the debt. He trusted us again, and we repaid him fivefold. He has laid up riches for you. They are all stowed, among cargo we carried, as if they were nothing.'

I went into the cabin and collapsed on the small bed. The old man, averting his eyes, brought a cover for me.

Slowly I realized something. I had fully expected them to betray me.

I had no words. I had no gestures or sentiments inside me. I turned my head to the wall. 'Sleep, lady,' he said.

A nightmare came to me, a dream such as I have never had in my life. I was near a river. I wanted to drink blood. I waited in high grass to catch one of the villagers, and when I had this poor man, I took him by his shoulders, and I sank two fang teeth into his neck. My mouth filled with delicious blood. It was too sweet and too potent to be described, and even in the dream I knew it. But I had to move on. The man was nearly dead. I let him fall. Others who were more dangerous were after me. And there was another terrible threat to my life.

I came to the ruins of a Temple, far from the marsh. Here it was desert – just with the snap of the fingers, from wetland to sand. I was afraid. Morning was coming. I had to hide. Besides, I was also being hunted. I digested this delicious blood, and I entered the Temple. No place to hide! I laid my whole body on the cold walls! They were graven with pictures. But there was no small room, no hiding place for me.

I had to make it to the hills before sunrise, but that wasn't possible. I was moving right towards the sun!

Suddenly, there came above the hills a great fatal light. My eyes hurt unbearably. They were on fire. 'My eyes,' I cried and reached to cover them. Fire covered me. I screamed. 'Amon Ra, I curse you!' I cried another name. I knew it meant Isis, but it was not that name, it was another title for her that flew from my lips.

I woke up. I sat bolt upright, shivering.

The dream had been as sharply defined as a vision. It had a deep resonance in me of memory. Had I lived before?

I went out on the deck of the ship. All was well enough. We could see the coastline clearly still, and the lighthouses, and the ship moved on. I stared at the sea, and I wanted blood.

'This is not possible. This is some evil omen, some twisted grief,' I said. I felt the fire. I could not shut out the taste of the blood, how natural it had seemed, how good, how perfect for my thirst. I saw the twisted body of the villager again in the marshes.

This was a horror; it was no escape from what I had just witnessed. I was incensed, and feverish.

Jacob, the tall young one, came to me. He had with him a young Roman. The young man had shaved his first beard, but otherwise he seemed a flushed and glistening child.

I wondered wearily if I were so old at thirty-five that everyone young looked beautiful to me.

He cried, 'My family, too, has been betrayed. My Mother made me leave!'

'To whom do we owe this shared catastrophe?' I asked. I put my hands on his wet cheeks. He had a baby's mouth, but the shaven beard was rough. He had broad strong shoulders, and wore only a light, simple tunic. Why wasn't he cold out here on the water? Perhaps he was.

He shook his head. He was pretty still and would be handsome later. He had a nice curl to his dark hair. He didn't fear his tears, or apologize for them.

'My Mother stayed alive to tell me. She lay gasping until I came. When the *Delatores* had told my Father that he plotted against the Emperor, my Father had laughed. He had actually laughed. They had accused him of plotting with Germanicus! My Mother wouldn't die until she'd told me. She said that all my Father was accused of doing was talking with other men about how he would serve under Germanicus again if they were sent North.'

I nodded wearily. 'I see. My brothers probably said the same thing. And Germanicus is the Emperor's heir and *Imperium Maius* of the East. Yet this is treason, to speak of serving Rome under a pretty general.'

I turned to go. To understand gave no consolation.

'We are taking you to different cities,' said Jacob, 'to different friends. Better that we not say.'

'Don't leave me,' said the boy. 'Not tonight.'

'All right,' I said. I took him into the cabin and closed the door, with a polite nod to Jacob, who was watching all with a guardian's conscience.

'What do you want?' I asked.

The boy stared at me. He shook his head. He flung his hands out. He turned and drew close to me and kissed me. We went into a rampage of kisses.

I took off my shift and sank into the bed with him. He was a man all right, tender face or no.

And when I came to the moment of ecstasy, which was quite easy, given his phenomenal stamina, I tasted blood. I was the blood drinker in the dream. I went limp, but it didn't matter. He had all he needed to finish the rites to his satisfaction.

He rose up. 'You're a goddess,' he said.

'No,' I whispered. The dream was rising. I heard the wind on the sand. I smelled the river. 'I am a god . . . a god who drinks blood.'

We did the rites of love until we could do them no more.

'Be circumspect and very proper with our Hebrew hosts,' I said. 'They will never understand this sort of thing.'

He nodded. 'I adore you.'

'Not necessary. What is your name?'

'Marcellus.'

'Fine, Marcellus, go to sleep.'

Marcellus and I made a night of every night after that until we finally saw the famous lighthouse of Pharos and knew we had come to Egypt.

It was perfectly obvious that Marcellus was

being left in Alexandria. He explained to me that his maternal grandmother was still alive, a Greek, and indeed her whole clan.

'Don't tell me so much, just go,' I said. 'And be wise and safe.'

He begged me to come with him. He said he had fallen in love with me. He would marry me. He didn't care if I bore no children. He didn't care that I was thirty-five. I laughed softly, mercifully.

Jacob noted all this with lowered eyes. And David looked away.

Quite a few trunks followed Marcellus into Alexandria.

'Now,' I said to Jacob, 'will you tell me where I'm being taken? I might have some thoughts on the matter, though I doubt I could improve on my Father's plan.'

I still wondered. Would they deal honestly with me? What about now that they had seen me play the whore with the boy? They were such religious men.

'You're headed to a great city,' Jacob said. 'It couldn't be a better place. Your Father has Greek friends there!'

'How could it be better than Alexandria?' I said.

'Oh, it is far and away better,' Jacob said.

'Let me talk to my Father before I talk to you further.'

We had put out to sea. The land was going away. Egypt. It was growing dark.

'Don't be afraid,' Jacob said. 'You look as though you are terrified.'

'I'm not afraid,' I said. 'It's only that I have to lie in my bed and think and remember and dream.' I looked at him, as he shyly looked away. 'I held the boy like a Mother, against me, night after night.'

This was about the biggest lie I've told in my life.

'He was a child in my arms.' Some child! 'And now I fear nightmares. You must tell me – what is our destination? What is our fate?'

3

'Antioch,' said Jacob, 'Antioch on the Orontes. Greek friends of your Father await you. And they are friends with Germanicus. Perhaps in time . . . but they will be loyal to you. You are to be married to a Greek of breeding and means.'

Married! To a Greek, a provincial Greek? A Greek in Asia! I stifled my laughter and my tears. That was not going to happen to me. Poor man! If he really was a provincial Greek, he was going to have to experience the conquest of Rome all over again.

We sailed on, from port to port. I mulled all this over.

It was nauseating trivia like this which of course protected me from my full and inevitable grief and shock over what happened. Worry about whether your dress is properly girdled.

Don't see your Father lying dead with his own dagger in his chest.

As for Antioch, I had been far too embroiled in the life of Rome to know or hear much about this city. If Tiberius had stationed his 'heir,' Germanicus, there to get him away from Roman popularity, then I thought: Antioch must be the end of the civilized world.

Why in the name of the gods had I not run away in Alexandria, I thought? Alexandria was the greatest city in the Empire, next to Rome. It was a young city, built by Alexander, for whom it was named, but it was a marvelous port. No one would ever dare raze the Temple of Isis in Alexandria. Isis was an Egyptian goddess, wife of the powerful Osiris.

But what had that to do with things? I must have been plotting in the back of my mind already, but I didn't allow any conscious plot to surface and blemish my highborn Roman moral character.

I quietly thanked my Hebrew guardians for this intelligence, for keeping it even from the young Roman Marcellus, the other man they had rescued from the Emperor's assassins, and I asked for frank answers to my questions regarding my brothers.

'All taken by surprise,' said Jacob. 'The

Delatores, those spies of the Praetorian Guard, are so swift. And your Father had so many sons. It was your eldest brother's slaves who jumped the wall at their Master's command and ran to warn your Father.'

Antony. I hope you shed their blood. I know you fought with your last breath. And my niece, my little niece Flora, had she run screaming from them, or did they do it with mercy? The Praetorian Guard doing anything with mercy! Stupid to even think so.

I didn't say anything aloud. Just sighed.

After all, when they looked at me, these two Jewish merchants beheld the body and face of a woman; naturally my protectors should think a woman was inside of me. The disparity between outward appearances and inner disposition had disturbed me all my life. Why disturb Jacob and David? On to Antioch.

But I had no intention of living in any old-fashioned Greek family, if such still existed in the Greek city of Antioch, a family in which women lived apart from the men, and wove wool all day, never going out, having no part in the life of the world whatsoever.

I'd been taught all the virtuous female arts by my nurses and I could indeed do anything with yarn or thread or loom that any other woman could do, but I knew well what the 'Old Greek Ways' had been, and I remembered vaguely my Father's Mother, who had died when I was very young – a virtuous Roman matron who was always making wool. So they had said of her in her Epitaph, and in fact, they had said in my Mother's Epitaph: 'She kept the House. She made wool.'

And so they had said of my Mother! The very same tiresome words.

Well, no one was going to say that on mine. (How humorous to reflect on the fact now, thousands of years later, that I have no Epitaph!)

What I failed to realize in my overall dejection was that the Roman world was enormous, and the Eastern portion of it differed dramatically from the Northern barbarian lands, where my brothers had fought.

The entire of Asia Minor, towards which we sailed, had been conquered by Alexander of Macedon hundreds of years before. As you know, Alexander had been the pupil of Aristotle. Alexander had wanted to spread Greek culture everywhere. And in Asia Minor Greek ideas and styles found not mere country towns or farmers, but ancient cultures, like the Empire of Syria, willing to receive the new ideas, the grace and beauty of the Greek enlightenment, and willing to bring in tune with it their own centuries-old literature, religion, styles of life and dress.

Antioch had been built by a general of Alexander the Great who sought to rival the beauty of other Hellenistic cities, with splendid Temples, administrative buildings and libraries of books in the Greek language, its schools where Greek philosophy was taught. A Hellenistic government was established – quite enlightened compared to ancient Eastern despotism, and yet there lay beneath all this the knowledge and customs and possibly the wisdom of the mysterious East.

The Romans had conquered Antioch early on because it was a huge trade center. It was unique in this way, as Jacob showed to me, drawing a crude map with his wet finger on the wooden table. Antioch was a port of the great Mediterranean because she was only twenty miles up the Orontes River.

Yet on the Eastern side she was open to the desert: all the old caravan routes came to Antioch, the camel merchants who brought fantastic wares from fabled lands – lands we know now to have been India and China – silk, carpet and jewels which never reached the markets of Rome.

Countless other traders came and went to
Antioch. Fine roads connected it in the East
with the Euphrates River and the Parthian
Empire beyond, and to the South you could go
to Damascus and Judea, and to the North, of
course, lay all the cities made by Alexander,
which had flowered under Roman rule.

Roman soldiers loved it there. It was an easy
and interesting life. And Antioch loved the
Romans because the Romans protected the
trade routes, and the caravans, and kept peace in
the port.

'You will find open places, arcades,
Temples, all that you seek and such markets
you would not believe. There are Romans
everywhere. I hope to One Most High that you
are not recognized by someone from your own
background! That is one danger of which your
Father had no time to plan.'

I waved it away.

'Does it have teachers now, and markets of
books?'

'From everywhere. You will find books
which no one can read. And Greek is spoken by
everyone. You have to go out in the country to
find some poor farmer who does not understand
Greek. Latin has now become common.

'The philosophers never stop; they speak of

97

Plato and Pythagoras, names that don't mean much to me; they talk about Chaldean magic from Babylon. Of course there are Temples to every imaginable god.'

He went on, reflecting as he spoke:

'The Hebrews? I think personally they are too worldly – they want to hang around in short tunics with the Greeks and go to the public baths. They are too interested in the Greek philosophy. It invades everything, all this thinking that Greeks did. Not good. But a Greek city is an inviting world.'

He glanced up. His Father was watching over us, and we were too close together, at this table on the deck.

He hastily filled me in on other facts:

Germanicus Julius Caesar, heir to the Imperial throne, the official adopted son of Tiberius, had been granted the *Imperium Maius* in Antioch. That is, he controlled all of this territory. And Gnaeus Calpurnius Piso was the governor of Syria.

I assured him that they would know nothing of me or my old-fashioned family or our quiet, old house on the Palatine Hill, squeezed between so many other extravagant new mansions.

'It's all Roman-style,' Jacob protested. 'You'll see. And you come with money! And forgive me, but you are still beautiful at your age; you have fresh skin and you move your limbs like a girl.'

I sighed and gave Jacob thanks. Time for him to break away unless we wanted his Father coming down upon us.

I watched the ever rolling blue waves.

I was thankful in secret that our family had withdrawn from the parties and banquets at the Imperial Palace, but then I blamed myself for such thankfulness, knowing that our reclusiveness must have paved the way for our downfall.

I'd seen Germanicus on his triumphal procession through Rome, a gorgeous young man, much as Alexander had been, and I knew from my Father and my brothers that Tiberius, fearing the popularity of his appointed heir, had sent him off to the East to get him away from the Roman crowds.

The Governor Piso? I had never laid eyes on him. The gossip was that he was sent East to devil Germanicus. Oh, such a waste of talent and thought.

Jacob returned to me.

'Well, you go nameless and unknown into this vast city,' said Jacob. 'And you have protectors of high character who are beloved of Germanicus. He's young and sets a tone of vitality and gaiety in the city.'

'And Piso?' I asked.

'Everyone hates him. Especially the soldiers, and you know what that means in a Roman province.'

You can look at the crashing, undulating sea from the railing of a deck forever, or just for so long.

That night I had my second blood dream. It was keenly similar to the first. I was thirsty for blood. And enemies were after me, enemies that knew I was a demon and must be destroyed. I was running. My own kind had forsaken me, thrust me out unprotected to the superstitions of the people. Then I saw the desert and knew I would die; I awoke, sitting up and crying out, but covering my mouth quickly so no one heard it.

What disturbed me so terribly was the thirst for blood. I could not imagine such a thing when I was awake, but in these dreams I was the monster that Romans called the Lamia. Or so it seemed. Blood was sweet, blood was all. Was the old Greek Pythagoras right? Souls do migrate from body to body? But my soul in this past life had been that of a monster.

During the day, I closed my eyes now and then and found myself dangerously on the edge of the dream, as if it were a trap in my mind, waiting to engulf my consciousness. But at night, that is when they came most strongly. *You have served me before!* What could this mean? *Come to me.*

Blood thirst. I closed my eyes, curled up in bed and prayed, 'Mother Isis, Cleanse my Mind of this Blood madness.'

Then I resorted to plain old ordinary eroticism. Get Jacob into bed! No such luck. Little did I know that Hebrews had been, and would be forever, the most difficult of men to seduce!

It was all made clear with great grace and tact.

I considered all the slaves. Out of the question. First off were the galley slaves, among whom no great 'Ben Hur' was chained, waiting for me to rescue him. They were just the dregs of the criminal poor, fastened Roman-style, so they would drown if the ship went down, and they were dying, as all galley slaves do from the monotony and the whip. It wasn't a pleasant sight to go down into the hold of a galley ship and see those men bending their backs.

But my eyes were as cold as those of an American watching color television pictures of the starving babies of Africa, little black skeletons with big heads screaming for water. News Break, Commercial Break, Sound Bite, CNN now switches to Palestine: rock throwing, rubber bullets. Television blood.

The rest on board were boring sailors, and two old pious merchant Hebrews who stared at me as if I were a whore, or worse, and turned their heads whenever I came out on deck in my long tunic with my long hair swinging free.

Such a disgrace I must have seemed! But what a fool I was then, really, living in numbness, and how pleasant that voyage – all because true grief and rage had not yet taken hold of me. Things had happened too fast.

I gloated over my last glimpse of my Father dispatching those soldiers of Tiberius, those cheap assassins sent by a cowardly, indecisive Emperor. And the rest – I banished it from my mind, affecting the attitude of the hardened Roman man or woman.

A modern Irish poet, Yeats, best characterizes the official Roman attitude towards failure and tragedy.

Cast a cold eye on life, on death.
Horseman, pass by!

There was never a Roman born who would not have agreed with that.

That was my stance – sole survivor of a great

house, commanded by her Father to 'live.' I didn't dare to dwell on the fate of my brothers, their lovely wives, their little children. I couldn't envision the slaughter of the children – little boys being run through by broadswords, or babies bashed against the wall. Oh, Rome, you and your bloody old wisdom. Be sure to kill the offspring. Kill the whole family!

Lying alone at night, I found myself amid more horrid blood dreams. They seemed fragments of a lost life, a lost land. Deep echoing vibrant tones of music dominated the dreams, as though someone were striking a gong, and others beside him beat solemnly on deep drums with soft coverings. I saw in a haze a world of stiff and flat alien paintings on the walls. Painted eyes around me. I drank blood! I drank it from a small shuddering human being, who knelt before me as if I were Mother Isis.

I woke to take the big jug of water by my bed and drink all of it down. I drank water to defy and satisfy this dream thirst. I was almost sick from drinking water.

I racked my mind. Had I ever had such dreams as a child?

No. And now these dreams had the heat of recollection! Of initiation into the doomed Temple of Isis, when it had been still the fashion. I had been intoxicated, and drenched in the blood of a bull, and dancing wildly in circles. My head was filled with the litanies of Isis. We were promised rebirth! 'Never tell, never tell, never tell . . .' How could an initiate tell anything of the rites, when you were so drunk you could hardly remember them?

Isis brought me memories now of lovely music of lyres, flutes, timbrels, of the high magical sound of the metal strings of the sistrum, which the Mother Herself held in her hand. There were only fleeting recollections of that naked blood dance, that night of rising into the stars, of seeing the scope of life in its cycles, of accepting perfectly just for a little while that the moon would always be changing, and the sun would set as it always rose. Embraces of other women. Soft cheeks and kissing and bodies rocking in unison. 'Life, death, rebirth, it's no series of miracles,' said the Priestess. 'To understand it and accept it, that is the miracle. Make the miracle within your own breast.'

Surely we had not drunk blood! And the bull – it was a sacrifice only for the initiation. We did not bring helpless animals to her flower-laden altars, no, our Blessed Mother did not ask that of us.

Now, at sea, alone, I lay awake to avoid

these blood dreams.

When exhaustion won out, a dream came with sleep as if it had been waiting for my eyes to close.

I lay in a gold chamber. I was drinking blood, blood from the throat of a god, or so it seemed, and choruses were singing or chanting – it was a dull, repetitive sound not quite worthy of being called music, and when I had had my fill of blood, this god or whoever this was, this silken-skinned proud thing, lifted me and placed me on an altar.

Vividly, I could feel the cold marble beneath me. I realized I wore no clothes. I felt no modesty. Somewhere far off, echoing through these great halls, came the weeping of a woman. I was full of blood. Those who chanted approached with little clay oil lamps. Faces around me were dark, dark enough to be from far faraway Ethiopia or India. Or Egypt. Look. Painted eyes! I looked at my hands and arms. They were dark. But I was this person who lay on the altar, and I say person now because it had come clear to me with no disturbance during the dream itself that I was a man lying there. Pain tore at me. The god said, 'This is merely the passage. You will now drink from each of us, only a little blood.'

Only when I woke did the brief transition in

the masculine gender leave me as puzzled as everything else. I was drenched with a sense of Egyptian art, Egyptian mystery – as I'd seen it in golden statues for sale in the marketplace, or when the Egyptian dancers performed at a banquet, like walking sculptures with their black-lined eyes, and black plaited wigs, whispering in that mysterious tongue. What had they thought of our Isis in Roman dress?

A mystery taunted me; something attacked my reason. The very thing the Roman Emperors had so feared in Egyptian cults and Oriental cults swept over me: mystery and emotion which claim a superiority to reason and law.

My Isis had been a Roman goddess, really, a universal goddess, the Mother of us all, her worship spreading out in a Greek and Roman world long before it had come into Rome itself. Our Priests were Greeks and Roman, poor men. We the congregation were all Greeks and Romans.

Something scratched at the back of my mind. It said, 'Remember.' It was a tiny desperate voice within my own brain that urged me to 'remember' for my own sake.

But remembering only led to confused and jumbled thoughts. Suddenly a veil would fall between the reality of my cabin on the ship, and the tumbling of the sea – between that and some dim and frightening world, of Temples covered in words that made magic! Long narrow beautifully bronzed faces. A voice whispered, 'Beware the Priests of Ra; they lie!'

I shivered. I closed my eyes. The Queen Mother was bound and chained to her throne! She wept! It had been her crying. Unspeakable. 'But you see, she has forgotten how to rule. Do as we say.'

I shook myself awake. I wanted to know and I did not want to know. The Queen wept beneath her monstrous fetters. I couldn't see her clearly. It was all in progress. It was busy. 'The King is with Osiris, you see. You see how he stares; each one whose blood you drink, you give to Osiris; each one becomes Osiris.'

'But why did the Queen scream?'

No, this was madness. I couldn't let this confusion overcome me. I couldn't deliberately slip from reason into these fantasies or recollections supposing they had a true root.

They had to be nonsense, twisted images of grief and guilt, guilt that I had not rushed to the hearth and driven the dagger into my breast.

I tried to remember the calming voice of my Father, explaining once how the blood of the gladiators satisfied the thirst of the dead, the *Manes*.

'Now, some say that the Dead drink blood,' spoke my Father from some long ago dinner talk. 'That's why we are so fearful on all these unlucky days, when the Dead are supposed to be able to walk the Earth. I personally think this is nonsense. We should revere our ancestors . . .'

'Where are the Dead, Father?' my brother Lucius asked.

Who had piped up from the other side of the table, to quote Lucretius in a sad little female voice that nevertheless commanded silence of all these men? Lydia:

Of earth return to earth, but any part
Sent down from heaven, must ascend again
Recalled to the high temples of the sky
And death does not destroy the elements
Of matter, only breaks the combinations.

'No,' my Father had replied to me quite gently. 'Rather quote Ovid: "The ghosts ask for but little; they value piety more than a costly gift."' He drank his wine. 'The ghosts are in the Underworld where they can't harm us.'

My eldest brother Antony had said, 'The Dead are nowhere and are nothing.'

My Father had raised his cup. 'To Rome,' he said, and it was he this time who had quoted

Lucretius: ' "Too many times, religion mothers crimes and wickedness." '

Shrugs and sighs all around. The Roman attitude. Even the Priests and Priestesses of Isis would have joined Lucretius when he wrote:

Our terrors and our darknesses of mind
Must be dispelled, then, not by sunshine's
    rays,
Not by those shining arrows of light,
But by insight into nature, and a scheme
Of systematic contemplation.

Drunk? Drugged? Bull's blood? Systematic? Well, it all came down to the same thing. Know! Twist the poetry as you will. And the phallus of Osiris lives forever in the Nile, and the water of the Nile inseminates the Mother Egypt eternally, death giving birth to life with the blessing of Mother Isis. Merely a particular scheme and a sort of systematic form of contemplation.

The ship sailed on.

I languished some eight more days in this torment, often lying awake in the dark, and sleeping only in the day to avoid the dreams.

Suddenly, in the early morning, Jacob pounded my door.

We were midway up the Orontes to the city.

Twenty miles now from Antioch. I did up my hair as best I could (I'd never done it without a slave) into a chignon on the back of my head, then covered my Roman gowns with a great black cloak and prepared to disembark – an Eastern woman, her face draped, protected by Hebrews.

When the city came into view – when the immense harbor greeted us and then embraced us with all its masts and racket and odors and cries, I ran to the deck of the ship and looked out at this city. It was splendid.

'You see,' Jacob said.

Taken from the ship by litter I found myself carried rapidly through vast waterfront markets, and then into a great open square, crowded with people. I saw everywhere the Temples, porticoes, booksellers, even the high walls of an amphitheater – all that I could have expected in Rome. No, this was no town.

The young men were crowded about the barbershops ready to have their obligatory shave and the inevitable fancy curls on their foreheads, which Tiberius with his own hairstyle had made fashionable. There were wine shops all over. The slave markets were jammed. I glimpsed the entrances to the streets devoted to crafts – the street of the tentmakers, the street of the silversmiths.

And there in all its glory, in the very center of Antioch, stood the Temple of Isis!

My goddess, Isis, with her worshipers coming and going, undisturbed, and in huge numbers. A few very proper-looking linen-clad Priests stood at the doors! The Temple was aswarm.

I thought, I can run away from any husband in this place!

Gradually I realized a great commotion had come upon the Forum, the center of the city. I heard Jacob ordering the men to hurry out of the broad market street and into the back streets. My bearers were running. The curtains were brought shut by Jacob's hand so I couldn't see out.

News was being shouted out in Latin, in Greek, in Chaldean: Murder, Murder, Poison, Treachery.

I peeped out of the curtain.

People were weeping and cursing the Roman Gnaeus Calpurnius Piso, cursing him and his wife, Placina. Why? I didn't much like either one of them, but what was all this?

Jacob shouted again at my bearer to hurry.

We were rushed through the gates and into the vestibule of a sizable house no different in design or color than my own in Rome, only much smaller. I could see the same refinements, the distant peristyle, clusters of weeping slaves.

The litter was promptly set down and I stepped out, deeply concerned that they had not stopped me at the doors to wash my feet, as was proper. And my hair, it had all fallen down in waves.

But no one noticed me. I turned round and round, amazed at the Oriental curtains and tassels that hung over the doorways, the caged birds everywhere singing in their little prisons. The woven carpets lying all over the floor, one heaped upon another.

Two obvious ladies of the house came towards me.

'What's the matter!' I asked.

They were as fashionable as any rich woman in Rome, drenched in bracelets and wearing gold-trimmed gowns.

'I implore you,' said one of the women, 'for your own sake, go! Get back into the litter!'

They tried to push me inside the curtained cell of the litter. I wouldn't go. I became furious.

'I don't know where I am,' I said. 'And I don't know who you are! Now, stop pushing me!'

The Master of the House, or someone who certainly appeared to be such, came dashing towards me, with tears streaming down his cheeks and his short tousled gray hair a mess – torn as if in mourning. He'd ripped his long tunic. He'd smeared dirt on his face! He was old with a bent back and a massive head, loaded with skin and wrinkles.

'Your Father was my young colleague,' he said to me in Latin. He grabbed me by the arms. 'I dined in your house when you were a baby. I saw you when you crawled on all fours.'

'Tender,' I said quickly.

'Your Father and I studied in Athens, slept under the same roof.'

The women stood panic-stricken with their hands over their mouths.

'Your Father and I fought with Tiberius on his first campaign. We fought those lurid barbarians.'

'Very brave,' I said.

My black outer cloak fell down, revealing my unkempt wild long hair and plain dress. Nobody cared.

'Germanicus dined in this house because your Father spoke of me!'

'Oh dear, I see,' I said.

One of the women motioned for me to get in the litter. Where was Jacob? The old man wouldn't let me go.

113

'I stood with your Father and with Augustus when news came to us of the massacre of our troops in the Teutoburg Forest, that General Varus and all his men were slain. My sons fought with your brothers in the legions of Germanicus when he punished those Northern tribes! Oh, God!'

'Yes, very marvelous, indeed,' I said gravely.

'Get back in the litter and get out,' said one of the women.

The old man clutched me.

'We fought the madman, King Arminius!' said the old man. 'We could have won! Your brother Antony wasn't for giving up and coming back, was he?'

'I . . . no . . .'

'Get her out of here!' screamed a young patrician man, who had also been weeping. He came forward and shoved me towards the litter.

'Stand back, you imbecile!' I said to him. I slapped his face.

All this while, Jacob had been talking to the slaves, getting the scoop.

Jacob appeared beside me, as the gray-haired Greek sobbed and kissed my cheeks.

Jacob took over, guiding me into the litter.

'Germanicus has just been murdered,' Jacob said in my ear. 'Everybody loyal to him is convinced that the Emperor Tiberius put the Roman Governor Piso up to the murder. It was done with poison. Word is spreading through the city like fire.'

'Tiberius, you idiot!' I whispered, rolling my eyes. 'One cowardly step after another!'

I sank back into the darkness. The litter was being lifted.

Jacob went right on: 'Gnaeus Calpurnius Piso has allies here, naturally. Everybody's fighting everybody else. Settling scores. Mayhem. This Greek family traveled with Germanicus to Egypt. There are riots already. We go!'

'Farewell, friend,' I cried to the old Greek, as I was carried from the house. But I don't think he heard me. He had gone down on his knees. He cursed Tiberius. He screamed of suicide and begged for the dagger.

We were outside once more, hurrying through the street.

I lay askew in the litter, thinking dully in the darkness. Germanicus dead. Poisoned by Tiberius!

I knew that this recent trip of Germanicus to Egypt had made Tiberius very angry. Egypt was like no other Roman province. Rome was so dependent upon it for grain that Senators could not go there. But Germanicus had gone, 'just to see the ancient relics,' his friends had said in the streets of Rome.

'A mere excuse!' I thought in desperation. 'Where was the trial? The sentence? Poison!'

My bearers were running. People were screaming and sobbing around us. 'Germanicus, Germanicus! Give us back our beautiful Germanicus!'

Antioch had gone mad.

At last, we were obviously in a small narrow street that was little more than an alleyway – you know the kind, for a grid of them was uncovered in the ruins of Pompeii in Italy. You could smell the male urine collected in the jugs on the corner. You could smell food cooking from high chimneys. My bearers were running and stumbling over rough cobblestones.

Once we were all thrown to the side as a chariot came crashing through the narrow place, its wheels no doubt finding the ruts in the stone intended for it.

My head had hit the wall. I was furious and frightened. But Jacob said, 'Lydia, we are with you.'

I covered up all over with the cloak, so that only one eye allowed me to see the seams of light between the curtains on either side of me. I had my hand on my dagger.

The litter was set down. It was a cool indoor place. I heard Jacob's father, David, arguing. I knew no Hebrew. And I wasn't even sure that he was speaking in Hebrew.

Finally, Jacob took over in Greek, and I realized that they were purchasing outright a proper house for me which came with all fine appointments, including much fine furniture, left recently by a rich widow who had lived there alone, but alas, the slaves had been sold off. No slaves. This was a quick cash deal.

Finally, I heard Jacob say in Greek:

'You damn well better be telling me the truth.'

As the litter was lifted I beckoned to him. 'I owe you my life twice over now. That Greek family who was to shelter me? They are truly in danger?'

'Of course,' he said. 'When a riot starts, who cares? They went with Germanicus to Egypt! Piso's men know that! Anybody with the slightest excuse will attack, murder and plunder someone else. Look, fire.' He told the men to hurry.

'All right,' I said. 'Never say my real name again. From now on say this name: My name is Pandora. I am a Greek from Rome. I paid you to bring me here.'

117

'You have it, my dear Pandora,' he replied. 'You are some strong woman. The Deed to your new house is made up in a fake name with less charm. But the Deed verifies you are widowed, emancipated and a Roman Citizen. We'll get the Deed when we pay up the gold, which we won't do until we are in the house. And if the man does not give me that Deed with everything written out in full to protect you, I'll strangle him!'

'You're very clever, Jacob,' I said wearily.

On and on went this dark bouncing journey in the litter until at last it came to a halt. I could hear the metal key turning in the lock of the gate, and then we were brought into the large vestibule of the house itself.

I should have waited out of consideration for my guardians, but frantically I climbed out of this miserable little black veiled prison, throwing off the cloak and taking a deep breath.

We were in the broad vestibule of a fine house, with great charm to it and much ingenuity in its decoration.

Even now, my thoughts scattered, I saw the lion-head fountain right near the gate through which we'd just come, and I washed my feet in the cool of the water.

The receiving room, or atrium, was huge, and

beyond it I saw the rich couches of the dining room on the far side of a rather large enclosed garden – the peristyle.

It was not my massive ancient opulent old home on the Palatine Hill, which had grown new corridors and rooms over many generations, penetrating its broad gardens.

It was a bit too glossy. But it was grand. All the walls were freshly painted with a more Oriental bent, I think – more swirls and serpentine lines. How could I judge? I could have fainted from relief. Would people really leave me alone here?

There sat the desk in the atrium, and near it books! Along the porticoes flanking the garden, I saw the many doors; I looked up and saw the second-story windows closed on the porches. Splendor. Safety.

The mosaic floors were old; I knew the style, the festive figures of the Saturnalia on parade. They had to have been brought here from Italy.

Little real marble, plastered columns, but so many well-executed murals full of the requisite happy nymphs.

I went out into the soft wet grass of the peristyle and looked up at the blue sky.

I wanted only to breathe, but now came the moment of truth regarding my belongings. I was too dazed to ask about what was mine. And as it turned out, no such thing was necessary.

Jacob and David first did an entire inventory of the household furnishings they were purchasing for me, as I stood there staring at them in near disbelief at their patience with detail.

And when they'd found every room quite fine, and a bedchamber down the hall to the right, and a small open garden somewhere to the left, beyond the kitchen, they went upstairs, found things proper and then unloaded my possessions. Trunk followed trunk.

Then to my utter shock, Jacob's father, David, drew out a scroll and actually started taking a full inventory of everything that belonged to me, from hairpins to ink and gold.

Jacob was meantime sent on an errand!

I could see the hasty writing of my Father on this inventory that David read under his breath.

'Personal toilet articles,' David said in final summation of one portion of this examination. 'Clothes, one, two, three trunks – to the largest bedroom, go! Household plate to the kitchen. Books here?'

'Yes, please.' I was too shocked at his honesty and meticulousness to speak.

'Ah, so many books!'

'Fine, don't count them!' I said.

'I cannot, you see, these fragile . . .'

'Yes, I know. Carry on.'

'You want your ivory and ebony shelves assembled here in the front room?'

'Magnificent.'

I slumped down on the floor, only to be lifted at once by two helpful Asian slaves and settled in an amazingly soft cross-legged Roman chair. I was given a cup of fresh clean-smelling water. I drank it down, thought of blood. Closed my eyes.

'Ink, writing materials on the desk?' asked the old man.

'If you will,' I sighed.

'Now, everybody out,' said the old man, dispensing coins quickly and generously to these Asian slaves, who bowed from the waist and backed out of the room, nearly stumbling over each other.

I was about to try to form some sensible words of gratitude when a fresh brace of slaves rushed in – nearly colliding with the departing crew – carrying baskets of everything edible that a marketplace could yield, including at least nine kinds of bread, jugs of oil, melons, green vegetables and much smoked food that would last for days – fish, beef and exotic sea creatures dried out to look like parchment.

At once to the kitchen, save for a plate of olives and cheese and bread at once for the lady on that table to her left. Fetch the lady's wine, which her Father has sent.

Oh, how incredible. My Father's wine.

Then everyone was ordered out again with lots of coins freely given and the old man at once returned to his inventory.

'Jacob, come here, count for me this gold as I read off the list to you! Plate, coin, more coin, jewels of exceptional value? Coin, bars of gold. Yes . . .'

On and on they went, rushing at it.

Where had my Father hidden all this gold? I couldn't imagine it.

What was I going to do with it? Were they really going to let me keep this? They were honest men but this was such a fortune.

'You must wait until everyone is gone,' said David, 'and then hide this gold yourself in various places about the house. You will find such places. We cannot do that for you, for then we would know where it was. Your jewels? Some I leave here to be hidden for they are much too valuable to be flashed abroad among the populace in your first days.' He opened a casket of gems. 'See this ruby? It is superb. Look at the size of it. This can feed you for the rest of your life if sold to a honest man for half of its worth. Every jewel in this box is exceptional. I know jewels. These are hand-picked from the finest. See these pearls? Perfection.' He returned the ruby and the pearls to the casket and shut the lid.

'Yes,' I said weakly.

'Pearls, more gold, silver, plate . . .' he muttered. 'It's all here! We should take more care but . . .'

'Oh, no, you have done wonders,' I declared.

I stared at the bread and the wine in the cup. My Father's wine bottle. My Father's amphorae around the room.

'Pandora,' said Jacob, addressing me most seriously. 'Here in my hand is the Deed to this house. And another paper which describes your official entry into the port under your new made-up name, Julia, La, La, La and so forth. Pandora, we have to leave you.'

The old man shook his head and bit his lip.

'We have to sail for Ephesus, child,' he said. 'I am ashamed that I must leave you, but the harbor will soon be blocked!'

'There are ships on fire already in the harbor,' said Jacob under his breath. 'They've pulled down the statue of Tiberius in the Forum.'

'The transaction is closed,' said the old man

to me. 'The man who sold the house has never laid eyes on you and does not know your real name, and there is no evidence of it remaining here. Those were not his slaves who brought you here.'

'You've done miracles for me,' I said.

'You are on your own, my beautiful Roman princess,' Jacob said. 'It hurts my soul to leave you like this.'

'We must,' said the old man.

'Don't go out for three days,' said Jacob, coming near to me, about as near as he could, as if he even meant to break all the rules and kiss my cheek. 'There are enough legions here to quell this riot, but they will let it burn itself out, rather than slaughter Roman citizens. And forget those Greek friends. Their house is already an inferno.'

They turned to leave!

'Were you well paid for all this?' I asked. 'If not, take from my gold now, freely. I insist!'

'Don't even think of such things,' said the old man. 'But for your peace of mind, know this: your Father staked me twice after my ships were captured by pirates in the Adriatic. Your Father put his money in with mine and I made profits for both of us. The Greek owed your Father money. Worry about those matters no more. But we must go!'

'God be with you, Pandora,' said Jacob.

Jewels. Where were the jewels? I leapt up and opened the casket. There were hundreds of them, flawless, dazzlingly clear and exquisitely polished. I saw their value, their clarity and the care of the polishing. I took the big egg-shaped ruby David had shown to me and then another just like it and thrust them at the two men.

They put up their hands to say No.

'Oh, but you must,' I said. 'Give me this respect. Confirm for me that I am a free Roman woman and that I shall live as my Father told me to do! It will give me courage! Take this from me.'

David shook his head sternly, but Jacob took the ruby.

'Pandora, here, the keys. Follow us and lock the gate at the street and then the doors to the vestibule. Don't fear. There are lamps everywhere. Plenty of oil –'

'Go!' I said as they passed over the threshold. I locked the gate and held to the bars, staring at them. 'If you can't get out, if you need me, come back here,' I said.

'We have our own people here,' Jacob said soothingly. 'Thank you from my heart for the beautiful ruby, Pandora. You will survive. Go back in, bolt the doors.'

I made it to the chair but I did not sit in it. Rather I collapsed and prayed, '*Lares familiares* . . . spirits of the house, I should find your altar. Welcome me, please, I bring no ill will to anyone. I will heap your altar with flowers and light your fire. Give me patience. Let me . . . rest.'

Yet I did nothing but sit in shock on the floor, my hands limp, for hours as the daylight waned. As the strange little house grew dark.

A blood dream began, but I wouldn't have it. Not that alien Temple. Not the altar, no! Not the blood. I banished it and imagined I was home.

I was a little girl. Dream of that, I told myself, of listening to my eldest brother, Antony, talk of war in the North, driving the mad Germans back to the sea! He had so loved Germanicus. So had my other brothers. Lucius, the young one, he was so weak by nature. It broke my heart to think of him crying out for mercy as soldiers cut him down.

The Empire was the world. All that lay beyond was chaos and misery and struggle and strife. I was a soldier. I could fight. I dreamt I was putting on my armor. My brother said, 'I am so relieved to discover you are a man, I always thought so.'

I didn't waken till the following morning.

And then it was that grief and pain made

themselves known to me as never before.

Note this. Because I knew the full absurdity of Fate and Fortune and Nature more truly than a human can bear to know it. And perhaps the description of this, brief as it is, may give consolation to another. The worst takes its time to come, and then to pass.

The truth is, you cannot prepare anyone for this, nor convey an understanding of it through language. It must be known. And this I would wish on no one in the world.

I was alone. I went from room to room of this small house, banging upon the walls with my fists and crying with my teeth clenched, and whirling. There was no Mother Isis.

There were no gods. Philosophers were fools! Poets sang lies.

I sobbed and tore at my hair; I tore at my dress as naturally as if it had been a newborn custom. I knocked over chairs and tables.

At times I felt a huge exhilaration, a freedom from all falsehoods and conventions, all means by which a soul or body can be held hostage!

And then the awesome nature of this freedom spread itself out around me as if the house did not exist, as if the darkness knew no walls.

Three nights and days I spent in this agony.

I forgot to eat food. I forgot to drink water.

I never lighted a lamp. The moon nearing her fullness gave enough light to this meaningless labyrinth of little painted chambers.

Sleep was gone from me forever.

My heart beat fast. My limbs clenched, then slackened, only to clench again.

At times, I lay on the moist good Earth of the courtyard, for my Father, because no one had laid his body on the moist good Earth, as it should have been done, right after his death and before any funeral.

I knew suddenly why this disgrace was so important, his body rent with wounds and not placed on the Earth. I knew the gravity of this omission as few have ever known the meaning of anything. It was of the utmost importance because it did not matter at all!

Live, Lydia.

I looked at the small leafy trees of the garden. I felt a strange gratitude that I had opened human eyes in this darkness on Earth long enough to see such things.

I quoted Lucretius:

'That which comes from Heaven ascends to Heaven'?

Madness!

Alas, as I said, I wandered, crawled, wept and cried for three nights and days.

4

Finally, one morning, when the sun came spilling down through the open roof, I looked at the objects in the room and I realized I didn't know what they were, or what they'd been made for. I didn't know their common names. I was removed from their definitions. I didn't even know this place.

I sat up and realized I was looking at the Lararium, the shrine of the household gods.

This was the dining room of course, and those were the couches, and there the glorious conjugal bed!

The Lararium was a high three-sided shrine, a little temple with three pediments, and inside stood figures of old household gods. No one in this profane city had even taken them away with the dead woman.

The flowers were dead. The fire had simply

gone out. No one had quenched it with wine, as should have been done.

On hands and knees I crawled in my torn dress around the garden of the peristyle, gathering flowers for these gods. I found the wood and made their sacred fire.

I stared at them. I stared for hours. It seemed I would never move again.

Night fell. 'Don't sleep,' I whispered. 'Keep watch with the night! They wait for you by dark, those Egyptians! The moon, look, it's almost full, only a night or so from being full.'

But the worst of my agony had passed and I was exhausted, and sleep rose to embrace me. Sleep rose as if to say 'Care no more.'

The dream came.

I saw men in gilded robes. 'You will be taken now in the sanctum.' But what's there? I didn't want to see. 'Our Mother, our beloved Mother of Sorrows,' said the Priest. The paintings on the walls were rows upon rows of Egyptians in profile, and words made of pictures. Myrrh burned in this place.

'Come,' said those who held me. 'All the impurities have gone from you now, and you will partake of the sacred Fount.'

I could hear a woman crying and moaning. I peeped into the great room before I entered it.

There they were, the King and the Queen on their thrones, the King still and staring as in the last dream, and the Queen struggling against her golden fetters. She wore the crown of Upper and Lower Egypt. And pleated linen. Her hair was not a wig but real plaits. She cried and her white cheeks were stained in red. Red stained her necklace and her breasts. She looked soiled and ignominious.

'My Mother, my goddess,' I said. 'But this is an abomination.'

I forced myself to wake.

I sat up and I laid my hand on the Lararium, and looked at the spiderwebs in the trees of the garden, made visible by the climbing sun.

I thought I heard people whispering in the ancient Egyptian tongue.

I was not going to allow this! I would not go mad.

Enough! The only man I had ever loved, my Father, said, 'Live.'

It was time for action. To get up and get going. I was suddenly all strength and purpose.

My long nights of mourning and weeping had been equivalent to the initiation in the Temple; death had been the intoxicant; comprehension had been the transformation.

It was over now, and the meaningless world

was tolerable and need not be explained. And never would it be, and how foolish I had ever been to think so.

The facts of my predicament warranted action.

I poured out a cup of wine, and took it with me to the front gate.

The city seemed quiet. People walked to and fro, casting their eyes away from a half-dressed, ragged woman in her vestibule.

At last a workman trudging under his burden of bricks.

I thrust forth the wine. 'I have been ill for three days,' I said. 'What of the death of Germanicus? How goes it in the city?'

The man was so grateful for the wine. Labor had made him old. His arms were thin. His hands shook.

'Madam, thank you,' he said. He drained the cup, as if he could not stop himself. 'Our Germanicus was laid out in the public square for all to see. How beautiful he was. Some compared him to the great Alexander. People could not determine. Had he been poisoned or not? Some said Yes, some said No.

'His soldiers loved him. Governor Piso, thank the gods, is not here and dares not come back. Germanicus's wife, the gracious

Agrippina, has the ashes of Germanicus in an urn she carries next to her breast. She sails for Rome, seeking justice for Tiberius.'

He handed me the cup. 'I humbly thank you.'

'The city is as usual again.'

'Oh, yes, what could stop this glorified marketplace?' he declared. 'Business goes on as always. The loyal soldiers of Germanicus keep the peace, waiting for justice. They will not let the murderous Piso return, and Sentius gathers to himself here all who served under Germanicus. The city is happy. The flame burns for Germanicus. If there is war, it won't be here. Don't worry.'

'Thank you, you have helped me marvelously much.'

I took the cup, locked the gate, shut the door and went into action.

Nibbling on enough bread to give me strength, and murmuring aloud the common sense of Lucretius, I surveyed the house. It had a large luxurious bath on the right side of the courtyard. Full of light. Water flowed steadily from the seashells of the nymphs into the plastered basin, and the water was fine. There was no need to light a fire for it.

In the bedchamber were my clothes.

Roman dresses were simple, as you know,

just long shifts or tunics, and we wore two or three of them, plus an outdoor cover-up tunic, the stola, and finally the palla, or mantle, which hung to the ankles and belted below the breasts.

I chose the finest tunics, composing three layers of gossamer silk, and then a brilliant red palla that covered me from head to toe.

In all my life, I had never had to put on my own sandals. This was hysterically funny and annoying!

All my toilet articles had been laid out on tables which held burnished mirrors. What a mess!

I sat down in one of the many gilded chairs, pushed the burnished metal mirror close, and tried to work with the paints as my slaves had always done.

I managed to darken my eyebrows, but my horror of the painted Egyptian eyes stopped me. I rouged my lips, put some white powder on my face, but that was it. I couldn't attempt powdering my arms, as would have been done for me in Rome.

I don't know what I looked like. Now I had to braid this damned hair, and I managed it, and fixed the braids in a big coil on the back of my head. I used enough pins for twenty women. Dragging down the loose curls around my face, on my forehead and cheeks, I saw in the mirror a Roman woman, modest and acceptable, I thought, her brown hair parted in the middle, her eyebrows black and her lips rosy red.

Gathering up all this drapery was the biggest nuisance. I attempted to match length with length. I tried to get the silk stola straight and then belt it tightly beneath my breasts. I mean, all this folding, all this drapery and fastening. I'd always had slave girls around me. Finally with two undertunics and a long, fine red stola, I snatched up a silk palla, a very large one, fringed and decorated all over with gold.

I put on rings, bracelets. But I intended to hide under this mantle as much as possible. I could remember my Father cursing every day of his life that he had to wear the toga, the official outer garment of the highborn Roman male. Well, only prostitutes wore togas. At least I didn't have to cope with that.

I headed straight for the slave markets.

Jacob was right about the population here. The city was filled with men and women of all nations. Many women walked in pairs, arm in arm.

Loose Greek cloaks were entirely acceptable here, and so were long exotic Phoenician or Babylonian gowns, both for men and women.

Long hair among the men was common, as were heavy beards. Some women went about in tunics no longer than a man's. Others were completely veiled, revealing only the eyes, as they walked, accompanied by guards and servants.

The streets were cleaner than they might have been in Rome, the sewage flowing to wider gutters in the center and more swiftly to its destination.

Long before I reached the Forum, or the central plaza, I had passed three different doors in which rich courtesans stood arguing sarcastically over price with wealthy young Greeks and Romans.

One said, as I passed, to a handsome young man, 'You want me in bed? You're dreaming. Any of the girls you can have, as I told you. If you want me, go home and sell everything you own!'

Rich Romans in their full togas stood at the corner wine shops, and respected my quick glance away with a simple nod as I passed.

Pray none of them would recognize me! It was not a likely thing, by any means, and we were so far from Rome, and I had lived so long in my Father's house, happily reprieved by him from banquets and suppers, and even ceremonial gatherings.

The Forum was far larger than I had remembered from my brief glimpse. When I came to the edge of it and beheld the huge square flooded with sun, flanked on all sides with porticoes or Temples or Imperial buildings, I was amazed.

In the canopied markets, everything was for sale, silversmiths grouped together, the weavers in their own place, the silk merchants in a row, and I could see down the side street that came in to my right that it was dedicated to the sale of slaves – the better slaves, who might never have to go to an auction block.

Far away I saw the high masts of the ships. I could smell the river. There stood the Temple of Augustus, its fires burning, its uniformed Legionnaires in lazy readiness.

I was hot and anxious, because my mantle kept slipping, in fact, all this silk seemed to slip and to slide, and there were many open wine gardens where women gathered in groups, chatting. I could have found a place near enough to someone to have a drink.

But I had to have a household. I had to have loyal slaves.

Now, in Rome, of course I had never gone to a slave market. I would never have had to do such a thing. Besides, we had so many families of slaves on our land in Tuscany and in Rome that we seldom if ever bought a new slave. On the contrary, my Father had a habit of inheriting the decrepit and wise from his friends, and we had often teased my Father about the Academy, which did nothing in the slaves' garden but argue about history.

But now I had to act the shrewd woman of the world. I inspected every quality household slave on display, quickly settled upon a pair of sisters, very young and very frightened that they were going to be auctioned at noon and go to a brothel. I sent for stools and we sat together.

We talked.

They came from a small fine family household in Tyre; they'd been born slaves. They knew Greek and Latin well. They spoke Aramaic. They were angelic in their sweetness.

They had immaculate hands. They demonstrated every skill I required. They knew how to dress hair, paint a face, cook food. They rattled off recipes for Eastern dishes of which I'd never heard; they named different pomades, rouges. One of them flushed with fear, and then said, 'Madam, I can paint your face for you, and very quickly and perfectly!'

I knew this meant I had made a mess of the job.

I also knew that, coming from a small household, they were far more versatile than our slaves at home.

I bought them both, the answer to their prayers; I demanded clean tunics of modest length for both of them, got the tunics, made of blue linen, though they weren't very fine, then found a roaming merchant with an armful of pallae. I brought each sister a blue mantle. They were in such happiness. They were reticent and wanted their heads covered.

I had no doubt of them. They would have died for me.

It didn't occur to me that they were starving until, while searching for other slaves, I heard a nasty slave dealer remind an impudent educated Greek that he would get no food until he was sold.

'Horrors,' I said. 'You girls, you're probably hungry. Go to the cookshop in the Forum. Look down the street. See there, the scattering of benches and tables.'

'Alone?' they said in dismay.

'Listen, girls. I have no time to feed you like birds from my hand. Don't look any man in the eye; eat and drink what you want.' I gave them a seemingly shocking amount of money. 'And don't leave the cookshop till I come for you. If a man comes to you, pretend to be in terror, bow your heads and protest as best you can that you don't speak his language. If worst comes to worst, go to the Temple of Isis.'

They ran together down the narrow street towards the distant banquet, their mantles such a beautiful blue as they ballooned in the breeze that I can see it even now, the color of the sky streaking through the tight sweaty crowds beneath the jumble of canopies. Mia and Lia. Not hard to remember, but I could not tell them apart.

A low derisive laughter surprised me. It was the Greek slave who had just been threatened with starvation by his Master.

He said to his Master:

'All right, starve me. And then what will you have to sell? A sickened and dying man, instead of an unusual and great scholar.'

Unusual and great scholar!

I turned and looked at the man. He sat on a stool and did not rise for me. He wore nothing but a filthy loincloth, which was plain stupidity on the part of the merchant, but this neglect certainly revealed that this slave was one very handsome man, beautiful in face, with soft brown hair and long almond-shaped green eyes, and a sarcastic expression to his pretty mouth. He was maybe thirty years old, perhaps a little younger. He was fit for his age, as Greeks like to be, having a sound musculature.

His brown hair was filthy, had been hacked off, and around his neck by a rope was the most wretched small board I ever beheld, crowded with tiny cramped letters in Latin.

Pulling up the mantle again, I stepped up very close to his gorgeous naked chest, a little amused by his audacious stare, and tried to read all this.

It seemed he could have taught all philosophy, all languages, all mathematics, could sing everything, knew every poet, could prepare whole banquets, was patient with children, had known military service with his Roman Master in the Balkans, could perform as an armed guard, was obedient and virtuous and had lived all his life in Athens in one house.

I read this a bit scornfully. He glared at me impertinently when he saw this scorn. Impudently, he folded his arms just below this little plaque. He leaned back against the wall.

Suddenly I saw why the merchant, hovering near, had not made the Greek rise. The Greek had only one good leg. The left leg below the knee was made of well-carved ivory, complete with carefully engraved foot and sandal. Perfect toes. Of course it had been pieced together, this

fine ivory leg and foot, but in three proportion-
ate sections, each girded with decorative work,
and separate parts for the feet, nails defined and
sandal straps exquisitely carved.

I had never seen such a false limb, such a sur-
render to artifice rather than a meager attempt to
imitate nature.

'How did you lose your leg?' I asked him in
Greek. No answer. I pointed to the leg. No
answer.

I asked again in Latin. Still no answer.

The slave trader was rising on his toes in his
anxiety and wringing his hands.

'Mistress, he can keep records, run any business; he writes in perfect hand, keeps honest
numbers.'

Hmmm. So no mention of tutoring children?
I did not look like a wife and mother. Not
good.

The Greek sneered and looked away. He said
softly under his breath in piercing Latin that if I
did spend money for him, I was spending it for
a dead man. His voice was soft and beautiful,
though weary and full of contempt, his enunci-
ation unaffected and refined.

I threw off all patience. I spoke quickly in
Greek.

'Learn from me, you arrogant Athenian

142

idiot!' I said, red in the face, and furious to be so misjudged both by a slave and a slave dealer. 'If you can write Greek and Latin at all, if you have in fact studied Aristotle and Euclid, whose name you misspelled, by the way, if you have been schooled in Athens and have seen battle in the Balkans, if even half of this great epic is true, why wouldn't you want to belong to one of the most keenly intelligent women you'll ever meet, who'll treat you with dignity and respect in exchange for your loyalty? What do you know of Aristotle and Plato that I don't? I've never struck a slave in my life. You pass up the one mistress to whom your loyalty might earn you any reward of which you could dream. That tablet is a pack of lies, isn't it?'

The slave was stunned, but not angered. He sat forward, trying to appraise me further, without being obvious. The merchant gestured furiously for the slave to rise to his feet, which the slave did, giving him an admirable height over me. His legs were sound and strong up to the ivory limb.

'What about telling me the real truth as to what you can do?' I said, switching to Latin.

I turned to the slave dealer. 'Get me a pen to correct this, the spelling of these names. If this man has any chance of becoming a teacher, these misspellings destroy it. He looks like a fool for writing such.'

'I didn't have space enough to write!' declared the slave suddenly, whispering in perfect Latin fury. He bent towards me, as if I should understand.

'Look at this little tablet, if you're so keenly intelligent! Do you realize the ignorance of this dealer here. He has not sense enough to know he has an emerald, and thinks it a piece of green glass! This is wretched. I crammed here what generalities I could.'

I laughed. I was seduced and thrilled. I couldn't stop laughing. This was too funny! The slave merchant was confused. Chastise the slave and lower his value? Or let the two of us work this out?

'What was I to do,' he demanded in the same confidential whisper, only this time in Greek, 'shout to every man passing, "Here sits a great teacher, here sits a philosopher!"?' He grew a little calm, having thus released this rage. 'The names of my grandfathers are carved on the Acropolis at Athens,' he said.

The merchant was mystified.

But I was so obviously delighted and interested.

My mantle slipped again and I gave it a hard

jerk. These clothes. Had no one ever told me silk slides on silk?

'And what about Ovid?' I said, taking a deep breath. I almost laughed myself into tears. 'You wrote Ovid's name here. Ovid. Is Ovid popular here? Nobody would dare write that on your card in Rome, I can tell you. You know, I don't even know if Ovid is still alive, and it's a shame. Ovid taught me to kiss when I was ten years old, when I read the *Amores*. You ever read the *Amores?*'

His entire demeanor altered. He softened and I could see he was just on the verge of hope, hope that I might be a good mistress for him. But he couldn't let himself believe it.

The merchant was waiting for the slightest signal as to what he might do. Clearly he could follow our exchanges.

'Look, you insolent one-legged slave,' I said. 'If I thought you could even read Ovid to me in the evenings, I'd buy you in a moment. But this tablet here makes you a glorified Socrates and Alexander the Great smashed in one. In what war in the Balkans did you carry arms? Why are you dumped in the hands of this lowly merchant rather than taken at once to some fine house? How could anyone believe all this? If blind Homer had sung such a preposterous tale, people would have gotten up and left the tavern.'

He grew angry, frustrated.

The merchant put out his hand in warning, as if to control the man.

'What the hell happened to your leg?' I asked. 'How did you lose it? Who made you this glorious replacement?'

Lowering his voice to an angry yet eloquent whisper, the slave declared slowly and patiently:

'I lost it in a boar hunt, with my Roman Master. He saved my life. We hunted often. It was on Pentelikon, the mountain . . .'

'I know where Pentelikon is, thank you,' I said.

His facial expressions were elegant. He was utterly confused. He licked his parched lips and said:

'Just make this merchant fetch the parchment and the ink.' He spoke his Latin with such beauty, the beauty of an actor or rhetorician, yet with no effort. 'I'll write the *Amores* of Ovid from memory for you,' he said, gently pleading through clenched teeth, which is no mean feat. 'And then I'll copy out all of Xenophon's history of the Persians for you, if you have the time, in Greek, of course! My Master treated me like a son; I fought with him, studied with him, learned with him. I wrote his letters for him. His education I made my education because he wanted it so.'

'Ah,' I said in proud relief.

He looked the full gentleman now, angered, caught in impossible circumstance yet dignified, and reasoning with just enough spirit to strengthen his own soul.

'And in bed? Can you do it in bed?' I asked. I can't say what rage or desperation prompted this question.

He was genuinely shocked. Good sign. His eyes really widened. He furrowed his brow.

Meantime the slave trader emerged with the table, stool, parchment, ink, and set it all down on the hot cobblestones.

'Here, write,' he said to the slave. 'Make letters for this woman. Add sums. Or I'll kill you and sell your leg.'

I broke again into helpless laughing. I looked at the slave, who still stood dazed. He broke away from my gaze to cast a disdainful look on the merchant.

'Are you safe around the slave girls?' I said patronizingly 'Are you a lover of boys?'

'I am completely trustworthy!' the slave said. 'I am not capable of crimes for any Master.'

'And what if I desire you in my bed? I'm the

Mistress of the house, twice widowed and on my own, and I am Roman.'

His face darkened. I couldn't name the emotions that seemed to pass over his expression, the sadness, indecision, confusion and ultimate perplexity that transformed him.

'Well?' I asked.

'Let's put it this way, Madam. You would be much more pleased with my recitation of Ovid than with any attempted enactment of his verses by me.'

'You like boys,' I said with a nod.

'I was born a slave, Madam. I made do with boys. I know nothing else. And I need neither.' His face was crimson now, and he had lowered his eyes.

Lovely Athenian modesty.

I gestured for him to sit down.

This he did with amazing simplicity and grace, considering the circumstances: the heat, the dirt, crowds, the fragile stool and the wobbling table.

He picked up the pen and quickly wrote in flawless Greek, 'Have I foolishly offended this great lady of learning and exceptional patience? Have I brought about, through rashness, my own doom?' He wrote on in Latin, 'Does Lucretius tell us the truth when he says that death is nothing to fear?' He thought for a moment, and then he wrote in Greek again, 'Are Virgil and Horace really equal to our great poets? Do the Romans truly believe this, or only hope it is true, knowing their achievements shine in other arts?'

I read this all very thoughtfully, smiling most agreeably. I had fallen in love with him. I looked at his thin nose, his cleft chin, and I looked into the green eyes that looked up at me.

'How did you come to this?' I asked. 'A slave shop in Antioch? You're Athenian-bred, just as you say.'

He tried to stand to answer. I pushed him to sit down.

'I can tell you nothing of that,' he said. 'Only that I was much beloved by my Master, that my Master died in his bed with his family around him. And that here I am.'

'Why didn't he set you free in his will?'

'He did, Madam, and with means.'

'What happened?'

'I can tell you no more.'

'Why not? Who sold you, why?'

'Madam,' he said, 'please place a value upon my loyalty to a house in which I served all my life. I cannot speak more. If I become your servant, you will have the same loyalty from me.

Your house will become my house, and sacred to me. What happens within your walls will remain within your walls. I speak of virtue and kindness in my Master because this is proper to say. Let me say no more.'

Sublime old-Greek morality.

'Write more, hurry!' said the slave merchant.

'Be quiet,' I told him. 'He's written quite enough.'

The handsome brown-haired slave, this enticingly beautiful one-legged man, had fallen into some deep pit of woe and looked towards the distant Forum, flash of figures back and forth over the mouth of the street.

'What would I do as a free man?' he said to me, looking up at me from a position of utter careless loneliness. 'Copy all day for a pittance at the booksellers? Write letters for coins? My Master risked his own life to save me from that boar. In battle I served under Tiberius in Illyricum, where with some fifteen legions he put down all revolts. I chopped the head off a man to save my Master. What am I now?'

I was filled with pain.

'What am I now?' he repeated the question.

'If I were free, I would live hand to mouth, and when I slept in some filthy tenement, my ivory leg would be severed and stolen!'

I gasped and put my hand to my lips.

His eyes filled with tears as he looked at me, and his voice became all the more softer, yet sharply articulate:

'Oh, I could teach philosophy beneath the arches out there, you know, prattle on about Diogenes, and pretend that I liked wearing rags, as do his followers these days. What a circus out there, have you seen it? I have never seen so many philosophers in my life as in this city! Take a look when you go back. You know what it takes to teach philosophy here? You have to lie. You have to fling meaningless words as fast as you can at young people, and brood when you can't answer, and make up nonsense and ascribe it to the old Stoics.'

He broke off, and tried to gain command of himself.

I was almost in tears as I looked down at him.

'But you see, I have no skill at lying,' he said. 'That has been my undoing with you, Great Lady.'

I was shattered inside, my wounds silently opened. The nerve which had carried me out of confinement was ebbing away But surely he saw my tears.

He looked towards the Forum again.

'I dream of an honorable Master or Mistress,

a house with honor. Can a slave through the contemplation of honor thereby have honor? The law says not. So any slave called to testify in a court trial must be tortured, for he has no honor! But reason says otherwise. I have learned and I can teach both bravery and honor. And yes, all of this tablet is true. I didn't have time or opportunity to temper its boastful style.'

He bowed his head and looked again towards the Forum, as though towards the lost world. He drew himself up in the chair, for bravery's sake. Again, he tried to stand.

'No, sit,' I said.

'Madam,' he said, 'if you seek my services for a house of ill repute, let me tell you now . . . if it is to torture and force young girls such as those you just purchased, if you order me to advertise their charms abroad, I won't do it. It is as dishonorable to me as to steal or to lie. Why do you want me?'

The tears were halted, merely resting between him and his vision of the world around him. His face was serene.

'Do I look as if I am a whore?' I asked him with shock. 'Yea gods, I wore all my best clothes. I'm doing my best to look revoltingly respectable in all these fancy silks! Do you see cruelty in my eyes? Can't you believe that it is perhaps the tempered soul that survives grief? One need not fight on a battlefield to have courage.'

'No, Madam, no!' he said. He was so very sorry.

'Then why fling these insults at me now?' I said, full of hurt. 'And no, I agree with you, what you've written there, our Roman poets are not the equals of the Greeks. I don't know our destiny as an Empire and this weighs as heavily on me as it ever did on my Father and his Father! Why? I don't know!' I turned as if to go, but I had really no intention of going! His insults had simply gone too far.

He bent towards me over the writing table.

'Madam,' he said whispering even lower and with greater solicitude. 'Forgive me my rash words. You are absolutely a paradox. Your face is eccentrically painted, and I think the lip rouge is not properly set. You have rouge on your teeth. You have no powder on your arms. You wear three dresses of silk and I can see through all of them! Your hair is in two barbarian-style braids lying on your shoulders, and you are raining little silver and gold pins galore. Look at these little pins falling. Madam, you will be hurt by these pins. Your mantle, more appropriate for evening, has fallen on the ground. Your hems drag in the dirt.'

Not missing a beat of his speech, he reached down deftly and picked up the palla, standing at once to offer it to me, coming round the table with a heavy shift of his leg, to lay the palla on my shoulders.

'You speak with miraculous speed, and stunning gibes,' he went on, 'yet you carry a huge dagger in your girdle. It should be hidden on your forearm under your mantle. And your purse. You take gold out of it to pay the girls. It's huge, carelessly visible. And your hands, your hands are beautiful, fine as your Latin and your Greek, but they are deeply creased with dirt as though you have been digging in the Earth itself.'

I smiled. I had stopped my tears.

'You are very observant,' I said cheerfully. I was charmed. 'Why did I have to cut you so deeply to find your soul? Why can't we simply reveal ourselves to one another? I need a strong steward, a guardian who can bear arms, run my house and protect it because I am alone. Can you really see through all this silk?'

He nodded. 'Well, now that the mantle is over your shoulders and hiding the . . . the dagger and the girdle –' He blushed. Then as I smiled at him, trying to regain my calm, trying to fight back the engulfing darkness that would take away all confidence from me, all faith in any task, he spoke on.

'Madam, we learn to hide our souls because we are betrayed by others. But I would entrust to you my soul! I know it, if you would reconsider your judgment! I can protect you, I can run your house. I will not molest your little girls. But mark, for all my time fighting in Illyricum I have one leg. I came home from three years of bloody constant battle to lose it to a boar because a spear, poorly tempered and made, broke as I thrust it into the boar.'

'What's your name?' I asked.

'Flavius,' he answered. This was a Roman name.

'Flavius,' I said.

'Madam, the palla is slipping again from your head. And these little pins, they are sharp, they are everywhere, they'll hurt you.'

'Never mind that,' I said, though I let him drape me again properly as if he were Pygmalion, and I his Galatea. He used the tips of his fingers. But the mantle was already soiled.

'Those girls,' I said, 'whom you glimpsed. They are my household, as of the past half-hour. You have to be their loving master. But if you lie in any woman's bed under my roof, the bed had better be mine. I am flesh and blood!'

He nodded, at a total loss for words.

I pulled open my purse and took out what I thought to pay, a reasonable price in Rome, I thought, where slaves were always bragging about how much they had cost. I laid down the gold, oblivious to the imprint of the coin, only gauging the value.

The slave stared at me with ever increasing fascination, then his eyes whipped the merchant.

The slimy, merciless, weasling slave trader puffed up like a toad and told me this priceless Greek scholar was to be auctioned for a high price. Several rich men had expressed interest. An entire school class was to question him within the hour. Roman officers had sent their stewards to inspect him.

'I have no more stamina for it,' I said, and reached in my purse again.

At once, my new slave Flavius put his hand out gently to prevent me.

He glared at the merchant with great authority and fearless contempt.

'For a man with one leg!' said Flavius between his teeth. 'You thief! You charge my Mistress that, here in Antioch, where slaves are so plentiful the ships take them on to Rome, for it's the only way to cut their losses!'

I was quite impressed. All had gone so well. The darkness flowed back away from me, and there seemed for the moment a divine meaning in the warmth of the sun.

'You cheat my Mistress and you know it! You're the scum of the Earth!' he went on. 'Madam, do we ever purchase from this scoundrel again? I advise never!'

The slave trader broke into an inane smile, a hideous grimace of cowardice and stupidity, bowed and gave me back a third of what I'd given him.

I could hardly keep from another burst of laughing. I had to fetch the mantle from the ground again. Flavius did it. This time, I knotted it properly in front.

I looked at the gold which had been returned, scooped it up, entrusted it to Flavius and off we went.

When we had plunged into the thick crowd in the center of the Forum I did laugh and laugh at the whole affair.

'Well, Flavius, you're protecting me already, saving me money, giving me excellent advice. If there were more men like you in Rome, the world might be better for it.'

He was choked up. He couldn't talk. It was an effort to whisper:

'Lady, you have on trust my body and soul forever.'

I went up on tiptoe and kissed his cheek. I realized that his nakedness, the filth of the loincloth, all this was a disgrace he bore without a sign of protest.

'Here,' I said, giving him some money. 'Take the girls home, put them to work, then you go to the baths. Get clean. Get Roman clean. Have a boy if you want. Have two. Then buy fine clothes for yourself, not slave clothes, mind you, but clothes that you would buy for a rich young Roman Master!'

'Madam, please hide that purse!' he said as he took the coins. 'And what is my Mistress's name? To whom shall I say I belong, if asked.'

'To Pandora of Athens,' I said. 'Though you shall have to fill me in on the current state of my birthplace, because I have never actually been there. But a Greek name serves me well. Now go. See, the girls watch!'

Lots of people were watching. Oh, this red silk! And Flavius was such a splendid figure of a male.

I kissed him again, and whispered in his ear, calculatingly, devil that I am, 'I need you, Flavius.'

He looked down at me, awestruck. 'I am

yours forever, Madam,' he whispered.

'Are you sure you can't do with me in bed!'

'Oh, believe me, I have tried!' he confessed, flushing again.

I made my hand into a fist and punched his muscular arm.

'Very well,' I said.

The damsels had already risen, at my gesture. They knew I sent him to them.

I gave him my key, the directions to my house, described the particularities of its gate, and the old bronze lion fountain right inside the gate.

'And you, Madam?' he asked. 'You're going in the crowd unaccompanied? Madam, the purse is huge! It's full of gold.'

'Wait till you see the gold in the house,' I said. 'Appoint yourself the only one who can open chests, and then hide them in obvious places. Replace all the furniture I've smashed in my . . . my solitude. There are many pieces stored in rooms above.'

'Gold in the house!' He was alarmed. 'Chests of gold!'

'Now, don't worry about me,' I said, 'I know where to seek help now. And if you betray me, if you steal my legacy and I find my house ruined when I return, I suppose I shall have deserved it. Cover up the chests of gold with carpets. The place has heaps of little Persian carpets. Look upstairs. And tend to the Shrine!'

'I shall do everything you ask and more.'

'So I thought. A man who cannot lie cannot steal. Now the sun is intolerable here. Go to the girls. They wait.'

I turned.

He caught me by coming round in front of me.

'Madam, there is something I must tell you.'

'What!' I said with an ominous face. 'Not that you're a eunuch,' I said. 'Eunuchs don't grow muscles in their arms and legs like that.'

'No,' he said. Then he took on a sudden gravity. 'Ovid, you spoke of Ovid. Ovid is dead. Ovid died two years ago in the wretched town of Tomis on the upper rim of the Black Sea. It was a miserable choice of exile, a barbarian outpost.'

'No one told me this. What a revolting silence.' I threw up my hands over my face. The mantle fell. He retrieved it. I scarce noticed. 'I had so prayed that Tiberius would let Ovid come back to Rome!' I told myself I had no time to stop for this. 'Ovid. No time to weep for him now . . .'

'His books are no doubt plentiful here,'

Flavius said. 'They are very easily found in Athens.'

'Good, perhaps you will have time to find some for me. Now, I'm off; pins or tumbled braids or sliding mantle, I do not care. And don't look so worried. When you leave the house, just lock up the girls and the gold.'

When I finally turned around he was making his way rather gracefully towards the girls. The sun rippled prettily on his well-muscled back. His hair was curly and brown, rather like my own. He stopped for one moment when a vendor attacked him with an armful of cheaply made tunics, cloaks and whatnot, more than likely stolen goods, full of dye that would run in the first rain, but who knows? He bought a tunic hastily and slipped it over his head, and purchasing a red sash, tied it around his waist.

Such a transformation. The tunic went halfway to his knees. That must have been a great relief to him, to have on something clean. I should have thought of this before I left him. Stupid.

I admired him. Naked or clothed, you can't carry such beauty and dignity unless you have been cherished. He wore the raiment of the affection bestowed on him and inscribed in the art of his ivory leg.

In our brief encounter, a bond had been forged forever.

He greeted the girls. With his arms around them, he guided them out of the crowd.

I went straight to the Temple of Isis, and thereby, unwittingly, took the first firm step towards a larcenous immortality, an inglorious and unearned supernature, a never ending and utterly useless doom.

5

As soon as I entered the Temple Compound I was received by several rich Roman women, who welcomed me generously. They were all properly painted with white on their arms and their faces, well-drawn eyebrows, lip color – all the details of which I'd made a hash that morning.

I explained that though I had means, I was on my own. They were for helping me in every way. When they heard I had been actually initiated in Rome, they were in awe.

'Thank Mother Isis they didn't discover you and execute you,' said one of the Roman women.

'Go in and see the Priestess,' they said. Many of them had not yet undergone the secret ceremonies and were waiting to be called by the goddess for this momentous event.

There were many other women here, some

Egyptian, some Babylonian perhaps. I could only guess. Jewels and silks were the order of the day. Fancy painted gold borders lined their mantles; some wore simple dresses.

But it seemed to me that all of them spoke Greek.

I couldn't bring myself to enter the Temple. I looked up and saw in my mind our crucified Priests in Rome.

'Thank God you were not identified,' said one.

'Quite a few people fled to Alexandria,' said another.

'I raised no protest,' I said dismally.

There came a chorus of sympathy. 'How could you, under Tiberius? Believe me, every one who could escaped.'

'Don't be laden with misery,' said a young blue-eyed Greek woman, very properly dressed.

'I'd fallen away from the worship,' I said.

Again came a comforting round of soft voices.

'Go in now,' said one woman, 'and ask to pray in the very sanctuary of Our Mother. You are an initiate. Most of us here are not.'

I nodded.

I went up the steps of the Temple and entered inside it.

I paused to shake from my mantle the mundane, that is, all the trivia I had discussed. My mind was focused upon the goddess, and desperate to believe in her. I loathed my hypocrisy, that I used this Temple and this worship, but then it didn't seem significant. My despair of the three nights had penetrated too deep.

What a shock awaited me as I found myself inside.

The Temple was far more ancient than our Temple in Rome, and Egyptian paintings covered its walls. A shiver at once went through me. The columns were in the Egyptian style, not fluted but smoothly round, and brightly painted in orange, and rising to giant lotus leaves at the capitals. The smell of the incense was overpowering and I could hear music emanating from the Sanctuary. I could hear the thin notes of the lyre, and of the wires of the sistrum being plucked, and I could hear a litany being chanted.

But this was a thoroughly Egyptian place, which enveloped me as firmly as my blood dreams. I almost fainted.

The dreams came back – the deep paralytic sense of being in some secret Sanctuary in Egypt, my soul swallowed within another body!

The Priestess came to me. This too was a shock.

In Rome, her dress would have been purely Roman, and she might have worn a small exotic headdress, a little cap to her shoulders, perhaps.

But this woman wore Egyptian clothes of pleated linen, in the old style, and she wore a magnificent Egyptian headdress and wig, the broad mass of long black braids falling down stiffly over her shoulders. She looked as extravagant perhaps as Cleopatra had ever looked, for all I knew.

I had only heard stories of Julius Caesar's love of Cleopatra, then her affair with Mark Antony and Cleopatra's death. All that was before my birth.

But I knew that Cleopatra's fabulous entrance into Rome had much affrighted the old Roman sense of morality. I had always known the old Roman families feared Egyptian magic. In the recent punitive Roman massacre, which I've described, there was a lot of shouting about license and lust; but beneath it, there had been an unspoken fear of the mystery and the power hidden behind the Temple doors.

And now as I gazed at this Priestess, at her painted eyes, I felt in my soul this fear. I knew it. Of course this woman seemed to have stepped from the dreams, but it was not that which struck me so much, for after all, what are dreams? This was an Egyptian woman – wholly alien and inscrutable to me.

My Isis had been Greco-Roman. Even her statue in the Roman Sanctuary had been clothed in a gorgeously draped Greek dress and her hair had been done softly in the old Greek style, with waves around her face. She had held her sistrum and an urn. She had been a Romanized goddess.

Perhaps the same had happened with the goddess Cybele in Rome. Rome swallowed things and made them Roman.

In a very few centuries, though I had no thought of it then – how could I – Rome would swallow and shape the followers of Jesus of Nazareth, and make of his Christians the Roman Catholic church.

I suppose you are familiar with the modern expression, 'When in Rome, do as the Romans do.'

But here, in this reddish gloom, among flickering lights and a deeper muskier incense than I had ever smelled, I resented my timidity in silence. Then the dreams did descend, like so many veils lowered one by one to enclose me. In a flash I saw the beautiful Queen weeping. No. She screamed. Cried for help.

'Get away from me,' I whispered to the air around me. 'Fly from me, all things that are impure and evil. Get away from me as I enter the house of my Blessed Mother.'

The Priestess took me in hand. I heard voices from my dream in violent argument. I strained to clear my vision, to see the worshipers coming and going towards the Sanctuary to meditate or to make sacrifice, to ask for some favor. I tried to realize it was a big busy crowd, very little different from Rome.

But the touch of the Priestess enfeebled me. Her painted eyes struck terror. Her broad necklace caused me to blink my eyes. Row upon row of flat stones.

I was taken into a private apartment of the Temple by her, offered a sumptuous couch. I lay back exhausted. 'Fly from me, all things evil,' I whispered. 'Including dreams.'

The Priestess sat beside me and enfolded me in her silken arms. I looked up into a mask!

'Talk to me, suffering one,' she said in Latin with a thick accent. 'Speak all that must come forth.'

Suddenly – uncontrollably – I poured out my whole family story, the annihilation of my family, my guilt, my travails.

'What if I was the cause of my family's downfall – my worship at the Temple of Isis? What if Tiberius had remembered it? What have I done? The Priests were crucified and I did nothing. What does Mother Isis want of me? I want to die.'

'That she does *not* want of you,' said the Priestess, staring at me. Her eyes were huge, or was it the paint? No, I could see the whites of her eyes, so glistening and pure. Her painted mouth let loose words like a tiny breeze in a monotone.

I was fast becoming delirious and totally unreasonable. I murmured what I could about my initiation, what details I could tell a Priestess, for all these things were highly secret, you know, but I confirmed for her that I had been reborn in the rites.

All the stored-up weakness in me was cut loose in a flood.

Then I laid down my guilt. I confessed that I had, early on, left the Cult of Isis, that in recent years, I had walked only in the public processions to the sea, when the goddess was carried to the shore to bless the ships. Isis, the goddess of Navigation. I had not lived a life of devotion.

I had done nothing when the Priests of Isis were crucified, except speak out with many others behind the Emperor's back. There had been a solidarity between me and those Romans who thought Tiberius was a monster, but we had not raised our voices in defense of Isis. My

Father had told me to remain silent. So I had. This was the same Father who had told me to live.

I turned over and slipped down off this couch and I lay on the tiled floor. I don't know why. I pressed my cheek to the cold tile. I liked the coldness against my face. I was in a state of madness, but not an uncontrollable state. I lay staring.

I knew one thing. I wanted to get out of this Temple! I didn't like it. No, this had been a very bad idea.

I hated myself suddenly for having become so vulnerable to this woman, whatever sort she was, and the atmosphere of the blood dreams beckoned to me.

I opened my eyes. The Priestess bent over me. I saw the weeping Queen of my nightmares. I turned away and shut my eyes.

'Be at peace,' she said in her calculated and perfected voice. 'You did nothing wrong,' said the Priestess.

It seemed preposterous that such a voice should issue from such a painted face and form, but the voice was definite.

'First,' the Priestess said, 'you must understand that Mother Isis forgives anything. She is the Mother of Mercy.' Then she said, 'You have been more fully initiated by your description than most here or anywhere. You made a long fast. You bathed in the sacred blood of the bull. You must have drunk the potion. You dreamed and saw yourself reborn.'

'Yes,' I said, trying to revive the old ecstasy, the priceless gift of belief in something. 'Yes. I saw the stars and great fields of flowers, such fields . . .'

It was no good. I was scared of this woman and I wanted to get out of there. I'd go home and confess all this to Flavius and make him let me weep on his shoulder.

'I am not pious by nature,' I confessed. 'I was young. I loved the free women who went there, the women who slept with whom they chose, the whores of Rome, the keepers of the houses of pleasure, I liked women who thought for themselves, and followed the goings-on of the Empire.'

'You can enjoy such company here as well,' said the Priestess, without batting an eye. 'And don't fear that your old ties to the Temple caused your downfall in Rome. We have plenty of news to confirm that the highborn were not persecuted by Tiberius when he destroyed the Temple. It is always the poor who suffer: the street whore and the simple weaver, the hairdresser, the bricklayer. No noble family was persecuted in the name of Isis. You know that. Some women fled to Alexandria because they would not give up the worship, but they were never in danger.'

The dreams approached. 'Oh, Mother of God,' I whispered.

The Priestess went on talking.

'You, like Mother Isis, have been the victim of tragedy. And you, like Mother Isis, must take strength and walk alone, as Isis did when her husband, Osiris, was slain. Who helped her when she searched all over Egypt for the body of her murdered husband, Osiris? She walked alone. She is the greatest of the goddesses. When she recovered the body of her husband, Osiris, and could find no organ of generation for him with which she might be impregnated, she drew the semen right from his spirit. Thus, the god Horus was born of a woman and a god. It was the power of Isis who drew the spirit from the dead man. It is Isis who tricked the god Ra into revealing his name.'

That was the old tale all right.

I looked away from the Priestess. I was unable to look at her decorated face! Surely she felt my revulsion. I must not hurt her. She meant well. It wasn't her fault that she looked to me like a monster. Why in hell had I come here!

I lay dazed. The room had a soft golden light coming mainly through its three doors, and they were cut Egyptian-style, these doors, wider at the base than at the top, and I let this light make a blur of my vision. I asked the light to do this.

I felt the Priestess's hand. Such silken warmth. So lovely, her touch, her sweetness.

'Do you believe all of it!' I suddenly whispered.

She completely ignored this question. Her painted mask gave forth the creed.

'You must be like Mother Isis. Depend on no one. You don't have the burden of recovering a lost husband or father. You are free. Receive into your house men with love as you choose. You belong to no one but Mother Isis. Remember, Isis is the goddess who loves, the goddess who forgives, the goddess of infinite understanding because she herself has suffered!'

'Suffered!' I gasped. I moaned, a very uncommon sound for me, most of my life. But I saw the weeping Queen of my nightmares, bound to her throne.

'Listen to this,' I said, 'the dreams I will now recount, and then tell me why it is happening.' I knew my voice sounded angry. I was sorry for it. 'These dreams don't come from wine or potions, or after long periods of wakefulness that twist the mind.'

Then I launched into another totally unplanned confession.

I told this woman of the blood dreams, the dreams of ancient Egypt in which I had drunk blood – the altar, the Temple, the desert, the sun rising.

'Amon Ra!' I said. This was the Egyptian name for the sun god, but I had never spoken it to my knowledge. I said it now. 'Yes, Isis tricked him into revealing his name, but he killed me and I was her blood drinker, do you hear me, a thirsty god!'

'No!' said the Priestess. She sat motionless.

She thought for a long while. I had scared her and now this scared me all the more.

'Can you read the ancient picture writing of Egypt?' she asked.

'No,' I said.

Then she said, in a more relaxed and vulnerable tone:

'You speak of very old legends, legends buried in the history of our worship of Isis and Osiris; that they once did indeed take the blood of their victims as sacrifice. There are scrolls here that tell of this. But nobody can really decipher them, except for one . . .'

Her voice trailed off.

'Who is the one?' I asked. I sat up on my elbows. I realized the plaits of my hair had come undone. Good. It felt good because it was free now and clean. I raked my hair with both hands.

What did it feel like to be entombed in paint and wig like this Priestess?

'Tell me,' I said, 'who is the one who can read these legends. Tell me!'

'These are evil tales,' she said, 'that Isis herself and Osiris live on, somewhere, in material form, taking blood even now.' She made an expression of denial and disgust. 'But this is not our worship! We sacrifice no humans here! Egypt was old and wise before Rome was born!'

Who was she trying to convince? Me?

'I've never had such dreams, in a string like this, with the same theme.'

She became very worked up with her declarations.

'Our Mother Isis has no taste for blood. She has conquered death and set her husband Osiris as King of the Dead, but for us, she is life itself. She didn't send you these dreams.'

'Probably not! I agree with you. But then who did? Where do they come from? Why did they pursue me at sea? Who is this one who can read the old writing?'

175

She was shaken. She had let go of me and she stared off, her eyes taking on a deceptive ferocity due to the black lining.

'Perhaps somewhere in childhood you heard an old tale, maybe an old Egyptian Priest told it to you. You forgot it, and now it flames in your tortured mind. It feeds on fires to which it has no right – your Father's death.'

'Yes, well, I certainly hope so, but I've never known an old Egyptian. At the Temple, the Priests were Roman. Besides, if we take the dreams and lay them out, what is the pattern there? Why is the Queen weeping? Why does the sun kill me? The Queen is in fetters. The Queen is a prisoner. The Queen is in agony!'

'Stop.' The Priestess shuddered. Then she put her arms around me, as if it was she who needed me. I felt her stiff linen and the thick hair of her wig, and beneath it the hurried pounding of her heart. 'No,' she said. 'You're possessed of a demon, and we can drive this demon out of you! Maybe the way was opened for this wretched demon when your Father was attacked at his own Hearth.'

'You really believe it's possible?' I asked.

'Listen,' she said as casually now as one of the women outside. 'I want you to be bathed, to have fresh garments. This money, what portion can you give me? If none, we will provide all for you. We are rich here.'

'Here's plenty. I don't care.' I pulled the purse loose from my girdle.

'I will have everything done for you. Fresh clothes. This silk is too fragile.'

'You are telling me!' I said.

'This mantle is torn. Your hair is uncombed.'

I spilled out a dozen or so gold coins, more than I had paid for Flavius.

It shocked her, but she covered up the shock very quickly. Suddenly she stared at me, and her painted mask managed to make a flexible expression, a frown. I thought it might crack.

I thought she might weep. I was becoming a regular expert in making people weep. Mia and Lia had wept. Flavius had wept. Now she was going to cry. The Queen in the dream was crying!

I laughed in madness, throwing back my head, but then I saw the Queen! I saw her in distant wavery recollection, and I felt such sorrow that I too could have cried. My mockery was blasphemy. It was a lie unto myself.

'Take the gold for the Temple,' I said. 'Take it for new clothes, for all I need. But my offering to the goddess, I want it to be flowers, and bread, warm from the oven, a small loaf.'

'Very good,' she said with an eager nod.

'That is what Isis wants. She wants no blood. No! No blood!'

She started to help me up.

I paused. 'In the dream, you understand that she weeps. She is not happy with these blood drinkers, she protests, she objects. She herself is not the one who drinks blood.'

The Priestess was confounded, and then she nodded. 'Yes, that is obvious, is it not?'

'I too protest and suffer,' I said.

'Yes, come,' she said leading me through a thick tall door. She left me in the hands of the Temple slaves. I was relieved. I was weary.

I was taken into the ceremonial bath, cleansed by Temple maidens and re-dressed carefully by Temple maidens.

What a pleasure to have it all done right.

For a little while I wondered helplessly if they would frame me in white pleats and black plaits but they used the Roman style.

My hair was properly done by these girls in a correct circlet that would hold, leaving a generous frame of ringlets around the face.

The clothes given me were new and made of fine linen. Flowers had been stitched along the borders. This finery, so precise, so minute, seemed more valuable than gold.

It certainly gave more joy to me than gold.

I felt so tired! I was so grateful.

The girls then made up my face more artfully than I could have done it, and more in the Egyptian style, and I flinched when I saw myself in the mirror. Flinched. It wasn't the full paint of the Priestess, but my eyes were rimmed with black.

'How dare I complain?' I whispered.

I put down the mirror. One doesn't have to see oneself, fortunately.

I emerged into the great hall of the Temple, a proper Roman woman, with the extravagant face paint of the East. A common sight in Antioch.

I found the Priestess with two others, as formally dressed as she, and a Priest who wore the same old-fashioned Egyptian headdress, only he wore no wig, just a striped hood. His tunic was short, pleated. He turned and glared at me as I came forward.

Fear. Crushing fear. Flee this place! Forget about the offering, or have them make it for you. Go home. Flavius is waiting. Get out!

I was struck dumb. I let the Priest draw me aside.

'Pay attention,' he said to me gently. 'I will take you now into the holy place. I will let you talk to the Mother. But when you come out, you must come to me! Don't leave without coming to me. You must promise me, you will return each day, and if you have more of these dreams, you will lay them before us. There is one to whom they should be told, that is, unless the goddess drives them from your mind.'

'Of course I will tell anyone who can help,' I said. 'I hate these dreams. But why are you so anxious? Are you afraid of me?'

He shook his head. 'I don't fear you, but there is something I must confide to you. I must talk to you either today or tomorrow. I must speak with you. Go now to the Mother, then come to me.'

The others led me to the chamber of the Sanctuary; there were white linen curtains before the shrine. I saw my sacrifice lying there, a great garland of sweet-smelling white flowers, and the warm loaf of bread. I knelt. The curtains were pulled back by unseen hands and I found myself alone in the chamber kneeling before the *Regina Caeli,* the Queen of Heaven.

Another shock.

This was an ancient Egyptian statue of our Isis, carved from dark basalt. Her headdress was long, narrow, pushed behind her ears. On her head she wore a great disk between horns. Her breasts were bare. On her lap sat the adult

Pharaoh, her son Horus. She held her left breast to offer him her milk.

I was struck with despair! This image meant nothing to me! I groped for the essence of Isis in this image.

'Did you send me the dreams, Mother!' I whispered.

I laid out the flowers. I broke the bread.

I heard nothing in the silence from the serene and ancient statue.

I prostrated myself on the floor, stretching out my arms. And from the depths of my soul, I struggled to say, I accept, I believe, I am yours, I need you, I need you!

But I wept. All was lost to me. Not merely Rome and my family, but even my Isis. This goddess was the embodiment of the faith of another nation, another people.

Very slowly a calm settled over me.

Is it so, I thought. The Cult of my Mother is in all places, North and South and East and West. It is the spirit of this Cult which gives it power. I need not literally kiss the feet of this effigy. That is not the point.

I raised my head slowly, then sat back on my heels. A real revelation came upon me. I cannot fully record it. I knew it, fully, in an instant.

I knew that all things were symbols of other

things! I knew that all rituals were enactments of other happenings! I knew that out of our practical human minds we devised these things with an immensity of soul that would not allow the world to be devoid of meaning.

And this statue represented love. Love above cruelty. Love above injustice. Love above loneliness and condemnation.

That was what mattered, that single thing. I stared up at the face of the goddess and I knew her! I stared at the little Pharaoh, the proffered breast.

'I am yours!' I said coldly.

Her stark primitive Egyptian features were no obstacle to my heart; I looked at the right hand which held her breast.

Love. This requires strength from us; this requires endurance; this requires an acceptance of all that is unknown.

'Take the dreams away from me, Heavenly Mother,' I said. 'Or reveal their purpose. And the path I must follow. Please.'

Then in Latin I said an old litany:

You are she who has separated the Heavens and the Earth.
You are she who rises in the Dog Star.
You are she who makes strong the right.

*You are she who makes the children to love
    their parents.*
*You are she who decreed mercy for all who
    ask for it.*

I believed these words, but in a wholly profane way. I believed them because I saw her
worship as having collected together from the
minds of men and women the best ideas of
which men and women were capable. That
was the function for which a goddess existed;
that was the spirit from which she drew her
vitality.

The lost phallus of Osiris exists in the Nile.
And the Nile inseminates the fields. Oh, it was
so lovely.

The trick was not to reject it, as Lucretius
might have suggested, but to realize what her
image meant. To extract from that image the
best in my own soul.

And when I looked down at the beautiful
white flowers, I thought, 'It is your wisdom,
Mother, that these bloom.' And I meant by that
only that the world itself was filled with so
much to be cherished, preserved, honored, that
pleasure itself was resplendent – and she, Isis,
embodied these concepts that were too deep to
be called ideas.

I loved her – this expression of goodness which was Isis.

The longer I looked at her stone face, the more it seemed she saw me. An old trick. The more I knelt there, the more it seemed she spoke to me. I allowed this to happen, fully aware that it meant nothing. The dreams were remote. They seemed a puzzle which would find its idiot resolution.

Then with true fervor, I crawled towards her and kissed her feet.

My worship was over.

I went out refreshed, jubilant.

I wasn't going to have those dreams anymore. There was still daylight. I was happy.

I found many friends in the courtyard of the Temple, and sitting down with them under the olive trees, I drew out of them all the information I needed for practical life, how to get caterers, hairdressers, all that. Where to buy this thing and the other.

In other words, I was armed by my rich friends with full equipment to run a fine house without actually cluttering it up with slaves I didn't want. I could stick with Flavius and the two girls. Excellent. Anything else could be hired or bought.

Finally, very tired, with my head full of

names to remember and directions to recall, and very amused by the jokes and stories of these women, delighted with their ease in speaking Greek – which I had always loved – I sat back and thought, I can go home now.

I can begin.

The Temple was still very busy. I looked at the doors. Where was the Priest? Well, I would come back tomorrow. I didn't want to revive those dreams now, that was certain. Many people were coming and going with flowers and bread and some with birds to be set free for the goddess, birds that would take wing out of the high window of her Sanctuary.

How warm it was here. What a blaze of flowers covered the wall! I had never thought there could be a place as beautiful as Tuscany, but maybe this place was beautiful too.

I went out of the courtyard, before the steps, and into the Forum.

I approached a man under the arches who was teaching a group of young boys all of what Diogenes has espoused, that we give up the flesh and all its pleasures, that we live pure lives in denial of the senses.

It was so much as Flavius had described it. But the man meant his words, and was well versed. He spoke of a liberating resignation. He caught my fancy. For this is what I thought had come to me in the Temple, a liberating resignation.

The boys who listened were too young to know this. But I knew it. I liked him. He had gray hair and wore a simple long tunic. He was not ostentatiously in rags.

I at once interrupted. With a humble smile I offered the counsel of Epicurus, that the senses wouldn't have been given us were they not good. Wasn't this so? 'Must we deny ourselves? Look, back at the courtyard of the Temple of Isis, look at the flowers covering the top of the wall! Is this not something to savor? Look at the roaring red of those flowers! Those flowers are in themselves enough to lift a person out of sorrow. Who is to say that eyes are wiser than hands or lips?'

The young men turned to me. I fell into discussions with several of them. How fresh and pretty they were. There were long-haired men from Babylon and even highborn Hebrews here, all with very hairy arms and chests, and many colonial Romans who were dazzled by the points I made, that in the flesh and in the wine, we find the truth of life.

'The flowers, the stars, the wine, the kisses of one's lover, all is part of Nature, surely,' I said. I was of course on fire, having just come from the Temple, having just unburdened all fears and having resolved all doubts. I was for the moment invincible. The world was new.

The Teacher, whose name was Marcellus, came from under the arch to greet me.

'Ah, Gracious Lady, you amaze me,' he said. 'But from whom did you really learn what you believe? Was it from Lucretius? Or was it from experience? You realize that we must not ever encourage people to abandon themselves to the senses!'

'Have I said anything about abandon?' I asked. 'To yield is not to abandon. It is to honor. I speak of a prudent life; I speak of listening to the wisdom of our bodies. I speak of the ultimate intelligence of kindness, and enjoyment. And if you will know, Lucretius didn't teach me as much as one might think. He was always too dry for me, you know. I learned to embrace the glory of life from poets like Ovid.'

The crowd of boys cheered.

'I learnt from Ovid,' came shout after shout.

'Well, that's fine, but remember your manners as well as your lessons,' I said firmly.

More cheering. Then the young men began tossing out verses from Ovid's *Metamorphoses*.

'That's splendid,' I declared. 'How many here? Fifteen. Why don't you come to my house for a supper?' I asked. 'Five nights from now, all of you. I need the time to prepare. I have many books I want to show you. I promise you, I will show you what a delicious feast can do for the soul!'

My invitation was accepted with amusement and laughter. I disclosed the location of my house.

'I am a widow. My name is Pandora. I invite you with all propriety, and the feast awaits you. Don't expect dancing boys and girls, for you will not find them under my roof. Expect delicious food. Expect poetry. Which of you can sing the verses of Homer? Truly sing them? Which of you sings them now from memory for pleasure!'

Laughter, conviviality. Victory. It seemed everybody could do this, and welcomed the opportunity. Someone made a soft mention of another Roman woman who would be most jealous when she discovered she had competition in Antioch.

'Nonsense,' said another, 'her table is over-crowded. Lady, may I kiss your hand?'

'You must tell me who she is,' I said. 'I'll welcome her. I want to know her, and what I can learn from her.'

The Teacher was smiling. I slipped him some money.

It was getting dusk. I sighed. Look. The rising stars of the tinted evening that precedes blackness.

I received the boys' chaste kisses and confirmed our feast.

But something had changed. It was as quick as the opening of one's eyes. Ah, painted eyes, no.

Perhaps it was only the awful pall of twilight.

I felt a shudder. *It is I who summoned you.* Who spoke those words? *Beware, for you would be stolen from me now and I will not have it.*

I was dumbstruck. I held the Teacher's hand warmly. He talked about moderation in living. 'Look at my plain tunic,' he said. 'These boys have so much money, they can destroy themselves.'

The boys protested.

But this was dim to me. I tried to listen. My eyes roved. Whence came that voice! Who spoke those words! Who summoned me and who would attempt the theft?

Then to my silent astonishment I saw a man, his head covered by his toga, watching me. I knew him immediately, by his forehead and his eyes. I recognized his walk now as he moved steadily away.

This was my brother, the youngest, Lucius, the one I despised. It had to be him. And behold the sly manner in which he fled from notice into the shadows.

I knew the whole person. Lucius. He waited at the end of the long portico.

I couldn't move, and it was getting dark. All the merchants who are open only in the day were gone. The taverns were putting out their lanterns or torches. One bookseller remained open, with great displays of books under the lamps above.

Lucius – my much detested youngest brother – not coming to welcome me with tears but gliding in the shadows of the portico. Why?

I feared I knew.

Meantime, the boys were begging me to go to the nearby wine garden with them, a lovely place. They were fighting over who would pay for my supper there.

Think, Pandora. This sweet little invitation is some keen test of the degree of my daring and freedom. And I should not go to a common tavern with the boys! But within moments I would be alone.

The Forum grew quiet. The fires blazed before the Temples. But there were great spaces of darkness. The man in the toga waited.

'No, I must be off now,' I said. Desperately I thought, what I shall I do for a torchbearer? Dare I ask these youths to see me home? I could see their slaves waiting about, some already lighting their torches or lanterns.

Singing came from the Temple of Isis.

It was I who summoned you. Beware . . . for me and my purpose!

'This is madness,' I muttered, waving good-night to those who left in pairs or trios. I forced smiles and kind words.

I glared at the distant figure of Lucius, who now slouched at the end of the portico in front of doors closed for the night. His very posture was furtive and cowardly.

Quite suddenly, I felt a hand on my shoulder. I brushed it off immediately, wishing to lay down limits to such familiarity, and then I realized a man was whispering in my ear:

'The Priest at the Temple begs for you to come back, Madam. He needs to talk with you. He did not mean for you to leave without talking.'

I turned to see a Priest there beside me, in full Egyptian headdress and impeccable white linen and wearing a medallion of the goddess around his neck.

Oh, thank Heaven.

But before I could recover myself or answer,

another man had stepped up boldly, heaving forward his ivory leg and foot. Two torch-bearers accompanied him. We were embraced by a warm light.

'Does my Mistress wish to talk to this Priest?' he asked.

It was Flavius. He had followed my commands. He was wonderfully dressed as a Roman gentleman in the long tunic and a loose cloak. As a slave, he couldn't wear a toga. His hair was neat and trimmed and looked as impressive as any free man's. He was shining clean and appeared completely confident.

Marcellus, the Philosopher-Teacher, lingered. 'Lady Pandora, you are most gracious, and let me assure you that the tavern these boys frequent may give rise to another Aristotle or Plato but it is not a fit place for you.'

'I know that,' I said. 'Don't worry.'

The Teacher looked warily at the Priest and at the handsome Flavius. I slipped my arm about Flavius's waist. 'This is my steward, who will welcome you the night you come to me. Thank you for letting me disrupt your teaching. You're a kind man.'

The Teacher's face stiffened. Then he leaned closer. 'There's a man under the portico; don't look at him now, but you need more slaves to protect you. This city is divided, dangerous.'

'Yes, so you see him too,' I said. 'And his glorious toga, the mark of his genteel birth!'

'It's getting dark,' Flavius said. 'I'll hire more torchbearers now and a litter. Right over there.'

He thanked the Teacher, who reluctantly slipped away.

The Priest. He was still waiting. Flavius gestured for two more torchbearers and they came trotting to join us. We now had a plenitude of light.

I turned to the Priest. 'I will come to the Temple directly, but I must first talk with that man over there! The man in the shadows?' I pointed quite visibly. I stood in a flood of light. I might as well have been on a stage.

I saw the distant figure cringe and try to fade into the wall.

'Why?' Flavius asked with about as much humility as a Roman Senator. 'Something is very wrong about that man. He's hovering. The Teacher was right.'

'I know,' I answered. I heard the dim, echoing laughter of a woman! Yea gods, I had to stay sane long enough to get home! I looked at Flavius. He had not heard the laughter.

There was one sure way to do this. 'You

torchbearers, all of you, come with me,' I said to the four of them. 'Flavius, you stand here with the Priest and watch as I greet this man. I know him. Come only if I call.'

'Oh, I don't like it,' said Flavius.

'Neither do I,' said the Priest. 'They want you in the Temple, Madam, and we have many guards to escort you home.'

'I won't disappoint you,' I said, but I walked straight towards the toga-clad figure, crossing yard after yard of paved squares, the torches flaring around me.

The toga-clad man gave a violent start, with his whole body, and then he took a few steps away from the wall.

I stopped, still out in the square.

He had to come closer. I wasn't going to move. The four torches gasped and blew in the breeze. Anybody anywhere near could see us. We were the brightest thing in the Forum.

The man approached. He walked slow, then fast. The light struck his face. He was consumed with rage.

'Lucius,' I whispered. 'I see you, but I can't believe what I see.'

'Nor can I,' he said. 'What the hell are you doing here?' he said to me.

'What?' I was too baffled to answer.

'Our family is in disgrace in Rome and you're making a spectacle of yourself in the middle of Antioch! Look at you! Painted and perfumed and your hair full of ointment! You are a whore.'

'Lucius!' I cried. 'What in the name of the gods are you thinking? Our Father is dead! Your own brothers may be dead. How did you escape? Why aren't you glad to see me? Why don't you take me to your house?'

'Glad to see you!' he hissed. 'We are in hiding here, you bitch!'

'How many of you? Who? What about Antony? What happened to Flora?'

He sneered with exasperation.

'They are murdered, Lydia, and if you do not get yourself to some safe corner where no roaming citizen of Rome can find you, you are dead too. Oh, that you would turn up here, spouting philosophy! Everybody in the taverns was talking about you! And that slave with the leg made of ivory! I saw you at noon, you wretched and infernal nuisance. Damn you, Lydia!'

This was pure unadulterated hate.

Again, came that distinct echoing laughter. Of course he did not hear it. Only I could hear it.

'Your wife, where is she. I want to see her! You *will* take me in!'

'I will not.'

'Lucius, I am your sister. I want to see your wife. You're right. I've been foolish. I didn't think things through very well. There are so many miles of sea between here in Rome. It never occurred to me –'

'That's just it, Lydia, you never really think of anything sensible or practical. You never did. You're an uncompromising dreamer, and stupid on top of it.'

'Lucius, what can I do?'

He turned from right to left, sizing up the torchbearers.

He narrowed his eyes. I could feel his hatred. Oh, Father, do not see this from Heaven or the Underworld. My brother wants me dead!

'Yes,' I said, 'four torchbearers and we are in the middle of the Forum. And don't forget about the man with the ivory leg over there and the Priest,' I said softly, 'And do regard the soldiers outside the Emperor's Temple. Take note. How goes it with your wife? I must see her. I'll come in secret. She'll be happy that I am alive, surely, for I love her like a sister. I will never connect myself with you in public. I've made a grevious error.'

'Oh, knock it off,' he said. 'Sisters! She's dead!' He looked from right to left again. 'They were all massacred. Don't you understand? Get away from me.' He took a few steps back but I moved forward, drawing the light around him again.

'But who is with you, then? Who escaped with you? Who else is alive?'

'Priscilla,' he said, 'and we were damned lucky to get away when we did.'

'What? Your mistress? You came here with your mistress? The children, they are all dead?'

'Yes, of course, they must be. How could they have escaped? Look, Lydia, I give you one night to get out of this city and away from me. I am lodged here comfortably and will not tolerate you. Get out of Antioch. Go by sea or land, I don't care, but go!'

'You left your wife and children to die? And came here with Priscilla?'

'How the hell did you get away, you stinking bitch in heat, answer me that! Of course you had no children, the great famous barren womb of our family!' He looked at the torchbearers. 'Get away from here!' he shouted.

'Stay right where you are.'

I put my hand on my dagger. I moved the mantle so that he could see the flash of the metal.

He looked genuinely surprised and then gave a ghastly false smile. Oh, revolting!

'Lydia, I wouldn't hurt you for the world!' he said as if insulted. 'I am only worried for us all. Word came from the house. Everyone had been killed. What was I to do, go back and die for nothing?'

'You're lying. And don't you call me a bitch in heat again unless you want to become a gelding. I know you lie. Somebody tipped you off, and you got out! Or it was you who betrayed us all.'

Ah, how sad for him that he was not more clever, more quick. He did not take umbrage at these loathsome charges as he should have. He just tilted his head and said:

'No, that's not true. Look, come with me now. Send these men away, get rid of that slave, and I will help you. Priscilla adores you.'

'She's a liar and slut! And how calm you have become in the face of my suspicions. Nothing as steamed as when you saw me! I just accused you of betraying our family to the *Delatores*. I accused you of abandoning your wife and children to the Praetorian Guard. Can you hear these words?'

'It's utter stupidity, I would never do such a thing.'

'You reek of guilt. Look at you. I should kill you now!'

198

He backed up. 'Get out of Antioch!' he said. 'I don't care how you judge me or what I had to do to save myself and Priscilla. Get out of Antioch!'

There were no words for my judgment. It was harsher than my soul could hold.

He backed away, and then walked fast into the darkness, disappearing before he reached the portico. I listened to his steps as they echoed down the street.

'Dear Heaven!' I whispered. I was about to cry. My hand was still on the dagger, however.

I turned around. The Priest and Flavius stood much closer than ordered. I was frankly utterly baffled, stopped.

I didn't know what to do.

'Come to the Temple at once,' said the Priest.

'All right,' I said. 'Flavius, you come with me, stand watch with the four torchmen, I want you right by the Temple guards, and keep an eye out for that man.'

'Who is he, Madam,' Flavius whispered as I strode towards the Temple, leading them both.

How regal he looked. He had the presence of a free man. And his tunic was beautiful thin wool, striped in gold, belted in gold, well fitted across his chest. Even his ivory leg had been polished. I was more than pleased. But was he armed?

Beneath his quiet demeanor, he was deeply protective of me.

In my misery, I couldn't form words to answer him.

Several litters were now crisscrossing the square, carried on the shoulders of hurrying slaves, and other slaves carried the torches beside them. A kind of soft glow rose from the commotion. People were on their way to dinners or private ceremonies. Something was happening in the Temple.

I turned to the Priest. 'You will guard my slave and my torchbearers?'

'Yes, Madam,' he said.

It was full night. The breeze was sweet. A few lanterns had been lighted under the long porticoes. We drew near to the braziers of the goddess.

'Now I must leave you,' I said. 'You have my permission to protect my property, as you so eloquently put it earlier, unto death. Don't move from these doors. I won't leave here without you. I won't stay long. I don't want to. But have you a knife?'

'Yes, Madam, but it's untried. It was among your possessions, and when you did not come home and it grew dark . . .'

'Don't recount the history of the world,' I

said. 'You did the right thing. You probably will always do the right thing.'

I turned my back to the square and said, 'Let me see it. I'll know if it's decorative or sharp.'

When he drew it from the forearm sling, I touched it with my finger and blood came from the cut. I returned it. This had belonged to my Father. So my Father had filled my trunk with his weapons as well as his wealth, so that I might live!

Flavius and I exchanged one last slow glance.

The Priest grew very anxious. 'Madam, please come inside,' he said.

I found myself ushered right through the tall doors into the Temple, and with the Priestesses and the Priest of that earlier afternoon.

'You want something of me?' I asked. I was out of breath. I was faint. 'I have much on my mind, things that must be done. Can this wait?'

'No, Lady, it cannot!' said the Priest.

I felt a shudder in my limbs as if I were being watched by someone. The tall shadows of the Temple were too concealing.

'All right,' I said. 'It's about those awful dreams, isn't it?'

'Yes,' said the Priest. 'And more than that.'

6

We were taken into another chamber, and this one had only one dim light.

I couldn't see well in the flickering of the flame and I realized I could not make out the faces of the other Priest and Priestess. An Oriental screen, a screen of worked ebony partitioned off the end of this room, and I felt certain someone was behind it.

But I felt nothing but gentleness emanating from all of these gathered here. I looked around. I was so miserable over my brother, and so impatient that I couldn't find polite words.

'Please, you must forgive me,' I said. 'A dire matter requires me to hurry.' I was becoming afraid for Flavius's safety. 'Do send guards to flank my slave outside, now.'

'Done, Lady,' said the Priest, the one I knew. 'I beg you to stay and recount your story again.'

'Who is there!' I pointed. 'Behind that screen. Why is this person concealed?' This was very rude and irreverent, but I was in a full state of alarm.

'That is one of our most devoted supporters,' said the Priest who had escorted me to the shrine of Isis earlier. 'This one often comes by night to pray at the shrine and has given much money to the Temple. He only wants to hear what we have to say.'

'Well, I'm not so sure of that. Tell him to come out!' I said. 'Besides, what is it we're supposed to say?'

I was infuriated suddenly that they might have betrayed my confidences. I hadn't told them my true Roman name, only of my tragedy, but the Temple was sacred.

They became all flustered in their gentleness.

The figure, draped in the toga, much taller than my brother, in fact, remarkably tall, stepped out from behind the screen. The toga was dark, but nevertheless the classical garment. His face was hidden by the toga. I could only see his lips.

He whispered:

'Don't be afraid. You told the Priest and Priestesses this afternoon of blood dreams.'

'This was in confidence!' I said indignantly.

I was completely suspicious, for I had told a good deal more than blood dreams to these people.

I tried better to see the figure. There was something distinctly familiar about the figure – the voice, even in a whisper . . . something else.

'Lady Pandora,' said the Priestess who had so consoled me earlier. 'You talked to me of an old legendary worship, worship which we oppose and condemn. A worship of our Beloved Mother which once involved human sacrifice. I told you that we abhor such things. And we do.'

'However,' said the Priest, 'there is someone afoot in the city of Antioch who does drink blood from humans, draining them until they are dead. Then he flings the bodies before dawn on our steps. The very steps of our Temple.' He sighed. 'Lady Pandora, I am entrusting you with a powerful confidence.'

All thought of my evil brother left me. The hound of the dreams bore down upon me with its evil breath. I tried to gather my wits. I thought again of the voice I'd heard in my head: *It is I who summoned you.* The feminine laughter.

'No, it was a woman's laughter,' I murmured.

'Lady Pandora?'

'You tell me there is someone afoot in Antioch who drinks blood.'

'By night. He cannot walk in the day,' said the Priest.

I saw the dream, the rising sun, knowing I the blood drinker would die in the rays of the sun.

'You're telling me that these blood drinkers I saw in my dream exist?' I asked. 'That one of them is here.'

'Someone wants us to believe this,' said the Priest, 'that the old legends have truth, but we don't know who it is. And we are leery of the Roman authorities. You know what happened in Rome. You came speaking of dreams in which the sun killed you, in which you were a blood drinker. Lady, I'm not betraying your confidences here. This one –' He gestured to the tall man. 'This is the one who reads the ancient writing. He's read the legends. Your dreams echo the legends.'

'I am sick,' I said. 'I need a chair. I have enemies to worry about.'

'I'll protect you from your enemies,' said the mysterious tall man in the toga.

'How can you? You don't even know who they are.'

There came a silent voice from the tall man in the toga:

Your brother Lucius betrayed the entire family. He did it out of jealousy of your brother Antony. He sold out everybody to the Delatores *for a guaranteed one-third of the family's wealth and left before the killing began. He had the cooperation of the Sejanus of the Praetorian Guard. He wants to kill you.*

I was shocked but also not about to let this person overwhelm me.

You speak just like the woman, I said silently. *You speak right to my thoughts. You speak like the woman who said to me in my head, 'It is I who summoned you.'*

I could feel his shock at this. But I too slumped as if dealt a mortal blow. So this creature knew all about my brothers, and Lucius had betrayed us. And this creature knew.

What are you? I fired off to the mind speaker, the tall one. *Are you a magician?*

No answer.

The Priest and Priestess, unable to hear this silent exchange, pursued their course.

'This blood drinker, Lady Pandora, he leaves human victims on the steps of the Temple before dawn. He writes an old name in Egyptian on his victims with their blood. Should the government discover this, our Temple might be held accountable. This is not our worship.

'Will you recount again for us – for our friend here – your dreams? We must protect the worship of Isis. We did not believe in these old legends . . . until this creature appeared and began his killing, then comes out of the sea a beautiful Roman woman who speaks of similar beings who are in her dreams.'

'What name does he write on his victims?' I asked. 'This blood drinker. Is it Isis?'

'It's meaningless, it's forbidden, it's old Egyptian. It is one of the names by which Isis was once called, but never by us.'

'What is it?'

None of them, including the silent one, answered me.

In the silence, I thought of Lucius and I almost wept. Then hatred came over me, deep hatred, as it had in the Forum when I spoke with him, saw his cowardly rage. Betrayed the entire family. To be weak is a dangerous thing. Antony and my Father had been such strong men.

'Lady Pandora,' said the Priest. 'Tell us what you might know of this creature in Antioch. Have you dreamed of him?'

I thought of the dreams. I tried to respond in depth to what these people in this Temple were telling me.

The tall distant Roman spoke:

'Lady Pandora knows nothing about this blood drinker. She is telling you the truth. She knows only the dreams and there have been no names spoken in her dreams. In her dreams she sees an earlier time of Egypt.'

'Well, thank you, Gracious Lord!' I said furiously. 'And just how have you arrived at that conclusion?'

'By reading your thoughts!' the Roman said, quite unruffled. 'The same as I have regarding those who would put you in danger here. I'll protect you from your brother.'

'Indeed. You had better leave that to me. It is I who will settle that score with him. Now, let us leave the question of my personal misfortune. And you explain to me, most clever one, why I am having these dreams! Fork up some useful magic from your mind reading. You know, a man with your gifts should post yourself at the courthouse, and determine cases for the judges if you can read minds. Why don't you go to Rome and become the advisor to the Emperor Tiberius?'

I could feel, positively feel, the little tumult in the heart of the distant concealed Roman. Again, there came that sense of something familiar about this creature. Of course I was no stranger to necromancers, astrologists or oracles. But this man had mentioned specific names – Antony, Lucius. He was an astounder.

'Tell me, oh, mysterious one,' I said. 'How close do my dreams come to what you've read in the old writing? And this blood drinker, the one that's roaming Antioch, is he a mortal man?'

Silence.

I strained to see the Roman more clearly but couldn't. He had in fact receded somewhat into the darkness. My nerves were on the breaking point. I wanted to kill Lucius; in fact, I had no choice.

The Roman said softly, 'She knows nothing of this blood drinker in Antioch. Tell her what you know of him – for it may be he, this blood drinker, who is sending her the dreams.'

I was confused. The woman's voice had been so clear in my head earlier, *It is I who summoned you*.

This was causing confusion in the Roman; I could feel it like a little turbulence in the air.

'We've seen him,' said the Priest. 'Indeed, we watch, in order to collect these poor drained corpses before anyone finds them and blames the deed on us. He is burned, burned all over his body, blackened. He cannot be a man. He is an old god, burnt black as if in an inferno.'

'Amon Ra,' I said. 'But why didn't he die? In the dreams, I die.'

'Oh, it is a horror to behold,' said the Priestess suddenly, as if she could contain herself no longer. 'This thing cannot be human. Its bones show through its blackened skin. But it is weak and its victims are weak. It barely staggers, yet it can drain the blood from the poor maimed souls upon whom it feeds. It crawls away in the morning as if it hasn't the strength to walk.'

The Priest seemed impatient.

'But he's alive,' said the Priest. 'Alive, god or demon or man, he lives. And each time he drinks blood from one of these weaklings, he grows a little stronger. And he is straight from the old legends, and you have dreamed of them. He wears his hair long in the old Egyptian style. He is in agony from his burns. He spits curses at the Temple.'

'What kind of curses?'

The Priestess interjected at once. 'He seems to think that Queen Isis has betrayed him. He speaks in old Egyptian. We barely understand him. Our Roman friend here, our benefactor, has translated the words for us.'

'Stop!' I demanded. 'My head is reeling.

Don't say any more. The man over there has told the truth. I know nothing of this bloody burnt creature. I don't know why I have the dreams. I think a woman is sending the dreams to me. It may be the Queen I described to you, the Queen on the throne, in fetters, who weeps, I don't know why!'

'You have never seen this man?' asked the Priest.

The Roman answered for me. 'She has not.'

'Oh, your marvelous talents as spokesman again!' I said to the Roman. 'I am so delighted! Why are you hiding behind your toga? Why do you stand over there, so far away that I can't see you? Have you seen this blood drinker?'

'Be patient with me,' he said. It was spoken with such charm that I couldn't bring myself to say more to him. I turned on the Priest and the Priestess.

'Why don't you lie in wait for this black burnt thing,' I said, 'this weakling? I am hearing voices in my head. But it's the words of a woman that come to me, warning me of danger. It's a woman laughing. I want to leave now. I want to go home. I have something that must be done, and must be done cleverly. I need to go.'

'I will protect you from your enemy,' said the Roman.

211

'That's charming,' I answered. 'If you can protect me, if you know who my enemy is, then why can't you lie in wait for this blood drinker? Catch him in a gladiator's net. Sink five tridents into him. Five of you can hold him. All you have to do is hold him till the sun rises, the rays of Amon Ra will kill him. It may take two days, even three, but they'll kill him. He'll burn like I did in the dream. And you, mind reader, why don't you help?'

I broke off, shocked and disoriented. Why was I so certain of this. Why was I using the name Amon Ra so casually, as if I believed in the god? I scarcely knew his fables.

'The creature knows when we are lying in wait,' said the Priest and Priestess. 'He knows when the tall friend is here, and does not come. We are vigilant, we are patient, we think we will see no more of him, and then he comes. And now you have come with the dreams.'

A vivid garish flash of the dream returned. I was a man. I argued and cursed. I refused to do something which I had been ordered to do. A woman was weeping. I fought off those who tried to stop me. But I had not foreseen that I would, as I ran away, come to a desert place where I could find no shelter.

If the others spoke, I took no note of it. I

heard the woman of the dream crying, the fettered Queen, and the woman was a blood drinker too. 'You must drink from the Fount,' said the man in my dream. And he wasn't a man. I wasn't a man. We were gods. We were blood drinkers. That's why the sun destroyed me. It was the force of a more powerful god. Layers upon layers of the dream lay below this polished bit of remembrance.

I came to my senses, or back to an awareness of the others, when someone placed a cup of wine in my hands. I drank it. It was excellent wine, from Italy, and I felt refreshed, though at once tired. It would make the walk home much too tiring if I drank any more. I needed my strength.

'Take this away,' I said. I looked at the Priestess. 'In the dream, I told you, I was one of them. They wanted me to drink from the Queen. They called her 'the Fount.' They said she did not know how to rule. I told you.'

The Priestess burst into tears and turned her back, hunching up her narrow shoulders.

'I was one of the blood drinkers,' I said. 'I was thirsty for blood. Listen, I am no lover of blood sacrifice. What do you know here? Does Queen Isis exist somewhere, within this Temple, bound in fetters –'

'No!' cried the Priest. The Priestess turned around, echoing the same horrified denial.

'All right, then, but you said there were legends that she did exist somewhere in material form. Now, what do you think is happening? She has summoned me here to assist this one, this burnt-up weakling? Why me? How can I do it? I'm a mortal woman. Remembering dreams of a past life does not enhance my power. Listen! It was a woman's voice, I told you, which spoke in my head to me, not an hour ago out there in the Forum, and she said 'It is I who summoned you,' I heard this, and she swore she would not have me stolen from her. Then up comes this mortal man who's more of a threat to me than anything in my head. The voice in my head had warned me of him! I don't want any of your mysterious Egyptian religion. I refuse to go mad. It is you, all of you – especially the talented mind reader – who must find this thing before he makes any more trouble. Allow me to go on.'

I stood up and began to walk out of the chamber.

The Roman spoke behind me, most gently, 'Are you really going out into the night alone, knowing full well what awaits you – that you have an enemy who wants to kill you, and that you have in your dreams knowledge that may draw this blood drinker to you?'

This was such a change of pace for the lofty mind reader, such a slip into semi-sarcastic vernacular, that I almost laughed.

'I'm going home now!' I said firmly.

They all pleaded, in different modes and tones. 'Stay in the Temple.'

'Absolutely not,' I said. 'If the dreams return I'll write them down for you.'

'How can you be so foolish!' said the Roman with genteel impatience. You would have thought *he* was my brother!

'That is an unforgivable impertinence,' I said. 'Are not magicians and mind readers bound by manners?' I looked to the Priest and Priestess. 'Who is this man?'

I went out and they followed me. I hurried to the door.

In the light I saw the Priestess's face. 'We know only that he's our friend. Please listen to his advice. He has never done anything but good for the Temple. He comes to read the Egyptian books we have here. He buys them up from the shops as soon as the sea brings them to us. He is wise. He can read minds, as you see.'

'You promised an escort of guards,' I said.

And I will be with you. The voice came from

the Roman, though I did not know where he was now at all. He was not in the great hall.

'Come, live within the Temple of Isis, and nothing can harm you,' said the Priest.

'I'm not quite the woman for living in the Temple Compound,' I said, trying to sound as humble and grateful as I could. 'I'd drive you mad in a week. Please open the door.'

I slipped out. I felt I had escaped from a dark corridor of spiderwebs, back into the Roman night, among Roman columns and Roman temples.

I discovered Flavius pressed against the column beside me, staring down into the stairs. Our four torchbearers were gathered next to us, very much alarmed.

There were men who were obviously Temple guards, but they stood cleaving to the doors, as did Flavius.

'Madam, go back in!' whispered Flavius.

At the foot of the stairs stood a group of helmeted Roman soldiers in full military dress with polished muscled breastplates and short red cloaks and tunics. They carried their deadly swords as if they were in battle. Their bronze helmets shone in the light of the Temple braziers.

Battle dress within the city. Everything but

shields. And who was the leader?

Lucius, my brother, stood beside the leader. Lucius wore his battle tunic of red, but no breastplate or sword. His toga was doubled and redoubled over his left arm. He was clean, with shining hair, exuding money. A jeweled dagger was on his forearm; another dagger was in his belt.

Trembling, he pointed at me.

'There she is,' said Lucius. 'Of the entire family, she escaped the order of Sejanus. It was a plot to kill Tiberius and somehow she bribed her way out of Rome!'

I quickly sized up the soldiers. There were two young Asiatics but the others were *old* and *Roman;* six in number. Yea gods, they must have thought I was Circe!

'Go back in,' said my beloved and loyal Flavius, 'seek sanctuary.'

'Be still,' I said. 'There's always time for that.'

The leader, he was the key, and I saw that he was an older man, older than my brother Antony, yet not as old as my Father. He had thick gray eyebrows and was impeccably clean shaven.

He wore battle scars proudly, one on his cheek, another on his thigh. He was exhausted.

His eyes were red and he shook his head as if to clear his vision.

This man's arms were very tanned, yet he was well muscled. This meant war – lots and lots of war.

Lucius declared, 'The entire family stands condemned. She should be executed on the spot!'

I decided my strategy as if I were Caesar himself. I spoke up at once, proceeding two steps down:

'You are the Legate, are you not? How tired you must be!' I took his hand in both of mine. 'Were you under the command of Germanicus?'

He nodded.

First blow struck!

'My brothers fought with Germanicus in the North,' I said. 'And Antony, the eldest, after the Triumphal March in Rome, lived long enough to tell us of the bones found in the Teutoburg Forest.'

'Ah, Madam, to see that field of bones, an entire army ambushed and the bodies left to rot!'

'Two of my brothers died in the battle. It was in a storm, in the North Sea.'

'Madam, you never saw such a disaster, but do you think the Barbarian God, Thor, could frighten our Germanicus?'

'Never. And you came here with the General?'

'Went everywhere with him, from the banks of the Elbe in the North to the South end of the River Nile.'

'How marvelous, and you are so tired, Tribune, look at you, you need sleep. Where is the famous Governor Gnaeus Calpurnius Piso? Why did it take him so long to quiet the city?'

'Because he's not here, Madam, and he doesn't dare to come back. Some say he makes a mutiny in Greece, others that he flees for his life.'

'Stop listening to her!' shouted Lucius.

'He was never much loved in Rome, either,' I said. 'It was Germanicus whom my brothers loved and my Father praised.'

'Indeed, and if we had been given one more year – one more year, Madam – we could have extinguished the fire of that bloody upstart King Arminius forever! We didn't even need that long! You spoke of the North Sea. We fought on all terrain.'

'Oh, yes, in the thick of the forest, and tell me this, were you there, Sir, when they found the lost standard of General Varus's legions? Is the story true!'

'Ah, Madam, when that golden eagle was

raised, you never heard such cries as from the soldiers.'

'This woman is a liar and a traitor,' shouted Lucius.

I turned on him. 'Don't push me too far! You're past all patience now. Do you even know the numbers of the Legions of General Varus who were ambushed in the Teutoburg Forest? I thought not! They were the Seventh, the Eighth and the Ninth.'

'Right, correct,' said the Legate. 'And we could have wiped out those tribes completely. The Empire would reach to the Elbe! But for some reason, and mine is not the place to question, our Emperor Tiberius called us back.'

'Hmmm, and then condemns your beloved leader for going to Egypt.'

'Madam, it was no trip to seize power, Germanicus's trip to Egypt. It was because of a famine.'

'Yes, and Germanicus had been declared *Imperium Maius* of all the Eastern provinces,' I said.

'And there was so much trouble!' said the Legate. 'You can not imagine the morale, the habits of the soldiers here, but our General never slept! He went directly when he heard of the famine.'

220

'And you with him?'

'All of us, his cohorts. In Egypt he delighted in seeing the old monuments. So did I.'

'Ah, how marvelous for him. You must tell me about Egypt! You know that I, as a Senator's daughter, cannot go to Egypt any more than can a Senator. I would so love –'

'Why is that, Madam?' asked the Legate.

'She's lying to you!' roared Lucius. 'Her whole family was murdered.'

'Very simple reason, Tribune,' I said to the Legate. 'It's no state secret. Rome is so dependent upon Egypt for corn that the Emperor wants to prevent the country from ever falling under the control of a powerful traitor. Surely you grew up as I did in dread of another Civil War.'

'I put my faith in our Generals,' said the Legate.

'You are right to do so. And you saw nothing from Germanicus but loyalty is that not so?'

'It is absolutely so. Ah, Egypt. We saw such Temples and statues!'

'The singing statues,' I asked, 'did you see them, the colossal man and woman who wail in the rising of the sun?'

'Yes, I heard it, Madam,' he said, nodding furiously. 'I heard the sound! It is magical. Egypt is full of magic!'

221

'Hmmm.' A tremor ran through me. I banished it. In a flash I saw two images mixed: that of the tall Roman in his toga, and that of a burnt and cunning creature! Think straight, Pandora!

'And in the Temple of Ramses the Great,' said the Legate, 'one of the Priests read the writing on the walls. All about victory? All about battle? We laughed because nothing really changes, Madam.'

'And Governor Piso, do you believe these rumors? Can we not speak safely of them, of rumors as if rumors were not things?'

'Everyone here despises him!' said the Legate. 'He was a bad soldier, plain and simple! And Agrippina the Elder, Germanicus's beloved wife, is on her way to Rome now with the General's ashes. She will officially accuse the Governor before the Senate!'

'Yes, how courageous of her, and that is how it should be done. If families are judged without trial, then we have fallen into tyranny, haven't we? Here, our friendly lunatic, don't you agree to that?'

Lucius was speechless. He turned red.

'And in the Teutoburg Forest,' I said tenderly, 'that gloomy arena for our doom, did you see all the bones of our lost legions, scattered about?'

'Buried them, Madam, with these hands!' The Legate held up his weathered callused palms. 'For who could tell what bones were ours and what bones were theirs? And Madam, the platform of that cowardly, sneaking King was still standing, from which the loathsome long-haired slob had ordered the sacrifice to his pagan gods of our men.'

Nods and noble mumbles came from the other soldiers.

'I was but a small child,' I said, 'when word came of the ambush of General Varus. But I remember our Divine Emperor Augustus – how he let his hair grow long in mourning and how he would pound his head on the walls, crying, "Varus, bring me back my legions."'

'You actually saw him this way?'

'Oh, many a time, and was present one night when he discussed his often mentioned thoughts – that the Empire must not try to push further. Rather it should police the states which it now contains.'

'Then Caesar Augustus did say this!' said the Legate in fascination.

'He cared about you,' I said to the Legate. 'How many years have you been in the field? Do you have a wife?'

'Oh, how I long to go home,' said the Legate.

'And now that my General has fallen. My wife is gray-haired as I am. I see her when we go to Rome for parades.'

'Yes, and compulsory service was only six years under the Republic, but now, you must fight for what? Twelve? Twenty? But who am I to criticize Augustus, whom I loved as I loved my Father and all my dead brothers?'

Lucius could see what was happening. He sputtered when he spoke:

'Tribune, read my Safe Conduct! Read it!'

The Legate looked truly annoyed.

My brother marshaled what he could of his rhetoric, which wasn't much. 'She lies. She is condemned. Her family is dead. I was compelled to bear witness to Sejanus because they sought to kill Tiberius himself!'

'You turned on your own family?' asked the soldier.

'Oh, don't wear yourself out with this,' I said. 'The man has harried me all day. He has discovered that I am a woman alone, an heiress, and thinks that this is some uncivilized outpost of the Empire where he can bring a charge against a Senator's daughter with no proof. Dear lunatic, do pay attention. Julius Caesar gave Antioch its municipal standing less than one hundred years ago. There are legions stationed here, are there not?'

I looked at the Legate.

The Legate turned and glowered at my trembling brother.

'What is this Safe Conduct?' I asked. 'This bears the name Tiberius.'

The Legate snatched it from Lucius before Lucius could respond and handed the scroll to me. I had to take my hand off my dagger to unroll the paper.

'Ah, Sejanus of the Praetorian Guard! I knew it. And the Emperor probably knows nothing of it. Tribune, do you know those palace guards make one and one half times what a Legionnaire makes? And now they have these *Delatores,* given incentive to charge others with crimes for one-third of the condemned man's property!'

The Legate was now sizing up my brother and every flaw in Lucius shone in the light; his cowardly posture, his trembling hands, his shifty eyes, his growing desperation in the pursing of his lips.

I turned to Lucius.

'Do you realize, you madman, whoever you are, what you are asking of this seasoned and wise Roman officer? What if he should believe your insane lies? What will become of him when the letter arrives from Rome inquiring into my whereabouts and the disposition of my fortune!'

'Sir, this woman is a traitor!' shouted Lucius. 'On my honor I swear –'

'What honor is that?' asked the soldier under his breath. His eyes fixed on Lucius.

'If Rome were such,' I said, 'that families as old as mine could be so easily dispatched as this man asks you now to do with me, then why would the widow of Germanicus dare to go before the Senate for a trial?'

'They are all executed,' said my brother, who was at his worst and most solemn, and seemed to have lost all touch with the effect of his words, 'every one of them, because they were in a plot to kill Tiberius and I was given Safe Conduct and passage out for reporting them, as was my duty, to the *Delatores,* and to Sejanus, with whom I spoke myself!'

The possibilities were making themselves known slowly to the Legate.

'Sir,' I said to Lucius, 'have you anything else on your person that identifies you?'

'I don't need anything else!' said Lucius. 'Your fate is death.'

'Same as it was for your Father?' asked the Legate, 'and your wife? Had you children?'

'Throw her into prison tonight, and write to Rome!' declared Lucius. 'You'll see that I speak the truth!'

'And where will you be, whoever you are, while I am in prison? Looting my house?'

'You slut!' shouted Lucius. 'Don't you see this is all feminine wiles and lurid distraction!'

There was shock among the soldiers, revulsion in the face of the Legate. Flavius moved next to me.

'Officer,' asked Flavius with tempered dignity, 'what am I allowed to do on behalf of my Mistress against this madman?'

'You use such words again, Sir,' I said firmly to Lucius, 'and I'll lose my patience.'

The Legate took Lucius's arm. Lucius's right hand went to his dagger.

'Just who are you?' the Legate demanded. 'Are you one of the *Delatores?* You tell me you turned on your whole family?'

'Tribune,' I said, laying the gentlest touch yet on his arm. 'My Father's roots went back to the time of Romulus and Remus. We know no origins other than those in Rome. It was the same with my Mother, who was herself the daughter of a Senator. This man is saying rather . . . horrible things.'

'So it seems,' said the Legate, narrowing his

gaze, as he inspected Lucius. 'Where are your friends here, your companions; where do you live?'

'You can't do anything to me!' said Lucius.

The Legate glared at Lucius's hand on the dagger.

'You prepare to draw that against me!' asked the Legate.

Lucius clearly was at a loss.

'Why did you come to Antioch?' I demanded of Lucius. 'Were you the bearer of the poison that killed Germanicus?'

'Arrest her!' shouted Lucius.

'No, I don't believe my own accusation. Not even Sejanus would put such treachery in the hands of a petty scoundrel like you! Come now, what else do you have on your person to connect you with this family, this Safe Conduct which you say came from the pen of Sejanus?'

Lucius was utterly baffled.

'I certainly have nothing belonging to me to connect me to your wild and bloody sagas and tales,' I said.

The Legate interrupted me. 'Nothing to connect you to this name?' He took the Safe Conduct from my hand.

'Absolutely nothing,' I said, 'nothing but this madman here who is spouting horrors, and would lead the world to believe that our Emperor has lost his wits. Only he connects me with his bloody plot without witness or verification, and hurls insults at me.'

The Legate rolled up the Safe Conduct. 'And your purpose here, Madam?' he asked in a whisper.

'To live in peace and quiet,' I said softly. 'To live in safety and under the true shelter of Roman rule.'

Now I knew the battle had been won. But something else was required to seal the victory. I took another gamble.

Slowly I reached for my dagger and slowly I brought it out of its sling.

Lucius leapt back at once. He drew his dagger and lunged at me. He was immediately stabbed by the Legate and at least two of the soldiers.

He hung there bleeding on their weapons, staring from right to left and then he spoke, but his mouth was too full of blood. His eyes widened; it seemed again he would speak. Then, as the soldiers withdrew their daggers, his body folded up on the cobblestones at the foot of the stairs.

My brother Lucius was quite mercifully dead.

I looked at him and shook my head.

The Legate looked at me. This was a significant moment, and I knew it.

'What is it, Tribune,' I asked, 'that separates
us from the long-haired barbarians of the
North? Is it not law? Written law? Traditional
law? Is it not justice? That men and women are
called to account for what they do?'

'Yes, Madam,' he said.

'You know,' I went on in a reverent voice,
staring at this heap of blood and clothes and flesh
that lay on the stones, 'I saw our great Emperor
Caesar Augustus on the day of his death.'

'You saw him? You did?'

I nodded. 'When they were certain he was to
die, we were rushed to him with a few other
close friends. It was his hope to put down
rumors in the capital that might lead to unrest.
He had sent for a mirror and combed his hair.
He was primly propped up. And he asked us as
we entered the room: Didn't we think he'd
played his part well in the comedy of life?

'I thought, what courage! And then he made
some further joke, the old theatrical line they
say after plays:

If I have made you happy, kindly let me know
your appreciation with a warm goodbye.

*

230

'I could tell you more, but –'

'Oh, please do,' said the Legate.

'Well, why not?' I asked. 'It was told to me that the Emperor said of Tiberius, his chosen successor, 'Poor Rome, to be chewed slowly by those sluggish jaws!'

The Legate smiled. 'But there wasn't anyone else,' he said under his breath.

'Thank you, Tribune, for all your assistance. Would you allow me to take from my purse sufficient funds to treat you and your soldiers to a fine dinner –'

'No, Madam, I wouldn't have it be said I or any man here was bribed. Now this dead man. Do you know anything more of him?'

'Only this, Officer, that his body probably belongs in the river.'

The soldiers all laughed among themselves.

'Good night, Gracious Lady,' said the soldier.

And off I went, striding across the blackness of the Forum, with my beloved one-legged Flavius at my side and the torchbearers round us.

Only now did I shake all over. Only now did the sweat cover my whole body.

When we had plunged deeply into the unbroken darkness of a small alleyway, I said,

'Flavius, let these torchbearers go. There is no reason for them to know where we are headed.'

'Madam, I don't have any lantern.'

'The night's full of stars and has a near full moon. Look! Besides, there are others from the Temple who are following us.'

'There are?' he asked. He paid off the torch-bearers and they ran back towards the mouth of the street.

'Yes. There is one watching. And besides, we can see well enough by the lighted windows and Heaven's light, don't you think? I am tired, so tired.'

I walked on, reminding myself again and again that Flavius could not keep up. I began to weep.

'Tell me something with your great philo-sophical knowledge,' I said as I walked on, determined to make the tears stop. 'Tell me why evil people are so stupid? Why are so many of them just plain stupid?'

'Madam, I think there are quite a few evil people who are quite clever,' he said. 'But never have I seen such skilled rhetoric on the part of anyone, either bad or good, as your talents revealed just now.'

'I'm delighted that you know that that is all it was,' I said. 'Rhetoric. And to think he had the same teachers as I, the same library, the same Father –' My voice broke.

He put his arm gingerly about my shoulder and this time I didn't tell him to move away. I let him steady me. We walked faster as a pair.

'No,' I said, 'Flavius, the majority of the evil are just plain dumb, I've seen it all my life. The true crafty evil person is rare. It's bumbling that causes most of the misery of the world, utter stupid bumbling. It's underestimation of one's fellow man! You watch what happens with Tiberius. Tiberius Caesar and the Guard. Watch what happens to that damned Sejanus. You can sow the seeds of distrust everywhere, and lose yourself in an overgrown field.'

'We are home, Madam,' he said.

'Oh, thank God, you know it. I could never have told you this was the house.'

Within moments, he stopped and turned the key in a lock. The smell of urine was everywhere overpowering, as it always was in the back streets of ancient cities. A lantern threw a dim light on our wooden door. The light danced in the jet of water which fell from the lion's mouth in the fountain.

Flavius gave a series of knocks. It sounded to me as if the women answering the inner door were crying.

233

'Oh, Lord, now what?' I said. 'I am too sleepy. Whatever it is, tend to it.'

I went inside.

'Madam,' squealed one of the girls. I couldn't remember her name. 'I didn't let him in. I swear I never unbolted the door. I have no key to the gate. We had this house, all this, ready for you!' She sobbed.

'What on Earth are you talking about?' I asked.

But I knew. I'd seen in the corner of my eye. I knew. I turned and saw a very tall Roman sitting in my newly refurbished living room. He sat relaxed with ankle on knee in a gilded wooden chair.

'It's all right, Flavius,' I said. 'I know him.'

And I did. Because it was Marius. Marius the tall Keltoi. Marius, who had charmed me in childhood. Marius, whom I had almost identified in the shadows of the Temple.

He rose at once.

He came towards me, where I stood in the darkness on the edges of the atrium, and he whispered, 'My beautiful Pandora!'

234

7

He stopped just short of touching me.

'Oh, do, please,' I said. I moved to kiss him, but he moved away. The room had scattered lamps. He played the shadows.

'Marius, of course, Marius! And you look not one day older than when I saw you in my girlhood. Your face is radiant, and your eyes, how beautiful are your eyes. I would sing these praises to the accompaniment of a lyre if I could.'

Flavius had slowly withdrawn, taking the distressed girls with him. He made not a sound.

'Pandora,' Marius said, 'I wish I could take you in my arms, but there are reasons why I cannot, and you mustn't touch me, not because I want it so much, but because I'm not what you think. You don't see the evidence of youth in me; it is something so far afield of the promises

235

of youth that I've only just begun to understand its agonies.'

Suddenly he looked off. He raised his hand for my silence and patience.

'That thing is abroad,' I said. 'The burnt blood drinker.'

'Don't think on your dreams just now,' he said to me directly. 'Think on our youth. I loved you when you were a girl of ten. When you were fifteen I begged your Father for your hand.'

'You did? He never told me this.'

He looked away again. Then he shook his head.

'The burnt one,' I said.

'I feared this,' he cursed himself. 'He followed you from the Temple! Oh, Marius! You are fool. You have played into his hands. But he is not as clever as he thinks.'

'Marius, was it you who sent me the dreams!'

'No, never! I would do anything in my power to protect you from myself.'

'And from the old legends?'

'Don't be quick of wit, Pandora. I know your immense cleverness served you well back there with your loathsome brother Lucius and the gentleman Legate. But don't think too much about . . . dreams. Dreams are nothing, and dreams will pass.'

'Then the dreams came from him, this hideous burnt killer?'

'I can't figure it!' he said. 'But don't think on the images. Don't feed him now with your mind.'

'He reads minds,' I said, 'just as you do.'

'Yes. But you can cloak your thoughts. It's a mental trick. You can learn it. You can walk with your soul locked up in a little metal box in your head.'

I realized he was in much pain. An immense sadness came from him. 'This cannot be allowed to happen!' he insisted.

'What is that, Marius? You speak about the woman's voice, you –'

'No, be quiet.'

'I will not! I will get to the bottom of this!'

'You must take my instructions!' He stepped forward and again he reached to touch me, to take me by the arms, as my Father might have done, but then he did not.

'No, it is you who must tell me everything,' I said.

I was amazed at the whiteness of his skin, its utter blemishless perfection. And once again the radiance of his eyes seemed almost impossible. Inhuman.

Only now did I see the full glory of his long

hair. He did look like the Keltoi, who had been his ancestors. His hair touched his shoulders. It was a gleaming gold, overly bright, yellow as corn and full of soft curls.

'Look at you!' I whispered. 'You're not alive!'

'No, take your last look, for you are leaving here!'

'What?' I said. 'Last look?' I repeated his words. 'What are you talking about! I've only arrived, laid my plans, rid myself of my brother! I am not leaving here. Do you mean to say you are leaving me?'

There was a terrible anguish in his face, a courageous appeal that I had never seen in any man, not even in my Father, who had worked swiftly in those last fatal moments at home, as if he were merely intent on sending me on an important appointment.

Marius's eyes were filmed with blood. He was crying, and his eyes were sore with the tears! No! These were tears like the tears of the magnificent Queen in the dream, who, bound to her throne, wept and stained her cheeks and her throat and her linen.

He wanted to deny it. He shook his head, but he knew I was quite convinced.

'Pandora, when I saw it was you,' he said,

'when you came into the Temple and I saw it was you who had had these blood dreams, I was beside myself. I must get you far from this, far from all danger.'

I separated myself from his spell, from the aura of his beauty. I beheld him with a cold eye, and I listened as he went on, noting all about him, from the glitter of his eyes to the way that he gestured.

'You have to leave Antioch at once,' he said. 'I will stay here the night with you. Then in the day, you pick up your faithful Flavius and your two girls, they are honest, and you take them with you. You put miles between you and this place by day, and this thing can't follow you! Don't tell me now where you mean to go. You can discuss all this at the docks in the morning. You have plenty of money.'

'You are the one who is dreaming now, Marius; I am not going. Who is it precisely that you want me to flee? The weeping Queen on her throne? Or the prowling, burnt one? The former reaches me over miles and miles of sea with her summons. She warns me against my evil brother. The other I can easily dispatch. I have no fear of him. I know what he is from the dreams, and I know how the sun has hurt him, and I will myself pin him to the wall in the sun.'

He was silent, biting his lip.

'I will do that for her, for the Queen in the dreams, to avenge her.'

'Pandora, I am begging you.'

'In vain,' I said. 'Do you think I have come so far only to run again? And the woman's voice –'

'How do you know it was this Queen of whom you dreamt? There could be other blood drinkers in this city. Men, women. They all want the same thing.'

'And you fear them?'

'Loathe them! And I must keep clear of them, not give them what they want! Never give them what they want.'

'Ah, I see it all,' I said.

'You do not!' he said, scowling down at me. So fierce, so perfect.

'You are one of them, Marius. You are whole. You are unburnt. They want your blood to heal themselves.'

'How could you think of such a thing?'

'In my dreams, they called the Queen "the Fount."'

I flew at him and imprisoned him in my arms! He was powerfully strong, solid as a tree! I never felt such hardness of muscle in a man. I lay my head on his shoulder, and his cheek against the top of my head was cold!

But he enfolded me gently with both arms, stroking my hair, pulling it down out of all the pins and letting it flow down my back. I felt a rich tingling all over the surface of my skin.

Hard, so hard, yet with no pulse of life. No warmth of human blood in his gentle, sweet gestures.

'My darling,' he said, 'I don't know the source of your dreams, but I know this. You will be protected from me and from them. You will never become part of this old tale that goes on verse by verse no matter how the world changes! I won't allow it.'

'Explain these things to me. I will not cooperate with you until you explain everything. Do you know the anguish of the Queen of the dream? Her tears are like yours. Look. Blood. You stain your tunic! Is she here, this Queen; has she summoned me?'

'And what if she has and she wants to punish you for this former life you dreamt in which the evil gods kept her fettered. What if that is so!'

'No,' I said. 'That is not her intention. Besides, I wouldn't do what the dark gods of the dream said. I wouldn't drink from "the Fount." I ran and that's why I died in the desert.'

'Ah!' He threw up his hands! And walked

away. He stared out into the dark peristyle. Only the stars lighted the trees there. I saw a faint glow coming from the far dining room on the other side of the house.

I looked at him, at his great height and the straightness of his back, and the way his feet were so firmly fixed on the mosaic floor. The lamps made his blond hair glorious.

I heard him, though he whispered with his back to me.

'How could this stupid thing have happened!'

'What stupid thing!' I demanded. I came to his side. 'You mean that I am here, in Antioch. I'll tell you how. My Father arranged my escape, that's how . . .'

'No, no, I don't mean that. I want you to be safe, alive, out of all danger, protected, so that you flower as you are meant to do. Your petals aren't even bruised at the edges, look at you, and your boldness heats your beauty! Your brother had no chance against your learning or your rhetoric. And yet you charmed the soldiers and made slaves of them with your superiority, never once rousing their resentment. You have years of life in you! But I must think of some way to make you safe. Look. This is the heart of it. You have to leave Antioch during the day.'

'"Friend of the Temple," that's what the

Priest and Priestess called you. They said you could read the old script. They said you bought up all the Egyptian books when they came into the port. Why? If you seek her, the Queen, then seek her through me, because it is she who said that she had summoned me.'

'She didn't speak in the dreams! You don't know who spoke the words! What if the dreams do have their root in your migrant soul? What if you have lived before? And now you come to the Temple and there is one of these loathed ancient gods on the prowl and you are in danger. You must get away, from here, from me, from this wounded hunter, whom I will find.'

'You're not telling me all you know! What happened to you, Marius! What happened! Who did this to you, this miracle of your radiance. This is no cloak; the light comes from within!'

'Damn it, Pandora, do you think I wanted my life foreshortened and my destiny extended forever!' He was suffering. He looked at me, unwilling to speak, and I felt such pain coming from him, such loneliness, that for a moment it was unbearable.

I felt a wave of my own anguish of the long night before, when the utter vacuity of all religions and creeds had struck me hard and the sheer effort of a good life seemed a fool's trap, and nothing more.

He suddenly closed his arms around me, surprising me, holding me firmly and rubbing his cheek gently against my hair, and kissing my head. Silken, polished, gentle beyond words. 'Pandora, Pandora, Pandora,' he said. 'The beautiful little girl grown into the marvelous woman.'

I held this hard effigy of the most spectacular and singular man I had ever known or seen: I held it and this time heard the beating of his heart, the distinct rhythm of it. I laid my ear on his chest.

'Oh, Marius, if only I could lay my head to rest next to yours. If I could only yield to your protection. But you are driving me away! You don't promise guardianship, you ordain flight for me, wandering and more nightmares, and mystery, and despair. No. I can't.'

I turned away from his caresses. I could feel his kisses on my hair.

'Don't tell me that I'll never see you again. Don't think I can bear that along with everything else that's happened. I have no one here, and then who comes but one who left such a stamp on my girlish heart that the details are as deep as the finest coin. And you say you will never see me again, that I must go.'

I turned around.

It was lust shining in his eyes. Yet he checked it. In a soft voice, he confessed with a little smile:

'Oh, how I admired your work with the Legate. I thought the two of you would plan out the whole conquest of the Germanic tribes on your own.' He sighed. 'You must find a good life, a rich life, a life where your soul and body are fed.' The color flared in his face. He looked at me, at my breasts, at my hips and then at my face. Ashamed and trying to conceal it. Lust.

'Are you a man still?' I asked.

He didn't answer me. But his expression grew chilly.

'You will never know the full extent of what I am!' he said.

'Ah, but not a man!' I said. 'Am I right? Not a man.'

'Pandora, you are deliberately taunting me. Why? Why do this?'

'This transformation, this induction into the blood drinkers; it's added no inches to your height. Did it add any inches anywhere else?'

'Please stop this,' he said.

'Want me, Marius. Say that you do. I see it. Confirm it in words. What does that cost you?'

'You are infuriating!' he said. His face colored

deeply with his rage, and pressed his lips together so hard that they went white. 'Thank the gods that I don't want you! Not enough to betray love for brief and bloody ecstasy.'

'The Temple people, they don't really know what you are, do they?'

'No!' he said.

'And you will not lay open your heart to me.'

'Never. You will forget me and these dreams will fade. I wager I can make them fade, myself, through prayer for you. I will do it.'

'That's a pious tack,' I said. 'What grants you such favor with the ancient Isis, who drank blood and was the Fount?'

'Don't say those words; it's all lies, all of it. You do not know that this Queen you saw was Isis. What did you learn in these nightmares? Think. You learned that this Queen was the prisoner of those who drank blood and she condemned them! They were evil. Think. Go back into the dream. Think. You thought them evil, evil then, and you think them evil now. In the Temple, you caught the scent of evil. I know you did. I watched you.'

'Yes. But you're not evil, Marius, you can't convince me of this! You have a body like marble, you're a blood drinker, but like a god, but not evil!'

He was about to protest when he stopped again. He looked out of the corner of his eye. And then slowly turned his head and let his gaze drift up through the roof of the peristyle.

'Is it the dawn coming,' I asked, 'the rays of Amon Ra?'

'You are the most maddening human being I've ever known!' he said. 'If I had married you, you would have put me in an early grave. I would have been spared all of this!'

'All of what?'

He called out for Flavius, who had been close all the while, listening to everything.

'Flavius, I'm leaving now,' he said. 'I must. But guard her. When night falls, I'll be here again, as quickly as I can. Should anything precede me, any badly scarred and frightening assailant, go for its head with your sword. The head, remember? And of course your Mistress here will no doubt be quite able to lend a hand in defending herself.'

'Yes, sir. Must we leave Antioch?'

'Watch your words, my faithful Greek,' I said. 'I am Mistress here. We are not leaving Antioch.'

'Try to persuade her to prepare,' said Marius. He looked at me.

A long silence fell between us. I knew he read my thoughts. Then a shudder of the blood dreams passed over me. I saw his eyes brighten. Something quickened in his expression. I shook off the dream, filled with terror. I am no hostess to terror.

'It's all interwound,' I murmured, 'the dreams, the Temple, you being there, their calling on you for help. What are you, some white god put on Earth to hunt the dark blood drinkers? Does the Queen live?'

'Oh, I wish I were such a god!' he said. 'I would be if I could be! That no more blood drinkers will ever be made, of that I am certain. Let them lay flowers on an altar before a statue of basalt!'

I felt such love for him and rushed to him suddenly. 'Take me with you now, wherever you are going.'

'I can't!' he said. He blinked as though something hurt his eyes. He couldn't fully lift his head.

'It's the coming light, isn't it? You are one of them.'

'Pandora, when I come to you, be ready to leave this place!' he said.

And he vanished.

Like that, he vanished. Like that, he was gone from my arms and from my living room and from my house.

I turned away and walked slowly about the shadowy living room. I looked at the murals on the walls; the happy dancing figures with their laurels and their crowns of leaves – Bacchus and his nymphs, so modestly covered for such a riotous crew!

Flavius spoke. 'Madam, a sword which I found among your possessions, may I have it in readiness?'

'Yes, and daggers galore, and fire, do not forget fire. It will run from fire.' I sighed. How did I know this? I did. So much for it. 'But Flavius.' I turned around. 'It won't come until dark. There is only a small margin of the night left. We can both sleep as soon as we see the sky turn purple.' I lifted my hand to my forehead. 'I am trying to remember . . .'

'What, Madam?' Flavius said. He looked no less splendid after the spectacle of Marius, simply a man of different proportion but equally fine, and with warm human skin.

'Whether the dreams ever came by day. Was it always night? Oh, I am sleepy and they summon me. Flavius, put a light in my bath. But I'm going to bed. I am drowsy. Can you watch?'

'Yes, Madam.'

'Look, the stars have all but faded. What is it like to be one of them, Flavius, to be admired only in the darkness, when men and women live with candles and lamps. To be known and described, only in the heaviness of night, when all the business of day has ended!'

'You are truly the most resourceful woman I've ever known,' he said. 'How you brought justice to the man who accused you.' He took my arm, and we moved towards the bedchamber where I had dressed that morning.

I loved him. An entire lifetime of crises could not have made it stronger.

'You will not sleep in the great bed of the house, in the dining room?'

'No,' I said. 'That is for the display of marriage, and I will never know marriage again. I want to bathe, but I'm so sleepy.'

'I can wake the girls.'

'No, to the bed. You have a chamber proper?'

'Yes,' he led the way. It was still quite dark. I thought I heard a rustling noise. Realized it was nothing.

And there lay the bed with its small lamp, and on the bed so many pillows in the Oriental style, a soft soft nest into which I fell, like a Persian.

At once, the dream:

We blood drinkers stood in a vast Temple. It was meant to be dark. We could see this dark, as certain animals must see in the dark. We were all bronze-skinned, or tanned, or golden. We were all men.

On the floor lay the Queen screaming. Her skin was white. Pure white. Her long hair was black. Her crown bore the horns and the sun! The crown of Isis. She was the goddess! It took five blood drinkers on either side to hold her down. She thrashed her head from side to side, her eyes seeming to crackle with Divine Light.

'I am your Queen! You cannot do this to me!' How purely white she was, and her screams grew ever more desperate and imploring. 'Great Osiris, save me from this! Save me from these blasphemers! Save me from the profane!'

The Priest beside me sneered at her.

The King sat motionless on the throne. But it was not to this King that she prayed. She prayed to an Osiris beyond.

'Hold her more tightly.'

Two more came to secure her ankles.

'Drink!' said the Priest to me. 'Kneel down and drink from her blood. Her blood is more powerful than any blood that exists in the world. Drink.'

She cried softly.

'Monsters, demon children!' she sobbed.

'I won't do it,' I said.

'Do it! You must have her blood!'

251

'No, not against her will. Not like this! She's our Mother Isis!'

'She is our Fount and our prisoner.'

'No,' I said.

The Priest shoved me forward. I knocked him down to the floor. I looked at her.

She looked at me as indiscriminately as she looked at the others. Her face was delicate and exquisitely painted. Her rage did not distort her features. Her voice was low and full of hatred.

'I will destroy you all,' she said. 'Some morning, I will escape and walk into the sun's light and all of you will burn! All of you will burn! As I burn! Because I am the Fount! And the evil in me will be burnt and extinguished in all of you forever. Come, you miserable fledgling,' she said to me. 'Do as they say. Drink, and wait my vengeance.

'The god Amon Ra will rise in the East and I will walk towards him, and his deadly rays will kill me. I shall be a sacrifice of fire to destroy every one of you who has been born of me, transformed by my blood! You greedy wanton gods who would use the power we possess for gain!'

Then a hideous transformation befell the entire dream. She rose to her feet. She was pristine and freshly adorned. Torches burst into flame around her, one and two and three and then many and more, flaring as if they'd just been ignited, till she was surrounded by flame. The gods were gone. She smiled and beckoned to me. She lowered her head; the white beneath her eyes shone as she looked up at me. She smiled. She was cunning.

I woke up screaming.

I was in my bed. Antioch. The lamp burned. Flavius held me. I saw the light shine on his ivory leg as it was stretched out. I saw the light shine on the carved toes.

'Hold onto me, hold me!' I said. 'Mother Isis! Hold me.'

'How long have I been asleep?'

'Only moments,' he said.

'No.'

'The sun has just risen. Do you want to go out, lie in the warm sun perhaps?'

'No!' I screamed.

He tightened his warm, desperate comforting grip. 'It was only a bad dream, my beautiful lady,' he said. 'Close your eyes. I'll sleep by your side, with my dagger here.'

'Oh, yes, please, please, Flavius. Don't let me go. Hold me,' I cried.

I lay down and he snuggled next to me, his knees behind mine, his arm over me.

My eyes opened. I heard Marius's voice again:

'Thank the gods that I don't want you! Not enough to betray love for brief and bloody ecstasy.'

'Oh, Flavius,' I said. 'My skin! Is my skin burning!' I started to rise. 'Put out the light. Put out the sun!'

'No, Madam, your skin is as beautiful as it always was. Lie down. Let me sing to you.'

'Yes, sing . . .' I said.

I followed his song, it was Homer, it was Achilles and Hector, and I loved the way he sang it, the pauses he made, I pictured those heroes, and the high walls of doomed Troy, and my eyes grew heavy. I drifted. I rested.

He placed his hand over my head, as if to keep the dreams out, as if to be a human dream catcher. And I sighed as he smoothed my hair.

I pictured Marius, the sheen of his skin. It had been so like that of the Queen, and the dazzle of his eyes, so truly like that of the Queen, and I heard him say, 'Damn it, Pandora, do you think I wanted my life foreshortened and my destiny extended forever!'

And there followed, before unconsciousness, the utter despair, the sense of worthlessness of all striving. Better that we be no more than beasts, like the lions in the arena.

8

I awoke. I could hear the birds. I wasn't sure. I calculated that it was still morning, midmorning.

I walked barefoot into the next room, and through it into the peristyle. I walked on the tiled edge of the Earth and looked up at the blue sky. The sun had not yet risen high enough to be seen directly above.

I unbolted the door and went barefoot to the gate. To the first man I saw, a man of the desert, wearing a long head veil, I said:

'What time is it? Noon?'

'Oh, no, Madam,' he said. 'Not by half. Have you overslept? How lucky for you.' He nodded and went on.

A lamp burned in the living room. I walked into the living room and saw that the lamp stood on the desk which my servants had prepared for me.

The ink was there and so were the pens, and so were sheets of clean parchment.

I sat down and I wrote down everything that I could remember of the dreams, my eyes straining to see by the miserable little lamp in the shadows, too far from the light that filled the fresh green garden of the peristyle.

My arm hurt finally from the speed with which I scratched at the parchment. In detail I described the last dream, the torches, the Queen's smile, her beckoning to me.

It was done. All the while, I had set aside the pages to dry all about me on the floor. There was no breeze or wind to threaten them. I gathered them up.

I went to the edge of the garden deliberately to look at the blue sky, this sheaf of papers close to my breast. Blue and clear.

'And you cover this world,' I said. 'And you are changeless, save for one light that rises and sets,' I said to the sky. 'Then comes the night with deceptive and seductive patterns!'

'Madam!' It was Flavius behind me, and very sleepy. 'You've scarcely slept at all. You need rest. Go back to bed.'

'Go get my sandals now, hurry,' I said.

And as he disappeared, so did I – out the front gate of the house, walking as fast as I could.

I was halfway to the Temple of Isis when I realized the discomfort of confronting this filthy street in bare feet. I realized I wore the rumpled linen dresses in which I'd slept. My hair streamed. I didn't slow my pace.

I was elated. I was not helpless as when I had fled my Father's house. I was not edgy and in deep danger as when Lucius had pointed me out to the Roman soldiers last night.

I was not gripped in fear as I had been when the Queen smiled to me in the dream. Nor shivering as I had been upon waking.

I walked on and on. I was in the grip of an immense drama. I would see it through to the last act.

People passed – laborers of the morning, an old man with a crooked stick. I barely saw these people.

I took a cold small delight in the fact that they noticed my loose, free hair and my wrinkled gowns. I wondered what it must be like to separate oneself from all civilization and never worry again about the position of a fastening or a pin, to sleep on grass, to fear nothing!

Fear nothing! Ah, that was so beautiful to me.

I came to the Forum. The markets were busy; the beggars were out in full force. Curtained litters were being carried every which way The philosophers were teaching under the porticoes. I could hear those huge strange noises that always come from a harbor – of the cargo being dropped, perhaps, I didn't know. I smelled the Orontes. I hoped Lucius's body was floating in it.

I went up the steps and right into the Temple of Isis.

'The High Priest and Priestess,' I said. 'I must see them.' I walked past a confused and distinctly virginal-looking young woman and went into the side chamber where they had first spoken to me. No table. Only the couch. I went into another apartment of the Temple. A table. Scrolls.

I heard feet rushing. The Priestess came to me. She was already painted for the day and her wig and ornaments were in place. I felt no shock as I looked at her.

'Look,' I said. 'I had another dream.' I pointed to the sheets which I had piled neatly on the table. 'I've written down everything for you.'

The Priest arrived. He approached the table and stared at the sheets.

'Read it all, every word. Read it now. Bear witness lest something happens to me!'

The Priest and Priestess stood on opposite sides of me, the Priest carefully lifting the pages to study each one, while not actually turning over the stack.

'I am a migrant soul,' I said. 'She wants some reckoning or favor of me, I don't know which, but she lives! She is no mere statue.'

They stared at me.

'Well? Speak up? Everyone comes to you for guidance.'

'But Madam,' said the Priest, 'we can't read any of this.'

'What?'

'It's written in the most ancient and ornate form of the old picture writing.'

'What!'

I stared down at the pages. I saw only my own words as they had flowed in a cadence from my mind, through my hand, through my pen. I couldn't make my eyes fix upon the form of the letters.

I lifted the last page and read aloud, 'Her smile was cunning. It filled me with fear.' I held out the page.

They shook their heads in firm denial.

Suddenly there was a little ruckus and Flavius, much out of breath and red in the face, was admitted to the room. He had my sandals. He took one look at me and rested back against the wall in great and obvious relief.

'Come here,' I said.

He obeyed.

'Now look at these pages, read them, are they not in Latin?'

Two slaves came timidly, hastily washing my feet and fastening on my sandals. Above me Flavius looked at the pages.

'This is ancient Egyptian writing,' Flavius said. 'The oldest form I've ever seen. This would fetch a fortune in Athens!'

'I just wrote it!' I said. I looked at the Priest, then the Priestess. 'Summon your tall blond-haired friend,' I said. 'Get him here. The mind reader, the one who can read the old script.'

'We can't, Madam.' The Priest looked help-lessly at the Priestess.

'Why not? Where is he? He only comes after dark, doesn't he?' I asked.

They both nodded.

'And when he shops for books, all the books on Egypt, he does this by the light of lamps too?' I asked. I already knew the answer.

They looked at one another helplessly.

'Where does he live?'

'Madam, we do not know. Please don't try to find him. He will be here as soon as the light fades. He cautioned us last night that you were most precious to him.'

'You don't know where he lives.'

I stood up.

'All right,' I said, I picked up the sheaf of my pages, my spectacular ancient writing.

'Your burnt one,' I said, as I walked out of the room, 'your murdering blood drinker. Did he come last night? Did he leave you an offering?'

'Yes,' said the Priest. He looked humiliated. 'Lady Pandora, rest and take some food.'

'Yes,' said my loyal Flavius, 'you must.'

'Not a chance,' I said. Clutching the pages, I walked across the great hall to the front doors. They pleaded with me. I ignored them.

I went out into the heat of the day. Flavius followed. The Priest and Priestess pleaded with us to remain.

I scanned the enormous marketplace. The good booksellers were all grouped at the far left end of the Forum. I walked across the square.

Flavius struggled to keep up. 'Madam, please, what are you going to do? You've lost your mind.'

'I have not and you know it,' I said. 'You saw him last night!'

'Madam, wait for him at the Temple, as he asked,' Flavius said.

'Why? Why should I do that?' I asked.

The bookshops were numerous, containing manuscripts in all languages. 'Egypt, Egypt!' I cried out, both in Latin and Greek. There was lots of noise, many buyers and sellers. Plato was everywhere, and Aristotle. There was a whole stack of the book of his life by Caesar Augustus, which he had completed in the years before his death.

'Egypt!' I cried out. Merchants pointed to old scrolls. Fragments.

The canopies flapped in the breeze. I looked into one room after another, at rows of slaves busily copying, slaves dipping their pens, who did not dare to look up from their work.

There were slaves outside, in the shade, writing letters dictated by humble men and women. It was all very busy.

Trunks were being brought into one shop. The owner, an elderly man, came forward.

'Marius,' I said. 'I come from Marius, the tall blond one who comes to your shop only by night.'

The man said nothing.

I went into the next shop. Everything was Egyptian, not merely the scrolls rolled out for display but the fragments of painting on the walls, the chunks of plaster holding still the profile of a King or Queen, rows of little jars, figures from some long-defiled tomb. How the Egyptians loved to make those tiny wooden figures.

And there I beheld just the sort of man I sought, the true antiquarian. Only reluctantly did he look up from his book, a gray-haired man, the book a codex in modern Egyptian.

'Nothing that would interest Marius?' I asked, walking into the shop. Trunks and boxes blocked me at each turn. 'You know, the tall Roman, Marius, who studies the ancient manuscripts, buys the most prized of them? You know the man I mean. Very blue eyes. Blond hair. He comes by night; you stay open for him.'

The man nodded. He glanced at Flavius and said with a lift of his eyebrows. 'Quite an ivory leg there.' Cultured Greek. Excellent. 'Grecian, Oriental and perfectly pale.'

'I come on Marius's behalf,' I said.

'I save everything for him, as he asks,' said the man with a little shrug. 'I sell nothing that isn't offered first to Marius.'

'I'm sure you do. I come on his behalf.' I looked around. 'May I sit down?'

'Oh, please do, forgive me,' said the man. He gestured to a sturdy trunk. Flavius stood perplexed. The man sat back down at his cluttered table.

'I wish I had a proper table. Where is my slave? I know I have some wine around here. I just . . . I was reading in this text the most amazing story!'

'Really,' I said. 'Well, take a look at this!' I thrust the pages into his hand.

'My god, but this is beautiful copying,' he said, 'and so fresh!' He whispered under his breath. He could make out many of the words. 'Marius will be very interested in this. This is about the legends of Isis, this is what Marius studies.'

I drew back the papers gently. 'I've written this for him!'

'You wrote it?'

'Yes, but you see, I want to surprise him with something, a gift! Something newly arrived, something he hasn't seen yet.'

'Well, there's quite a lot.'

'Flavius, money.'

'Madam, I don't have any'

'That's not true, Flavius; you wouldn't leave the house without the keys and some money. Hand it over.'

'Oh, I'll take it on credit if it's for Marius,' said the old man. 'Hmmm, you know, several things came onto the market this very week. It's because of the famine in Egypt. People were forced to sell, I suppose. You never know where an Egyptian manuscript comes from. But here –' He reached up and took a fragile papyrus from its niche in the dusty crisscross of wooden shelves.

He laid it down reverently and most cautiously opened it. The papyrus had been well preserved, but it was flaking at the edges. The thing would disintegrate if not handled with care.

I stood to look at it over his shoulder. A dizziness overcame me. I saw the desert and a town of huts with roofs of palm branches. I strained to open my eyes.

'This is,' said the old man, 'positively the oldest manuscript in Egyptian which I have ever seen! Here, steady yourself, my dear. Lean upon my shoulder. Let me give you my stool.'

'No, not necessary,' I said gazing at the letters. I read aloud, 'To my Lord, Narmer, King of Upper and Lower Egypt, who are these enemies of me that say I do not walk in righteousness? When has Your Majesty ever known me not to be righteous? Indeed I seek to do always more than what is asked of me or expected. When have I not heard every word of the accused so that he may be judged in fairness, as would Your Majesty? . . .'

I broke off. My head swam. Some brief recollection. I was a child and we were all going up into the mountains over the desert to ask the god Osiris, the blood god, to look into the heart of the evildoer. 'Look,' said those around me. The god was a man of perfection, bronze of skin and under the moon; he took the condemned and slowly drew out his blood. Beside me a woman whispered that the god had made his judgment and rendered punishment and the evil blood would go back now to be cleansed and reborn in another in which it would do no harm.

I tried to banish this vision, this sense of enclosing remembrance. Flavius was greatly concerned and held me by the shoulders.

I stood suspended in two worlds. I gazed out at the bright sun striking the stones of the Forum, and I lived somewhere else, a young man running up a mountain, declaring my innocence. 'Summon the old blood god! He will look into my husband's heart and see that the man lies. I never lay with another.' Oh, sweet darkness, come, I needed it to shroud the mountains because the blood god slept by day hidden, lest Ra, the sun god, find him and destroy him out of jealousy.

'Because she had conquered them all,' I whispered. I meant Queen Isis. 'Flavius, hold me.'

'I have you, Madam.'

'There,' said the old man, who had risen and pushed me down on his stool.

The night over Egypt filled with stars. I saw it as distinctly as I saw this shop around me in Antioch at midday. I saw the stars and knew I had won. The god would rule. 'Oh, come forth, please, from this mountain, our beloved Osiris, and look into my husband's heart and my heart, and if you find me in the wrong, then my blood is yours, I pledge it.' He was coming! There he was, as I had seen him in childhood before the Priests of Ra had forbidden the old worship. 'Righteousness, righteousness, righteousness!' the crowd chanted. The man who was my husband cowered as the god pointed his finger in judgment at him. 'Give me this evil blood and I shall devour it,' said the god. 'Then bring back my offerings. Do not be cowards in the face of a rich priesthood. You stand before a god.' He pointed at each of the villagers and pronounced his or her name. He knew trades. He could read their minds! He drew back his lips and showed his fangs. The vision dissolved. I stared at common objects as though they had life and venom.

'Oh, ye gods,' I said in genuine distress. 'I must reach Marius. I must reach him now!' When he heard these things, Marius would draw me into the truth with him. He had to do it.

'Hire a litter for your Mistress,' said the old bookseller to Flavius. 'She is overtired, and it's too long a walk up that hill!'

'Hill?' I perked up. This man knew where Marius lived! I quickly went faint again, bowing my head, and with a weary gesture said, 'Please, old gentleman, tell my steward precisely how to reach the house.'

'Of course. I know two short cuts, one slightly more difficult than another. We deliver books to Marius all the time.'

Flavius was staring aghast.

I tried to suppress my smile. This was going much better than I had ever hoped. But I was torn and bruised from the visions of Egypt. I hated the look of the desert, the mountains, the thought of blood gods.

I rose to go.

'It's a pink villa on the very edge of the city,' said the old man. 'It's just within the walls, overlooking the river, the last house. Once it was a country house outside the walls. It is on a mountain of stones. But no one will answer Marius's gate by day. All know how he wants to sleep all day and study all night, as is his custom. We leave our books with the boys.'

'He'll welcome me,' I said.

'If you wrote that, most likely he will,' said the old man.

Then we were off. The sun had fully risen. The square was filled with shoppers. Women carried baskets on their heads. The Temples were thriving. It was a game, darting through the crowd, one way and then another.

'Come on, Flavius,' I said.

It was a torture keeping to Flavius's slow pace as we mounted the hill, turn by turn, drawing ever closer.

'You know this is madness!' said Flavius. 'He can't be awake during the light of day; you've proven this to me and to yourself! I, the incredulous Athenian, and you the cynical Roman. What are we doing?'

Up and up we climbed, passing one sumptuous house after another. Locked gates. The bark of guard dogs.

'Hurry up. Must I listen to this lecture forever? Ah, there, look, my beloved Flavius. The pink house, the last house. Marius lives in style. Look at the walls and the gates.'

At last I had my hands on the iron bars. Flavius collapsed on the grass across the small road. He was spent.

I pulled on the bell rope.

Trees laid down heavy limbs over the top of

the walls. Through the mesh of leaf, I could make out a figure that came out on the high porch of the second floor.

'No admittance!' he cried out.

'I have to see Marius,' I said. 'He's expecting me!' I cupped my hands and shouted. 'He wants me to come. He told me to come.'

Flavius said a quick prayer under his breath. 'Oh, Mistress, I hope you know this man better than you knew your own brother.'

I laughed. 'There is no comparison,' I said. 'Stop complaining.'

The figure had disappeared. I heard running feet.

Finally two dark-headed young boys appeared before me, little more than children, beardless, with long black curls, and beautifully dressed in gold-trimmed tunics. They looked Chaldean.

'Open the gate, hurry!' I said.

'Madam, I can't admit you,' said the speaker of the two. 'I cannot admit anyone to this house until Marius himself comes. Those are his orders.'

'Comes from where?' I asked.

'Madam, he appears when he wishes, then he receives who he will. Madam, please, tell me your name and I will tell him that you have called.'

'You either open the gate or I will climb over the wall,' I said.

The boys were horrified. 'No, Madam, you can't do that!'

'Well? Aren't you going to shout for help?' I asked.

The two slaves stared amazed. They were so pretty. One was slightly taller than the other. Both wore exquisite bracelets.

'Just as I thought,' I said. 'There's no one else here but you.' I turned and tested the thick snaggle of vine that rose over the plastered brick. I leapt up and planted my right foot as high as I could in the thick mesh and rose in one leap to throw my arms over the top of the wall.

Flavius had risen from the grass and rushed to me.

'Madam, I beg you not to do this,' said Flavius. 'Madam, this is bad, bad, bad! You can't just climb this man's wall.'

The servants within were chattering frantically with one another. I think it was in Chaldean.

'Madam, I fear for you!' cried Flavius. 'How can I protect you from such a man as this Marius? Madam, the man will be angry with you!'

I lay on the top of the wall, on my stomach,

catching my breath. The garden inside was vast and lovely. Ah, what marble fountains. The two slaves had backed up and were staring at me as if I were a powerful monster.

'Please, please!' both boys pleaded with me at once. 'He'll exact a terrible vengeance! You don't know him. Please, Madam, wait!'

'Hand me the sheets of paper, Flavius, hurry. I have no time for disobedience!'

Flavius complied. 'Oh, this is wrong, wrong, wrong!' he said. 'Nothing can come of this but the most fearful misunderstandings.'

Then I slid down the inside of the wall, tickled all over by the thick overlay of bristling and brilliant leaves, and I laid my head in the matted tendrils and blossoms. I didn't fear the bees. I never have. I rested. I held tight to my written pages. Then moved to the gate so I could see Flavius.

'You let me handle Marius,' I said. 'Now, you didn't come out without your dagger.'

'No, I did not,' he said, lifting his cloak to reveal it, 'and with your permission I would like to plunge it through my heart now so that I will be most assuredly stone-cold dead before the Master of this house arrives home to find you running rampant in his garden!'

'Permission denied,' I said. 'Don't you dare.

Haven't you heard all that has been said? You are on guard not against Marius but against a shriveled limping demon of burnt flesh. He'll come at dark! What if he reaches here before Marius?'

'Oh, yea gods, help me!' His hands flew to his face.

'Flavius, straighten up. You are a man! Do I have to remind you of this perpetually? You are watching for this dreaded burnt bag of bones, and he is weak. Remember what Marius said. Go for his head. Stab him in the eyes, just cut him and cut him and shout for me, and I will come. Now go to sleep until dark. He can't come till then, if he even knows to come here! Besides, I think Marius will arrive first.'

I turned and walked towards the open doors of the villa. The beautiful long-haired boys were in tears.

For a moment the tranquillity and moist cool air of the garden lulled all fear in me, and I seemed safe, among patterns I understood, far far from dark Temples, safe in Tuscany in our own family gardens there, which had been so rich like this.

'Let me beg you one last time to come back out of this man's garden!' Flavius shouted.

I ignored him.

All the doors of this lovely plastered villa stood open to the porches above or the outdoors below. Listen to the trickling of the fountains. There were lemon trees, and many a marble statue of a lazy sensuous god or goddess, round which flowers grew in rich purple or blue. Diana, the huntress, rose from a bed of orange blossoms, the marble old and pitted. And there, a lazy Ganymede, half-covered in green moss, marked some path that had been overgrown. Far off, I could see the naked bending Venus at her bath on the edge of a pool. Water flowed into the pool. I glimpsed fountains all around me.

The small common white lilies had gone wild, and there stood old olive trees with marvelously twisted trunks, so wondrous to climb in childhood.

A pastoral sweetness hung over all, yet nature had been kept at bay The stucco of the walls was freshly painted, and so were the wooden shutters, opened wide.

The two boys were crying. 'Madam, he'll be so angry.'

'Well, not with you,' I said, as I entered the house. I had come across the grass and left scarcely any footprint on the marble floor.

'Boys, do stop sobbing! You don't even have to plead with him to believe you. Isn't that true?

He'll read the truth in your thoughts?'

This startled each in his own way. They looked at me warily.

I stopped just past the threshold. Something emanated from the house, not loud enough to be called a sound, but very like the rhythmic precursor of a sound. I had heard this very soundless rhythm before. When was it? In the Temple? When first I entered the room where Marius had hidden behind the screen?

I walked on marble floors from room to room. Breezes everywhere played with the hanging lamps. There were many lamps. And the candles. How many candles. And lamps on stands. Why, when this place was lighted up, it must have been bright as day!

And gradually I realized the entire lower floor was a library, except for the inevitable sumptuous Roman bath, and an enormous wardrobe of clothes.

Every other room was filled with books. Nothing but books. Of course there were couches for lying and reading, and desks for writing, but every wall had its prodigious stack of scrolls or shelves of bound books.

Also there were strange doors. They appeared to open onto concealed stairwells. But they had no locks and seemed to be made of polished granite. I found at least two of these! And one chamber of the first floor was totally enclosed in stone and locked in the same way, by impenetrable doors.

As the slaves trembled and sobbed I went outside and up the stairs to the second floor. Empty. Every room simply empty, except the room that obviously belonged to the boys! There were their beds, and their little Persian altars and gods, and rich rugs and tasseled pillows and the usual Oriental swirl of design.

I came down.

The boys sat at the main door, as if positioned like marble statues, each with his knees up, head down, weeping softly, perhaps getting a bit worn out.

'Where are the bedrooms of this house? Where is Marius's bedroom? Where is the kitchen? Where is the household shrine?'

One of them let out a soft choking cry. 'There are no bedrooms.'

'Of course not,' I said.

'Our food is brought to us,' wailed the other. 'Cooked and most delicious. But I fear that, unwittingly, we have enjoyed our last meal.'

'Oh, do take it easy. How can he blame you for what I've done? You're merely children and he's a gentle being, is he not? Here, put these

pages on his desk, and weight them down so
that they don't fly away.'

'Yes, he is most gentle,' said the boy. 'But
most set in his ways.'

I closed my eyes. I sensed the sound again,
the emanating encroaching sound. Did it want
to be heard? I couldn't tell. It seemed imper-
sonal, like the beat of a sleeping heart or the
flow of the water in the fountains.

I walked over to a large beautiful couch,
draped in fine silk with Persian designs. It was
very wide and seemed to bear, despite much
straightening, the imprint of a man's form.
There was the pillow there, all fluffed and fresh,
yet still I could see the indentation of the head,
where the man had lain.

'Does he lie here?'

The boys leapt to their feet, curls flying.

'Yes, Madam, that is his couch,' said the
speaker of the two. 'Please, please, don't touch
it. He lies there for hours and reads. Madam,
please! He is most particular that we do not lie
on it playfully in his absence, though he gives
us free rein in every other regard.'

'He'll know if you even touch it!' said the
other boy, speaking up for the first time.

'I'm going to sleep on it,' I said. I lay down
and closed my eyes. I rolled over and brought

up my knees. 'I am tired. I want only sleep. I feel safe for the first time in so long.'

'You do?' asked one of the boys.

'Oh, come here and lie by me. Bring pillows for your heads, so that he will see me before he sees you. He knows me well. The pages I have brought, where are they, yes, on the desk, well, they will make it clear why I have come in. It's all changed now. Something is wanted from me. I have no choice. There is no road home. Marius will understand. I've come as close to him as possible for my protection.'

I lay back right in the hollow of the pillow where he lay. I took a long deep breath. 'The breeze is like music here,' I whispered, 'do you hear it?'

I slept the deep exhausted sleep which I had held off now for so many hours of both night and day.

Hours must have passed.

I woke with a start. The sky was purple. The slaves were curled up next to the couch, just beneath me, like terrified little animals.

I heard the noise again, the sound, distinct, a pulse. I thought oddly of something I used to like to do as a child. It was this: I would put my ear to my Father's chest. And when I heard his heart, then I would kiss it. It had always made him happy.

I rose, realizing that I was not fully awake but certain this was no dream. I was in the beautiful villa of Marius in Antioch. The marble rooms opened one upon another.

I went to the last room, the room enclosed in stone. The doors were impossibly heavy. But suddenly, silently, they opened as if pushed from within.

I entered a massive chamber. Another pair of doors lay ahead of me. They too were made of stone. They had to lead to a stairwell, for the house ended just beyond.

These doors too suddenly opened, as if released by a spring!

Light from below.

A stairway went down from the threshold of the door. It was white marble, and newly made, with no wear of feet on it. So smooth, each slab, so clean.

A soft series of flames burned below, sending their antic shadows up the stairwell.

The sound now seemed louder. I closed my eyes. Oh, that all the world were these polished chambers and all that exists could be explained within.

Suddenly, I heard a loud cry.

'Lady Pandora!'

I spun around.

'Pandora, he is over the wall!'

The boys came screaming through the house, echoing Flavius's cry, 'Lady Pandora!'

A great darkness gathered itself right before my eyes and then descended on me, throwing the helpless, beseeching boys to the side. I was almost pitched down the stairwell.

Then I realized I was in the grasp of the burnt thing. I looked down to see the black wrinkled arm, like old leather, that held me. Strong spices filled my nostrils. Fresh clothing covered the hideously thin leg I saw, the dried-up foot.

'Boys, get the lamps, set it on fire!' I shouted. I fought desperately, driving us both back from the stairwell, but I couldn't get loose from the creature. 'Boys, the lamps downstairs!'

The boys clung to each other.

'I have you!' this creature said tenderly in my ear.

'No, you don't!' I said, and gave him one fine blow with my right elbow. It drove him off balance. He nearly toppled. But he didn't let me go. The whiteness of his tunic glowed in the shadows as he once more enclosed my arms, and rendered me almost helpless.

'Boys, downstairs, lamps full of oil!' I said. 'Flavius!'

The creature hugged me as if he were a giant snake. I could scarce breathe.

'We can't go downstairs!' one of the boys cried.

'We're not allowed,' said the other.

The creature laughed in my ear, a rich deep laugh. 'Not everyone is so bound to rebellion as you are, beautiful woman, outwitting your brother at the foot of the Temple steps.'

It was shocking to hear this clear articulate voice coming from a body which seemed burnt beyond all hope of life. I watched the blackened fingers moving over my own. I felt the touch of something cold on my neck. Then I felt the punctures. His fangs.

'No!' I cried. I thrashed back and forth in his grip, then threw all of my weight against him so that he almost toppled again but didn't fall.

'Stop it, bitch, or I'll kill you now.'

'Why don't you?' I demanded.

I twisted to see his face. It was like that of a long-dead corpse dried in the desert, burnt black with a spine of a nose, and arched lips that seemed quite unable to close over white teeth and the two fangs he bared now as he looked at me.

His eyes were full of blood, as Marius's eyes had been. His hair was a fine black mop, very thick, fresh and clean, as though it had sprung from his body, renewing itself like magic.

'Yes,' he said confidently. 'That is just what happened. And very soon I will have the blood I need to renew all of me! I won't be this hideous monster you see. I'll be what I was before those Egyptian fools put her in the sun!'

'Hmmm, so she kept her promise,' I said. 'She walked into the rays of Amon Ra so you would all burn up.'

'What do you know of it? She hasn't moved or spoken in a thousand years. I was that old when they removed the stones that enclosed her. She couldn't have walked into the sun. She is a great sacred vial of blood, an enthroned source of power, that's all, and I will have that blood, which your Marius has stolen out of Egypt.'

I pondered, searching desperately for a means to free myself.

'You came to me as a gift,' said the burnt one. 'You were all I needed to take on Marius! He wears his affections and weakness for you like bright silk garments for me to see!'

'I see,' I said.

'No, you don't!' he said. My head was pulled back by my hair. I screamed in annoyance.

His sharp teeth went into my neck. A series of heated wires threaded me through and through.

I swooned. An ecstasy rendered me motionless. I tried to resist, but I saw visions. I saw him in his glory, a golden man of an Eastern land, in a Temple of skulls. He was dressed in bright green silk breeches with an ornamented band around his forehead. Face delicate of nose and mouth. Then I saw him, without explanation, burst into flames that sent his slaves screaming. He twisted and turned in these flames, not dying but suffering exquisitely.

My head was swimming, and I was weakening. My blood flowed from all parts of my body into his wretched form. I thought of my Father, of my Father saying, 'Live, Lydia!' I wrenched my neck away from him and turned, poking him hard with my shoulder, and then pushed him with two hands so that he slid backwards on the floor. I brought my knee up against him. Nothing could get him off me!

I tried to reach for my dagger, but I was too dizzy, and besides, I didn't have my dagger. My only chance lay with the burning oil in the lamps at the foot of the stairs. I turned, reeling, and the monster caught me again with both hands by my long hair. He yanked me back.

'You demon!' I said. His strength had worn me out. He tightened his grip slowly. I knew that soon my arms would break.

'Ah,' he said, twisting free of me, and holding tight as ever. 'My purpose is served.'

A brighter light suddenly filled up the stairway.

A torch was placed at the foot of the steps. Then Marius stepped into view.

He appeared utterly calm and he appeared to be looking past me into the eyes of my captor.

'And what will you do now, Akbar?' Marius asked. 'Hurt her, violate her but one more time, and I shall kill you. Kill her, and you will die in agony. Let her go and you can run.'

He mounted the steps one by one.

'You underestimate me,' said the burnt thing, 'you arrogant Roman bumbler, you think I don't know you keep the Queen and the King, that you stole them out of Egypt? It is known. The word is spread through the world, through the Northern woods, through the wild lands, through the lands of which you know nothing. You killed the Elder who guarded the King and the Queen and stole them! The King and Queen have not moved or spoken in a thousand years. You took our Queen from Egypt. You think you are a Roman Emperor? You think she is a Queen you can take captive, like Cleopatra! Cleopatra was a Greek whore. This is our Isis, our Akasha! You blaspheming fool. Now let me into Akasha's presence. Stand against me, and this woman, the only mortal whom you truly love, dies.'

Marius came up step by step towards us.

'Akbar, did your informants tell you that it was the Elder in Egypt, her long keeper himself who left the Royal Pair to stand in the sun?' asked Marius. He took another step upward. 'Did they tell you that it was the Elder that caused the sun to strike them, the fire which destroyed hundreds of us, and spared the oldest only so they could live in agony as you do?'

Marius made a quick gesture. I felt the fangs deep in my neck. I couldn't get away. Again, I saw this creature in his former splendor, taunting me with his beauty, his jeweled feet as he danced, surrounded by painted women.

I heard Marius right beside me, but I couldn't make out the words.

The folly of it all went through my mind. I had led this creature to Marius, but was that what the Mother wanted? Akasha, that was the ancient name written on the bodies dumped on the steps of the Temple. I knew her name. I knew it in the dreams. I was losing consciousness. 'Marius,' I called out with all my strength.

My head fell forward, free of the fangs. I fought this total captivating weakness. I deliberately pictured the Emperor Augustus receiving us on his deathbed. 'I shall not see the end of this comedy,' I whispered.

'Oh, yes, you shall.' It was Marius's calm voice right near us. I opened my eyes. 'Akbar, don't risk it again, you've shown your determination.'

'Don't reach for me again, Marius,' said the burnt creature. 'My teeth caress her neck. But one more drop and her heart is silent.'

The rich dark of night brightened the torch below. That was all I could see. The torch. 'Akasha,' I whispered.

The burnt thing took a deep breath, his chest heaving against me. 'Her blood is beautiful,' he said. He kissed my cheek with the parched burnt lips. I closed my eyes. It was becoming harder and harder for me to breathe. I couldn't open my eyes.

He went on talking.

'You see, I have no fear to take her into death with me, Marius, for if I must die by your hand, why not with her as my consort?'

These words were distant, echoing.

'Pick her up in your arms,' said Marius. He was very close to us. 'And carry her gently, as if she were your only beloved child, and come down with me into the Shrine. Come and see the

286

Mother. Kneel before Akasha and see what she will allow!'

I swooned again, but I heard the creature laugh. He did lift me now, under the knees, and my head fell back. We went down the steps.

'Marius,' I said, 'he's weak. You can kill him.' My face fell against the chest of the burnt one as we descended. I could feel the bones of his chest. 'Really, very weak,' I said, scarcely able to remain conscious. Akasha, yes, her true name.

'Carefully, my friend,' said Marius. 'She dies and I destroy you. You've almost overplayed your hand. She narrows your chances with every labored breath. Pandora, be silent, please. Akbar is a great blood drinker, a great god.'

I felt a cold firm hand clasp mine.

We had reached the lower floor. I tried to lift my head. I saw rows of lamps, splendid wall paintings hammered with gold, a ceiling veiled in gold.

Two great stone doors were opened. A chapel lay within, a chapel full of dense fluttering devotional light and the overpowering scent of lilies.

The blood drinker who held me let out a cry. 'Mother Isis,' he said piteously. 'Oh, Akasha!'

He released me, setting me down on my feet, as Marius at once took hold of me, and the blistered and damaged one rushed towards the altar.

I stared, amazed. But I was dying. I couldn't breathe. I was falling to the floor. I tried to swallow air but I could not. I could not stand without Marius.

But oh, to leave the Earth and all its miseries with such a vision:

There they sat, The Great Goddess Isis and the King Osiris, or so it seemed, bronzed in skin, not white like the poor captive Queen in my dreams, but perfectly arrayed in garments of spun gold pleated and sewn in the fixed Egyptian style. Their black hair was long, plaited, real. The paint on their faces was fresh, the dark eyelining and mascara, the reddened lips.

She wore no crown of the horns and sun disk. Her collar of gold and jewels was superb, shimmering and alive in my eyes.

'I must get the crown, restore the crown!' I said aloud, hearing this voice come from me as if it had been born elsewhere to instruct me. My eyes closed.

The black thing knelt before the Queen.

I couldn't see clearly. I felt Marius's arms, and then a gush of hot blood come into my mouth. 'No, Marius, protect her!' I tried to speak. My words were washed away in this infusion of blood. 'Protect the Mother!' Again it came filling my mouth so that I had to swallow. Immediately I felt the strength, the power of this blood, infinitely stronger than the pull of Akbar. The blood rushed like so many rivers to the sea, through my body. It would not be stopped. Another gush followed, as if a giant storm had driven the river even faster into its delta, its broken and random streams seeking every morsel of flesh.

A wide and wondrous world opened and would have welcomed me, sunlight in the deep forest, but I wouldn't see it. I broke free. 'The Queen, save her from him!' I whispered. Did the blood drip from my lips? No, it was gone inside me.

Marius wouldn't listen to me. Again a bloody wound was pressed to my mouth, and the blood was driven ever faster. I felt the air fill my lungs. I could feel the length of my own body, sturdy, standing on its own. The blood brightened inside me like light, as though it had enflamed my heart. I opened my eyes. I was a pillar. I saw Marius's face, his golden eyelashes, his deep blue eyes. His long hair parted in the middle fell to his shoulders. He was ageless, a god.

'Protect her!' I cried. I turned and pointed.

A veil was lifted that had all my life hung between me and all things; now in their true color and shape, they gave forth their deliberate purpose: the Queen stared forward, immobile as the King. Life could not have imitated such serenity, such utter paralysis. I heard water dropping from the flowers. Tiny drops striking the marble floor, the fall of a single leaf. I turned and saw it, curled and rocking on the stones, this tiny leaf. I heard the breeze move under the golden canopied ceiling. And the lamps had tongues of flame to sing.

The world was a woven song, a tapestry of song. The multicolored Mosaics gleamed, then lost all form, then even pattern. The walls dissolved into clouds of colored mist which welcomed us, through which we could roam forever.

And there she sat, The Queen of Heaven, reigning over all in supreme and unperturbed stillness.

All the yearning of my childish heart was fulfilled. 'She lives, she is real, she reigns over Earth and Heaven.'

The King and the Queen. They didn't stir. Their eyes beheld nothing. They did not look at us. They did not look at the burnt thing as he drew closer and closer to their throne.

The arms of the Royal Pair were covered in many inscribed and intricate bracelets. Their hands rested on their thighs. It was the manner of many an Egyptian statue. But there never has been a statue to equal either of them.

'The crown, she would have her crown,' I said. With astonishing vigor I walked forward towards her.

Marius took my hand. Keenly, he watched the progress of the burnt one.

'She was before all such crowns,' Marius said, 'they do not mean anything to her.'

The thought itself burst with the sweetness of a grape on my tongue. Of course she was there before. In my dreams, she had had no crown. She was safe. Marius kept her safe.

'My Queen,' said Marius from behind me. 'You have a supplicant. It is Akbar from the East. He would drink the royal blood. What is your will, Mother?'

His voice was so tranquil! He had no fears.

'Mother Isis, let me drink!' cried this burnt creature. He stood up, threw up his arms and created another dancing vision of his former self. He wore human skulls hanging from his belt. He wore a necklace of blackened human fingers! Another of blackened human ears! It was grisly and revolting, yet he seemed to think it seductive and overpowering. At once the image left him. The god from the faraway land was on his knees.

'I am your servant and always was! I slew only the evildoer, as you commanded. I never abandoned your true worship.'

How fragile and insignificant seemed this pleading one, so revolting, so easy to clear away now from her presence. I looked at the King Osiris, as remote and indifferent as the Queen.

'Marius,' I said, 'the corn for Osiris; doesn't he want the corn? He's the god of the corn.' I was filled with visions of our processions in Rome, of people singing and bearing the offerings.

'No, he doesn't want the corn,' said Marius. He laid his hand on my shoulder.

'They are true, they are real!' I cried out. 'It is all real. Everything is changed. Everything is redeemed.'

The burnt thing turned and glared at me. But I was quite beyond all reason. He turned back to the Queen and reached out for her foot.

How her toenails flashed in the light with the golden flesh beneath them. But she was stone-still, as was the crownless King, without seeming judgment or power.

The creature suddenly sprang up and tried to seize the Queen by the neck!

I screamed.

'Shameless, despicable.'

Swiftly the frozen right arm of the Queen rose, her hand surrounding the burnt thing's skull and crushing it, the blood gushing down her as the monster gave his last fractured cry for mercy. She caught his body as it dropped over her waist. She hurled it in the air, and all its limbs broke loose from it, crashing to the floor like so much timber.

A gusting wind caught each remnant and gathered them all in one as a lamp fell from its three-legged stand to spill its burning oil on the remains.

'The heart, look,' I said. 'I can see its heart. The heart beats.'

But the fire quickly consumed the heart, consumed the flexing fingers and the writhing toes. There was a great stirring, a dance in the fire of bones, bones whirling in the flames, and then the bones blackened, thinned, snapped to pieces, became fragments; all of this thing was reduced at last to smoking cinders, crisping and skittering on the floor.

Then came the breeze again, full of the breath of the garden, lifting these cinders and carrying them away, like so many fragile tiny black insects, into the shadows of the antechamber.

I was spellbound.

The Queen was as before, her hand in its old place. She and the King stared at nothing, as if nothing had taken place. Only the wretched stain on her gown bore witness.

Their eyes took no heed of Marius or of me.

Then there was only quiet in the chapel. Only sweet perfumed quiet. Golden light. I breathed deeply. I could hear the oil in the lamps turned to flame. The Mosiacs were peopled with finely made worshipers. I could see the slow minute beginnings of decay of the various flowers, and it seemed but another strain of the same song that expressed their growth, their browning edges but another color in no contradiction to their brilliant colors.

'Forgive me, Akasha,' Marius said softly, 'that I let him come so close. I was not wise.'

I cried. Great gushing tears came from me.

'You summoned me,' I said to the Queen through my tears. 'You called me here! I will do all you want of me.'

Slowly her right arm rose; it rose from her thigh and extended itself and her hand very gently curved in the beckoning gesture of the dream, but there was no smile, no change in her frozen face.

I felt something invisible and irresistible

wrap itself around me. It came from her out-stretching welcoming arm. It was sweet and soft and caressing. It made a flush of pleasure through all my limbs and my face.

I moved forward, wound up in its will.

'I beg you, Akasha!' Marius said softly. 'I beg you under the name of Inanna, under the name of Isis, under the name of all goddesses, don't hurt her!'

Marius simply didn't understand! Marius had never known her worship! I knew. I knew that her blood drinker children had meant to be judges of the evildoer, and drink only from the condemned, according to her laws. I saw the god of the dark cave, whom I'd seen in my vision. I understood all.

I wanted to tell Marius. But I couldn't. Not now. The world was reborn, all systems built upon skepticism or selfishness were as fragile as spiderwebs and meant to be swept away. My own moments of despair had been nothing more than detours into an unholy and self-centered blackness.

'The Queen of Heaven,' I whispered. I knew I was speaking in the ancient tongue. A prayer came to my lips.

'And Amon Ra, the Sun God, for all his power, shall never conquer the King of the

Dead or his bride, for she is the ruler of the starry heavens, of the moon, of those who would bring the sacrifice of the evildoer. Cursed be those who misuse this magic. Cursed be those who seek to steal it!'

I felt myself, a human, held together by the intricate threads of blood which Marius had given me. I felt the design of its support. It had no weight, my body.

I was lifted towards her. Her arm came around me and pulled my hair back from my face. I put out my arms to embrace her neck because I could do nothing else. We were too close for any other possible sign of love.

I felt the soft silk of her real plaited hair, and the coldness and firmness of her shoulders, her arm. Yet she did not look at me. She was a petrified thing. Could she look at me? Did she choose to remain silent, staring forward? Did some evil spell hold her helpless, a spell from which a thousand hymns might waken her?

In my delirium I saw the words engraved in gold pieces among the jewels of her collar: 'Bring to me the evildoer and I shall drink his blood.'

It seemed I was in the desert and the necklace was tumbling over and over in the sand, in the wind, rather like the body of the burnt one had tumbled. Fallen, lost, to be remade.

I felt my head drawn to her neck. She had opened her fingers over my hair. She directed it, that my lips should feel this skin.

'It's what you want, isn't it?' I asked. But my words seemed remote from me, a pathetic expression of the fullness of my soul. 'That I am to be your daughter!'

She tipped her head slightly, away from me, so that I saw her neck. I saw the vein displayed, the vein from which she wanted me to drink.

Her finger rose gently through my hair, never pulling it or hurting it, merely embracing my head, sending rampant ecstasy through me, and urging my head gently down so that my lips could no longer avoid her shimmering skin.

'Oh, my adored Queen,' I whispered. I had never known such certainty, such ecstasy without limits or mundane cause. I had never known such bursting, triumphant faith as my faith in her.

I opened my mouth. Nothing human could bite through this hard flesh! Yet it gave, as though it were thin, and the blood pumped into me, 'the Fount.' I heard her heart driving it, a deafening force that vibrated in the drums of my ears. This was not blood. This was nectar. This was all that any created being could ever desire.

9

With the nectar flowing into me, there came another realm. Her ringing laughter filled the corridor; she ran ahead of me, girlish, feline, unencumbered by grandeur. She beckoned for me to follow. Out under the stars, Marius sat alone in his soft shapeless garden. She pointed to him. I saw Marius rise and take me in his arms. His long hair was such a fine adornment. I saw what she wanted. It was Marius I kissed in this vision as I drank from her; it was Marius with whom I danced.

A shower of flower petals descended upon us as upon a bridal couple in Rome, and Marius held my arm as though we had just been wed, and all around us people sang. There was a flawless happiness, a happiness so keen that perhaps there are those born who never even have the capacity for it.

She stood atop a broad black altar of diorite.

It was night. This was an enclosed place, filled with people, but it was dark and cool with the sandy wind off the valley floor, and she looked down at the one they offered up to her. He was a man, his eyes closed, his hands were bound. He didn't struggle.

She showed her teeth; a gasp rose from the worshipers who filled the place, and then she took the man by the throat and drank his blood. When she had finished, she let him fall and she held up her arms.

'All things are cleansed in me!' she cried out. Once again the petals fell, petals of all colors, and peacock feathers waved about us, and branches of palm, and there was singing in great lusty bursts, and the sound of a riotious drum, and she smiled looking down from where she stood, her face remarkably flushed and mobile and human, her black-painted eyes sweeping over her worshipers.

All began to dance, save she, who watched, and then her eyes rose slowly and she looked over their heads, out the high rectangular windows of this place, at the twinkling firmament. Pipes played. The dance had become a frenzy.

A weary and secretive darkness crept into her face, a distraction, as though her soul had traveled out of doors towards Heaven, and then she looked sadly down. She looked lost. Anger overcame her.

Then she cried out in a deafening voice, 'The rogue blood drinker!' The crowd fell silent. 'Bring him to me.'

The crowd parted to let this struggling furious god be forced to her altar.

'You dare judge me!' he cried. He was Babylonian, with full long curly locks and beard and mustache. It took ten mortals to hold him.

'Into the burning place, in the mountains, in the sun, in the strongest fetters!' she cried. He was dragged away.

Once again she looked up. The stars grew big and age-old patterns were clear. We floated under the stars.

A boy in a delicate gilded chair argued with those around him. The men were old, half-invisible in the darkness. The lamp shone on the boy's face. We stood in the door. The boy was frail, his little limbs like sticks.

'And you say,' said the incredulous boy, 'that these blood drinkers are worshiped in the hills!'

I knew he was the Pharaoh by the sacred lock of hair that grew from his bald head, by the manner in which the others waited upon him. He looked up in horror as she approached. His guardians fled.

'Yes,' she said, 'and you will do nothing to stop it!'

She lifted him, this small fragile boy, and tore at his throat as an animal might do it, letting the blood flood from the fatal wound. 'Little King,' she said. 'Little Kingdom.'

The vision ended.

Her cold white skin was closed beneath my lips. I kissed her now. I no longer drank.

I felt my own form, felt myself fall back over her arm, felt myself slipping out of her embrace.

In the dim radiance, her profile remained as it had before, silent and without feeling. Stark, a face without a blemish or a line. I sank back into Marius's arms. Her arm and hand returned to their former rigid position.

Everything was brilliantly clear, the motionless King and Queen, the artful figures fixed in lapis lazuli in the gold mosaics.

I felt a sharp pain in me, in the heart, in the womb, as if someone had stabbed me. 'Marius!' I cried out.

He picked me up and carried me from the chamber.

'No, I want to kneel at her feet,' I said. The pain took the breath out of me. I tried not to scream from this pain. Oh, the world had just

301

been reborn. And now this agony.

He set me down on the high grass, letting it be crushed under me. A flood of sour human fluid came out of my womb, even out of my mouth. I saw flowers right near me. I saw the friendly Heavens, vivid as in my vision. The pain was unspeakable.

I knew now why he had removed me from the Shrine.

I wiped at my cheek. I couldn't bear this filth. The pain devoured me. I struggled to see again what she had revealed to me, remember what she said, but there was too much obstruction in this pain.

'Marius!' I cried.

He covered me and kissed my cheek. 'Drink from me,' he said, 'drink until the pain goes away. It's only the body dying, drink. Pandora, you are immortal.'

'Fill me, take me,' I said. I reached down between his legs.

'It doesn't matter now.'

But it was hard, this organ I sought, the organ forever lost to the god Osiris. I guided it, hard and cold as it was, into my body. Then I drank and drank, and when I felt his teeth again on my neck, when he began to draw from me the new mixture that filled my veins, it was sweet suckling, and I knew him and loved him and knew all his secrets in one flash which meant nothing.

He was right. The lower organs meant nothing. He fed on me. I fed on him. This was our marriage. All around us, the grass was waving softly in the breeze, a majestic conjugal bed, and the smell of the green flooded me.

The pain was gone. I flung out my arm and felt the softness of flowers.

He tore off my fouled dress and lifted me. He carried me into the pool where the marble Venus stood forever with back bent, and one foot raised above the cool water.

'Pandora!' he whispered.

The boys stood at his side, offering him pitchers.

He dipped a pitcher and poured the water over me. I felt beneath my feet the tile at the bottom of the pool as the water ran down my skin. I had never known such sensation! Another pitcherful washed over me, deliciously. I feared for one instant the pain would return, but no, it was gone.

'I love you with all my heart,' I said. 'All my love belongs to them and to you, Marius. Marius, I can see in the darkness, I can see in the deep dark beneath the trees.'

Marius held me. The boys slowly bathed us both, dipping their pitchers and pouring the silvery water over us.

'Oh, to have you with me,' Marius said, 'to have you here; not to be alone, but to be with you, my beauty, you of all souls! You.' He stood back, and I gloried in him, drenched as I was, reached to touch his long wild foreign hair. He sparkled all over with droplets.

'Yes,' I said. 'It was exactly what she wanted.'

His face stiffened. He scowled. He stared at me. Something had changed altogether, and for the worse. I could feel it.

'What?' he asked.

'It is what she wanted. She made it plain to me in the visions. She wanted me to be with you, so you wouldn't be alone.'

He stood back. Was this anger?

'Marius, what is the matter with you? Can't you see what she's done?'

He stepped back again, away from me.

'You didn't realize that's what was happening?' I asked.

The boys thrust forth towels. Marius took one and wiped his face and his hair.

I did the same.

He was furious. He shook with anger.

This was a moment of mingled and inexplicable beauty and horror – his white body there, the shimmering pool, the lights falling gracefully from the open doors of the house, and above, the stars, her stars. And Marius angry and bristling, his eyes full of outrage.

I looked at him.

'I am her Priestess now,' I said. 'I'm to restore her worship. That's what she wants. But she brought me also for you, because you were alone,' I said. 'Marius, I saw all this. I saw our own wedding in Rome, as if it were the old days and our families were with us. I saw her worshipers.'

He was plainly horrified.

I didn't want to see this. Surely I was misunderstanding him.

I stepped up on the grass. I let the boys dry my body. I looked up at the stars. The house with all its warm lamps seemed crude and fragile, a bumbled attempt to make an order of things, which could not compare to the making of one complete flower.

'Oh, how spectacular is the simple night,' I said. 'It seems an insult to the night to speak of purpose and intent, when this common moment is so brimming full of blessed design and tranquillity All things follow their course.'

I stood back and spun around, letting the water fly from me. I was so strong. No dizziness overcame when I stopped. I had a sense of infinite power.

One of the boys held out a tunic for me. It was a man's, but as I've said so often here, Roman clothes are very simple. It was just a short tunic. I put it on and let him tie the sash around my waist. I smiled at him. He trembled and stepped back from me.

'Dry my hair,' I told him. Ah, such sensations.

Slowly I looked up. Marius too was dried and dressed. He was still looking at me with violent protest, and downright indignation.

'Someone has to go in,' I said, 'to change her golden gown. That blasphemer, he left her bloody.'

'I will do that!' Marius said in plain anger.

'Oh, so it comes to this,' I said. I looked around me, seduced by beauty to forget his altogether, to come back to him at some later hour after I had roamed beneath the olive trees and consorted with the constellations.

But his anger hurt me. The hurt was strange, and deep, without the various stages mortal flesh and mind command of pain.

'Oh, isn't it splendid!' I said. 'I learn that the goddess reigns, that she is real, that she has made all things! That the world is not just a giant graveyard! But I learn this as I find myself in an arranged marriage! And behold the groom! How he nurses his own temper.'

He sighed and bowed his head. Was I to see him cry again, this flawless familiar and beloved god among crushed flowers?

He looked up. 'Pandora,' he said. 'She's not a goddess. She didn't make the world.'

'How dare you say this!'

'I have to say it! I would have died for the truth when I was alive and will die for it now. But she will not let this happen. She needs me and she needs you to make me happy!'

'So very well!' I threw my hands. 'I am happy to do it. And we will restore her worship.'

'We will not!' he said. 'How can you even think of such a thing.'

'Marius, I want to sing it from the tops of mountains; I want to tell the world that this miracle exists. I want to run through the streets singing. We are to restore her to her throne in a great Temple in the very middle of Antioch!'

'You're talking madness!' he shouted.

The boys had run away.

'Marius, have you stopped up your ears to her commands? We are to hunt down and kill her renegade gods and see that new gods are born from her, gods who look into souls, gods who seek justice, not lies, gods who are not fantastical, lustful idiots or the drunken whimsical creatures of the Northern sky who hurl thunderbolts. Her worship is founded in the good, in the pure!'

'No, no, no,' he said. He stepped back as if that would make it all the more emphatic. 'You're talking rot!' he said. 'Stupidity, rank superstition!'

'I don't believe you said those words!' I cried. 'You are a monster!' I said. 'She deserves her throne! So does the King, who sits beside her. They deserve their worshipers bringing flowers to them. Did you think you had the power to read minds for no good reason!' I came forward. 'Do you remember when I first mocked you in the Temple? When I said you ought to station yourself at the courts and look into the minds of the accused? I had hit the mark in my ridicule!'

'No!' he roared. 'This is absolutely not true,' he said.

He turned his back on me, rushing into the house.

I followed him.

He rushed down the stairway and into her sanctum, stopping short before her. She and her King sat as before. Not an eyelash moved. Only the flowers clung to life in the perfumed air.

I looked down at my hands, so white! Could I die now? Would I live centuries like the burnt one?

I studied their seemingly divine faces. They did not smile. They did not dream. They looked, and nothing more.

I fell down on my knees.

'Akasha,' I whispered. 'May I call you this name? Tell me what you want.'

There was no change in her. None whatsoever.

'Well, speak, Mother!' declared Marius, his voice thick with sadness. 'Speak! Is it what you've always wanted?'

Suddenly he dashed forward, mounted the two steps of her dais and pounded on her breasts with his fists.

I was horrified.

She didn't move, she didn't blink. His fist struck a hardness he could not budge. Only her hair, struck by his arm, gave a little sway.

I ran to him and tried to pull him away.

'Stop it, Marius, she'll destroy you!'

I was amazed at my strength. Surely it equalled his. But he allowed me to pull him back, his face flooded with tears.

'Oh, what have I done!' he said staring at her. 'Oh, Pandora, Pandora! What have I done! I've made another blood drinker when I swore that there would never, never be another made, not so long as I survived!'

'Come upstairs,' I said calmly. I glanced at

the King and Queen. No sign of response or recognition. 'It isn't proper, Marius, that we argue here in the Shrine. Come upstairs.'

He nodded.

He let me lead him slowly out of the room. His head was bowed.

'Your long barbarian hair is most becoming,' I said. 'And I have eyes now to see you as never before. Our blood is intertwined as it might be in a child born to us.'

He wiped at his nose, and didn't look at me.

We walked into the large library.

'Marius, is there nothing in me that fills your eye, nothing you find beautiful?'

'Oh, yes, my dear, there is everything!' he said. 'But for the love of Heaven, bring your wits with you into this! Don't you see! Your life's been stolen not for a sacred truth but for a degraded mystery! Reading minds doesn't make me any wiser than the next man! I kill to live! As she once did, thousands and thousands of years ago. Oh, and she knew she had to do this. She knew the time had come.'

'What time? What did she know?'

I stared at him. I was gradually realizing that I could no longer read his thoughts, and surely he couldn't read mine. But the hovering boys, they were just open books in their fear, thinking themselves the servants of kindhearted but very loud-voiced demons.

Marius sighed. 'She did it because I had almost gained the courage to do what I had to do! To place them both and myself in the sun and finish forever what the Egyptian Elder had sought to do – rid the world of the King and Queen and all the fanged men and women who glut themselves on death! Oh, she is too clever.'

'You really planned to do that?' I asked. 'To immolate them and yourself?'

He made a small sarcastic sound. 'Yes, of course, I planned it. Next week, next month, next year, next decade, after another hundred years, maybe in two hundred, maybe after I'd read all the books in the world and seen all the places, maybe in five hundred years, maybe . . . maybe soon in my loneliness.'

I was at first too stunned to speak

He smiled at me wisely and sadly. 'Oh, but I cry like a child,' he said softly.

'Where comes the confidence,' I asked, 'to put an end so swiftly to such bold and complex evidence of divine magic!'

'Magic!' he cursed.

'I'd rather if you did not do this,' I said. 'I don't mean the crying, I mean burning up the Mother and Father and . . .'

311

'I'm sure you would!' he answered. 'And do you think I could bear to do it against your will, subject you to the fire? You innocent desperate idiot of a woman! Restore her altars! Oh! Restore her worship! Oh! You are out of your mind!'

'Idiot! You dare sling your insults at me! You think you've brought a slave into your household? You haven't even brought a wife.'

Yes. Our minds were locked now to each other, and later I would find out that it was because of our heavy exchange of blood. But all I knew then was that we had to content ourselves with words like mortal men and women.

'I did not mean to use petty insults!' he said. He was stung.

'Well, then sharpen your great male reason and your lofty elegant patrician mode of expression!' I said.

We glowered at each other.

'Yes!' he said. 'Reason,' he said. He held up his finger. 'You are the most clever woman I've ever known. And you listen to reason. I will explain and you will see. That is what must be done.'

'Yes, and you are hotheaded and sentimental and give way to tears again and again – and you pound upon the Queen herself like a child throwing a tantrum!'

His face went red with immediate anger. It sealed his lips against his words.

He turned and went away.

'Do you cast me out?' I said. 'Do you want me gone!' I shouted. 'This is your house. Tell me now if you want me gone. I'll go now!'

He stopped. 'No,' he said.

He turned around and looked at me, shaken, and caught off guard. In a raw voice, he said, 'Don't go, Pandora!' He blinked as if to clear his vision. 'Don't go. Please, don't.' And then he let fall a final whisper. 'We have each other.'

'And where do you go now, to get away from me?'

'Only to change her dress,' he said with a sad bitter smile. 'To clean and recostume "such bold evidence of complex and divine magic."'

He disappeared.

I turned to the violet outdoors. To the clouds stirred in a cauldron by the moon, to defy the darkness. To the big old trees that said, Mount our limbs, we will embrace you! To the scattered flowers everywhere that said, We are your bed. Lie down with us.

And so the two-hundred-year brawl began.

And it never really ended.

10

With my eyes still closed, I heard voices of the city, voices from nearby houses; I heard men talking as they passed on the road outside. I heard music coming from somewhere, and the laughter of women and children. When I concentrated I could understand what they said. I chose not to do this, and their voices melded with the breeze.

Suddenly, the state seemed unbearable. There seemed nothing to do but rush back to the chapel and kneel there and worship! These senses I had been given seemed fit for nothing else. If this was my destiny, then what was to become of me?

Through it all, I heard a soul weeping in agony; it was an echo of my own, a soul broken from a course of great hope, who could scarce believe that such fine beginnings should end in terror!

It was Flavius.

I leapt into the old gnarled olive tree. It was as simple as taking a step. I stood among the branches, and then leapt to the next, and then to the top of the wall, encrusted with vine. I walked along the wall towards the gate.

There he stood, his forehead pressed to the bars, both hands clutching at the iron. He bled from several slash marks on his cheek. He gnashed his teeth.

'Flavius!' I said.

He looked up with a start. 'Lady Pandora!'

Surely by the light of the moon, he saw the miracle wrought in me, whatever its cause. For I saw the mortality in him, the deep wrinkles of his skin, the painful flutter of his gaze, a thin layer of soil clinging to him all over in the natural moisture of his mortal skin.

'You must go home,' I said, climbing to sit on the wall, with legs on the outside. I bent down so he could hear me. He didn't back away but his eyes were huge with fascination. 'Go see to the girls, and sleep, and get those marks attended to. The demon's dead, you needn't worry anymore about him. Come back here tomorrow night at sundown.'

He shook his head. He tried to speak but he

couldn't. He tried to gesture but he couldn't. His heart thundered in his chest. He glanced back down the road to the small far-flung lights of Antioch. He looked at me. I heard his heart galloping. I felt his shock, and his fear, and it was fear for me, not him. Fear that some awful fate had befallen me. He reached for the gate and clung to the bars, right arm hooked around and left hand clasping it as if he wouldn't be moved.

I saw myself as he saw me in his mind – in a boy's sashed tunic, my hair wildly free, sitting atop the wall, as if my body were young and pliant. All lines of age had gone from me. He saw a face on me no one could have ever painted.

But the point was this. The man had reached his limit. He could go no further. And I knew most fully how I loved him.

'All right,' I said. I stood up and leaned over with both my hands. 'Come on, I'll lift you over the wall if I can.'

He raised his arms, doubtful, eyes still drinking up every detail of my transformation.

He weighed nothing. I lifted him up and deposited him on his feet within the gate. I dropped down on the grass beside him and put my arm around him. How hot was his alarm. How strong his courage.

'Still your heart,' I said. I led him towards the house, as he looked down at me, his chest heaving as though he were out of breath, but it was mere shock. 'I'll take care of you.'

'I had the thing,' he said, 'I had it by its arm!' How opaque his voice sounded, how filled with living fluid and effort. 'I sank my dagger into it over and over, but it just slashed at my face and it was gone over the wall like a swarm of gnats, just darkness, immaterial darkness!'

'Flavius, it's dead, burnt to cinders!'

'Had I not heard your voice, oh, I was going mad! I heard the boys crying. I couldn't climb the wall with this damned leg. Then I heard your voice, and I knew, knew you were alive!' He was filled with happiness. 'You were with your Marius.' The ease with which I could feel his love was sweet, and awe inspiring.

A sudden sense of the Shrine came back to me, of the Queen's nectar and the shower of flower petals. But I had to maintain my equilibrium in this new state. Flavius was also profoundly baffled.

I kissed him on the lips, warm, mortal lips, and then quickly like an artful cat I licked all the blood from the slash marks on his cheeks, feeling a shiver run through me.

I took him into the library, which in this house

was the main room. The boys hovered somewhere about. They had been lighting lamps
everywhere, and now they cowered. I could
smell their blood and their young human flesh.

'You'll stay with me, Flavius. Boys, can you
make a bedroom for my steward on this floor?
You have fruit and bread, don't you? I can smell
it. Have you enough furniture to make him a
comfortable place to the far right, where he is
out of the way?'

They came rushing out of their respective
hiding places, and they too struck me as vividly
human. I was distracted. The smallest natural
things about them seemed precious, their thick
black eyebrows, their round little mouths, their
smooth cheeks.

'Yes, Madam, yes!' they said almost in one
voice. They hurried forward.

'This is Flavius, my steward. He will stay
with us. For now, take him to the bath, heat the
water and attend to him. Get him some wine.'

They took Flavius in hand at once. But he
paused.

'Don't abandon me, Madam,' he said suddenly with the most serious and thoughtful
expression. 'I am loyal in all respects.'

'I know,' I said. 'Oh, how clearly I understand. You cannot imagine.'

Then it was off to the bath with the Babylonian boys, who seemed delighted to have something to do.

I found Marius's huge closets. He had enough clothes for the Kings of Parthia, Armenia, the Emperor's Mother, Livia, the dead Cleopatra, and an ostentatious patrician who paid no attention to Tiberius's stupid sumptuary laws.

I put on a much finer, long tunic, woven of silk and linen, and I chose a gold girdle. And with Marius's combs and brushes, I made a clean free mantle of my hair, free of all tangles, rippled and soft as it had been when I was a girl.

He had many mirrors, which, as you know, in those days were only polished metal. And I was rendered somber and mystified by the single fact that I was young again; my nipples were pink, as I had said; the lines of age no longer interrupted the intended endowments of my face or arms. Perhaps it is most accurate to say that I was timeless. Timeless in adulthood. And every solid object seemed there to serve in me my new strength.

I looked down at the blocks of marble tile which made up the floor and saw in them a depth, a proof of process wondrous and barely understood.

I wanted to go out again, speak to the flowers, pick them up in handfuls. I wanted to talk urgently with the stars. I dared not seek the Shrine for fear of Marius, but if he had not been around I would have gone there and knelt at the Mother and merely looked at her, looked at her in silent contemplation, listening for the slightest articulation, though I knew, quite certainly after watching Marius's behavior, that there would be none.

She had moved her right arm without the seeming knowledge of the rest of her body. She had moved it to kill, and then to invite.

I went into the library, sat down at the desk, where lay all my pages, and I waited.

Finally, when Marius came, he too was freshly dressed, his hair parted in the middle and combed to his shoulders. He took a chair near me. It was ebony and curved and inlaid with gold, and I looked at him, realizing how very like the chair he was – a great preserved extension of all the raw materials which had gone into it. Nature did the carving and inlay and then the whole had been lacquered.

I wanted to cry in his arms, but I swallowed my loneliness. The night would never desert me, and it was faithful in every open door with its intruding grass, and the veined olive branches rising to catch the light of the moon.

'Blessed is she who is made a blood drinker,' I said, 'when the moon is full, and the clouds are rising like mountains in the transparent night.'

'Probably so,' he said.

He moved the lamp that stood on the desk between us, so that it didn't flicker in my eyes.

'I made my steward at home here,' I said. 'I offered him bath, bed and clothes. Do you forgive me? I love him and will not lose him. It's too late now for him to go back into the world.'

'He's an extraordinary man,' Marius said, 'and most welcome here. Tomorrow perhaps he can bring your girls. Then the boys will have company and there will be some discipline by day. Flavius knows books, among other things.'

'You're most gracious. I was afraid you would be angry. Why do you suffer so? I cannot read your mind; I did not obtain that gift.' No, this wasn't correct. I could read Flavius's mind. I knew the boys at this very moment were very relieved by Flavius's presence as they helped him dress for bed.

'We are too closely linked by blood,' he said. 'I can never read your thoughts again either. We are thrown back on words like mortals, only our senses are infinitely keener, and the detachment we know at some times will be as cold as the ice in the North; and at other times feelings will enflame us, carry us on waves of burning sea.'

'Hmmm,' I said.

'You despise me,' he said softly, contritely, 'because I quenched your ecstasy, I took from you your joy, your convictions.' He looked quite genuinely miserable. 'I did this to you right at the happiest moment of your conversion.'

'Don't be so sure you quenched it. I might still make her Temples, preach her worship. I'm an initiate. I have only begun.'

'You will not revive her worship!' he said. 'Of that I assure you! You will tell no one about her or what she is or where she is kept, and you will never make another blood drinker.'

'My, if only Tiberius had such authority when he addressed the Senate!' I said.

'All Tiberius ever wanted was to study at the gymnasium at Rhodes, to go every day in a Greek cloak and sandals and talk philosophy. And so the propensity for action flowers in men of lesser mettle, who use him in his loveless loneliness.'

'Is this a lecture for my improvement? Do you think I don't know this? What you don't know is that the Senate won't help Tiberius govern. Rome wants an Emperor now to worship and to like. It was your generation, under

Augustus, which accustomed us to forty years of autocratic rule. Don't talk to me of politics as though I were a fool.'

'I should have realized that you understood it all,' he said. 'I remember you in your girlhood. Nobody could match your brilliance. Your fidelity to Ovid and his erotic writings was a rare sophistication, an understanding of satire and irony. A well-nourished Roman frame of mind.'

I looked at him. His face too had been wiped clean of discernible age. I had time now to relish it, the squareness of his shoulders, the straightness and firmness of his neck, the distinct expression of his eyes and well-placed eyebrows. We had been made over into portraits of ourselves in marble by a master sculptor.

'You know,' I said, 'even under this crushing and annoying barrage of definition and declaration which you make to me, as if I were weeping for your ratification, I feel love for you, and know full well that we are alone in this, and married to one another, and I am not unhappy.'

He appeared surprised, but said nothing.

'I am exalted, bruised in the heart,' I said, 'a hardened pilgrim. But I do wish you would not speak to me as if my full indoctrination and education were your primary concern!'

'I have to speak this way!' he said gently. His voice was all kindness in its heat. 'It *is* my primary concern,' he said. 'If you can understand what happened with the end of the Roman Republic, if you can understand Lucretius and the Stoics, whole, then you can understand what we are. You have to do this!'

'I'll let that insult pass,' I answered. 'I'm not in the mood for listing for you every philosopher or poet I have read. Nor for recounting the level of talk around our nighttime table.'

'Pandora, I don't mean any offense! But Akasha is not a goddess! Remember your dreams. She is a vial of precious strength. Your dreams told you she could be used, that any unscrupulous blood drinker could pass on the blood to another, that she is a form of demon, host to the power we share.'

'She can hear you!' I whispered, outraged.

'Of course, she can. For fifteen years I've been her guardian. I've fought off those renegades from the East. And other connivers from the African hinterlands. She knows what she is.'

No one could have guessed his age, save from the seriousness of his expression. A man in perfect form, that was what he seemed. I tried not to be dazzled by him, by the pulsing night behind him, and yet I wanted so to drift. 'Some wedding feast,' I said. 'I have things to say to the trees.'

'They will be there tomorrow night,' he said.

The last image I had of her passed before my eyes, colored in ecstasy; she took the young Pharaoh from his chair and broke him into sticks. I saw her before that revelation, at the beginning of the swoon, running down the corridor laughing.

A slow fear crept over me.

'What is it?' Marius asked. 'Confide in me.'

'When I drank from her, I saw her like a girl, laughing.' I recounted then the marriage, the flood of rose petals, and then her strange Egyptian Temple full of frenzied worshipers. At last I told him how she had entered the chamber of the little King, whose advisors warned him of her gods.

'She broke him up as if he were a boy of wood. She said, 'Little King, little Kingdom.'

I picked up my pages, which earlier I had placed on this desk. I described the last dream I had had of her, when she threatened, screaming, to walk into the sun and destroy her disobedient children. I described all the things I had seen – the many migrations of my soul.

My heart hurt so much. Even as I explained,

I saw her vulnerability, the danger that was embodied in her. I explained finally how I had written all this in Egyptian.

I was weary and wished truly that I had never opened eyes on this life! I feel the keen and total despair again of those nights of weeping in my little house in Antioch when I had pounded on walls, and driven my dagger into the dirt. If she had not run, laughing down that corridor! What did the image mean? And the little boy King, broken so helplessly?

I made a sum of it easily enough. I waited for Marius's belittling remarks. I hadn't much patience for him now.

'How do you interpret it?' he asked gently. He tried to take my hand but I withdrew it.

'It's bits and pieces of her recollection,' I said. I was heartbroken. 'It's what she remembers. There is but one suggestion of a future in it all,' I said. 'There is only one comprehensible image of a wish: our wedding, that we be together.' My voice was full of sadness, yet I asked him.

'Why do you weep again, Marius?' I asked. 'She must gather recollections like flowers picked at random from the garden of the world, like leaves falling into her hands, and from these recollections she fastened for me a garland! A wedding garland! A trap. I have no migrant soul. I think not. If I did have a migrant soul, then why would she alone, one so archaic, helpless, irrelevant to the world itself, so out of fashion and out of power, be the one to know this? To make it known to me? The only one to know?'

I looked at him. He was engaged yet crying. He showed no shame in it, and would obviously render no apology.

'What was it you said before?' I asked. '"That I can read minds makes me no wiser than the next man?"' I smiled. 'That is the key. How she laughed as she led me to you. How she wanted me to behold you in your loneliness.'

He only nodded.

'I wonder how she knew to cast her net so far,' I said, 'to find me across the rolling sea.'

'Lucius, that's how she knew. She hears voices from many lands. She sees what she wants to see. One night here I badly startled a Roman, who appeared to recognize me and then slunk away as if I were a danger to him. I went after him, thinking vaguely that there was something to this, his excessive fear.

'I soon realized a great weight distorted his conscience and twisted his every thought and movement. He was terrified to be recognized by someone from the capital. He wanted to leave.

'He went to the house of a Greek merchant, pounding on the door late, by torchlight, and demanded the payment of a debt owed to your Father. The Greek told him what he had told him before, that the money would be repaid only to your Father himself.

'The next night I sought Lucius out again. This time the Greek had a surprise for him. A letter had just come from your Father by military ship. This was perhaps four days before your own arrival. The letter plainly stated that a favor was being asked of the Greek by your Father in the name of Hospitality and Honor. If the favor was granted, all debts were canceled. Everything would be explained by a letter accompanying a cargo destined for Antioch. The cargo would take some time, as the ship had many stops to make. The favor was of crucial importance.

'When your brother saw the date of this letter, he was stricken. The Greek, who was thoroughly sick of Lucius by this time, slammed the door in his face.

'I accosted Lucius only steps away. Of course he remembered me, the eccentric Marius of long ago. I pretended surprise to see him here and asked after you. He was in a panic and made up some story about your being married and living in Tuscany, and said that he was on his way out of town. He hurried off. But the moment's contact had been enough to see the testimony he'd given the Praetorian Guard against his family – all lies – and to imagine the deeds that had resulted from it.

'The next time, on waking, I couldn't find him. I kept watch on the house of the Greeks. I weighed in my mind a visit to the old man, the Greek merchant, some way to lay down a friendship with him. I thought of you. I pictured you. I remembered you. I made up poems in my head about you. I didn't hear or see anything of your brother. I presumed he'd left Antioch.

'Then one night I awoke and came upstairs and looked out to see the city full of random fires.

'Germanicus had died, never retracting his accusations that Piso had poisoned him.

'When I reached the house of the Greek merchant, it was nothing but burnt timbers. I caught no sight or sound of your brother anywhere. For all I knew they were all dead, your brother, and the Greek merchant family.

'All through the nights after, I searched for sight or sound of Lucius. I had no idea you were here, only an obsessive longing for you. I tried to remind myself that if I mourned for every mortal tie I had had when alive, I would go mad long before I had learnt anything about my gifts from our King and Queen.

'Then, I was in the bookseller's and it was early evening and the Priest slipped up to me. He pointed to you. There you stood in the Forum, and the philosopher and students were bidding you farewell. I was so close!

'I was so overcome with love I didn't even listen to the Priest until I realized he was speaking of strange dreams as he pointed to you. He was saying that only I could put it all together. It had to do with the blood drinker who had recently been in Antioch, not an uncommon occurrence. I have slain other blood drinkers before. I've vowed to catch this one.

'Then I saw Lucius. I saw you come together. His anger and guilt were nearly blinding to me with this blood drinker's vision. I heard your words effortlessly from a great distance, but would not move until you were safely away from him.

'I wanted to kill him then, but the wiser course seemed to stay right with you, to enter the Temple and stay by your side. I was not certain of my right to kill your brother for you, that it was what you wanted. I didn't know that until

330

I'd told you of his guilt. Then I knew how much you wanted it done.

'Of course I had no idea how clever you had become, that all the talent for reason and words I'd loved in you when you were a girl was still there. Suddenly you were in the Temple, thinking three times faster than the other mortals present, weighing every aspect of what faced you, outwitting everyone. And then came the spectacular confrontation with your brother in which you caught him in the most clever net of truths, and thereby dispatched him, without ever touching him, but instead drawing three military witnesses into complicity with his death.'

He broke off, then said, 'In Rome, years ago, I followed you. You were sixteen. I remember your first marriage. Your Father took me aside, he was so gentle. "Marius, you're destined to be a roaming historian," he said. I didn't dare tell him my true estimation of your husband.

'And now you come to Antioch, and I think, in my self-centered manner, as you will promptly note – if ever a woman was created for me, it is this woman. And I know as soon as I leave you in the morning, that I must somehow get the Mother and Father out of Antioch, get them away, but then this blood drinker has to be destroyed, and then and only then can you be safely left.'

'Safely abandoned,' I said.

'Do you blame me?' he asked.

The question caught me off guard. I looked at him for a seemingly endless moment, allowing his beauty to fill my eyes, and sensing with intolerable keenness his sadness and desperation. Oh, how he needed me! How desperately he needed not just any mortal soul in which to confide, but me.

'You really did want to protect me, didn't you?' I asked. 'And your explanation of all points is so completely rational; it has the elegance of mathematics. There is no need for reincarnation, or destiny, or any miraculous allowance for any part of what's happened.'

'It's what I believe,' he said sharply. His face grew blank, then stern. 'I would never give you anything short of truth. Are you a woman who wants to be humored?'

'Don't be fanatical in your dedication to reason,' I said.

These words both shocked and offended him.

'Don't cling to reason so desperately in a world of so many horrid contradictions!'

He was silenced.

'If you so cling to reason,' I said, 'then in the

passage of time reason may fail you, and when it does you may find yourself taking refuge in madness.'

'What on Earth do you mean?'

'You're made of reason and logic religion. It's obviously the only way you can endure what's happened to you, that you're a blood drinker and custodian, apparently, of these displaced and forgotten dieties.'

'They aren't dieties!' He grew angry. 'Thousands of years ago, they were made, through some mingling of spirit and flesh that rendered them immortal. They find their refuge obviously in oblivion. In your kindness you characterize it as a garden from which the Mother gathered flowers and leaves to make a garland for you, a trap, as you said. But this is your sweet girlish poetry. We do not know that they string very many words together.'

'I am no sweet girl,' I said. 'Poetry belongs to everyone. Speak to me!' I said. 'And put aside these words, "girl" and "woman." Don't be so frightened of me.'

'I am not,' he said angrily.

'You are! Even as this new blood races through me still, eats at me and transforms me, I cling to neither reason nor superstition for my safety. I can walk through a myth and out of it!

You fear me, because you don't know what I am. I look like a woman, I sound like a man, and your reason tells you the sum total is impossible!'

He rose from the table. His face took on a sheen like sweat but far more radiant.

'Let me tell you what happened to me!' he said resolutely.

'Good, do tell me,' I said. 'In straightforward manner.'

He let this go by. I spoke against my heart. I wanted only to love him. I knew his cautions. But for all his wisdom, he displayed an enormous will, a man's will, and I had to know the source of it. I concealed my love.

'How did they lure you?'

'They didn't,' he said calmly. 'I was captured by the Keltoi in Gaul, in the city of Massilia. I was brought North, my hair allowed to grow long, then shut up amid barbarians in a great hollow tree in Gaul. A burnt blood drinker made me into a "new god" and told me to escape the local Priests, go South to Egypt and find out why all the blood drinkers had been burnt, the young ones dying, the old one suffering. I went for my own reasons! I wanted to know what I was!'

'I can well understand,' I said.

'But not before I saw blood worship at its

most grisly and unspeakable – I was the god, mind you, Marius, who followed you adoringly all over Rome – and it was to me that these men were offered.'

'I've read it in Caesar's history.'

'You've read it but you haven't seen it. How dare you throw at me such a trivial boast!'

'Forgive me, I forgot your childish temper.'

He sighed. 'Forgive me, I forgot your practical and naturally impatient intellect.'

'I'm sorry. I regret my words. I had to witness executions of Rome. It was my duty. And that was in the name of law. Who suffers more or less? Victims of sacrifice or the law?'

'Very well. I escaped these Keltoi and went to Egypt, and there I found the Elder, who was the keeper of the Mother and the Father, the Queen and the King, the first blood drinkers of all time, from which this enhancement of our blood flows. This Elder told me stories that were vague but compelling. The Royal Pair had once been human, no more. A spirit or demon had possessed one or both, lodging itself so firmly that no exorcism could oust it. The Royal Pair could transform others by giving the blood. They sought to make a religion. It was overthrown. Again and again it was overthrown. Anyone who possesses the blood can make another! Of course this Elder claimed ignorance of why so many had been burnt. But it was he who had dragged his sacred and royal charges into the sun after centuries of meaningless guardianship! Egypt was dead, he said to me. 'The granary of Rome,' he called it. He said the Royal Pair had not moved in a millennium.'

This filled me with the most remarkable and poetic sense of horror.

'Well, one day's hot light was not enough anymore to destroy the ancient parents, but all over the world the children suffered. And this cowardly Elder, given only pain for his reward, a burned skin, lost the courage required to continue the exposure of the Royal Pair. He had no cause, one or another.

'Akasha spoke to me. She spoke as best she could. In images, pictures of what had happened since the beginning, how this tribe of gods and goddesses had sprung from her, and rebellions had occurred, and how much history was lost, and purpose was lost, and when it came to the forming of words, Akasha could make but only a few silent sentences: "Marius, take us out of Egypt!"' He paused. '"Take us out of Egypt, Marius. The Elder means to destroy us. Guard us or we perish here."'

He took a breath; he was calmer now, not so

angry, but very much shattered, and in my ever increasing vampiric vision, I knew more about him, how very courageous he was, how very determined to hold to principles in which he believed, in spite of the magic that had swallowed him whole before he had had time even to question it. His was an attempt at a noble life, in spite of all.

'My fate,' he said, 'was directly connected to hers, to them! If I left them, the Elder would sooner or later put them in the sun again, and I, lacking the blood of centuries, would burn up like wax! My life, already altered, would have been ended. But the Elder did not ask me to install a new priesthood. Akasha did not ask me to install a new religion! She did not speak of altars or worship. Only the old burnt-out god in the Northern grove among the barbarians had asked me to do such a thing when he sent me to the South, to Egypt, the motherland of all mysteries.'

'How long have you kept them?'

'Over fifteen years. I lose count. They never move or speak. The wounded ones, those burnt so badly that time will take centuries to heal them, they learn that I am here. They come. I try to extinguish them before their minds can give forth a flash of a confirming image to other distant minds. She doesn't guide these burnt children to where she is, as she once guided me! If I am tricked or overwhelmed, she moves only as you saw, to crush the blood drinker. But she has called you, Pandora, reached out for you. And we know now to what exact purpose. And I've been cruel to you. Clumsy.'

He turned to me. His voice grew tender. 'Tell me, Pandora,' he asked. 'In the vision you saw, when we were married, were we young or old? Were you the girl of fifteen I sought too early perhaps, or the mature full blossom of a creature you are now? Are the families happy? Are we comely?'

I was hotly embraced by the sincerity of his words. The anguish and the pleading that lay behind them.

'We were as we are now,' I said, cautiously answering his smile with my own. 'You were a man fixed in the prime of life forever, and I? As I am at this hour.'

'Believe me,' he said with sweetness in his voice, 'I would not have spoken so harshly on this of all nights, but you have now so many other nights to come. Nothing can kill you now, but the sun or fire. Nothing in you will deteriorate. You have a thousand experiences to discover.'

'And what of the ecstasy when I drank from her?' I asked. 'What of her own beginnings and her suffering? Does she in no way connect herself to the sacred?'

'What is sacred?' he asked, shrugging his shoulder. 'Tell me. What is sacred? Was it sanctity you saw in her dreams?'

I bowed my head. I couldn't answer.

'Certainly not the Roman Empire,' he said, 'Certainly not the temples of Augustus Caesar. Certainly not the worship of Cybele! Certainly not the cult of those who worship fire in Persia. Is the name Isis sacred anymore, or was it ever? The Elder in Egypt, my first and only instructor in all this, said that Akasha invented the stories of Isis and Osiris to suit her purposes, to give a poetry to her worship. I think rather she grafted herself upon old stories. The demon in those two grows with each new blood drinker made. It must.'

'But to no purpose?'

'That it may know more?' he said. 'That it may see more, feel more, through each of us which carries its blood? Perhaps it is such a creature as that and each of us is but a tiny part of it, carrying all its senses and capacities and returning our experiences to it. It reaches out through us to know the world!

'I can tell you this,' he said. He paused and put his hands on the desk. 'What burns in me does not care if the victim is innocent or guilty of any crime. It thirsts. Not every night, but often! It says nothing! It does not talk of altars to me in my heart! It drives me as though I were the battle steed and it the mounted General! It is Marius who weeds the good from the bad, according to the old custom, for reasons you can well understand, but not this ravening thirst; this thirst knows nature but no morality.'

'I love you, Marius,' I said. 'You and my Father are the only men I've ever really loved. But I must go out alone now.'

'What did you say!' He was amazed. 'It's just past midnight.'

'You've been very patient, but I have to walk alone now.'

'I'll come with you.'

'You will not,' I said.

'But you can't simply roam around Antioch on your own, alone.'

'Why not? I can hear mortal thoughts now if I want to. A litter just passed. The slaves are so drunk it's a wonder they don't drop the thing and heave the Master into the road, and he himself is fast asleep. I want to walk alone, out there, in the city in the dark places and the dangerous places and the evil places and the places where even . . . where even a god would not go.'

'This is your vengeance on me,' he said. I walked towards the gate and he followed. 'Pandora, not alone.'

'Marius, my love,' I said, turning, taking his hand. 'It is not vengeance. The words you spoke earlier, "girl" and "woman," they have always circumscribed my life. I want only now to walk fearlessly with my arms bare and my hair down my back, into any cavern of danger I choose. I am drunk still from her blood, from yours! Things shimmer and flicker that should shine. I must be alone to ponder all you've said.'

'But you have to be back before dawn, well before. You have to be with me in the crypt below. You can't merely lie in some room somewhere. The deadly light will penetrate—'

He was so protective, so lustrous, so infuriated.

'I will be back,' I said, 'and well before dawn, and for now, my heart will break if we are not, as of this moment, bound together.'

'We are bound,' he said. 'Pandora, you could drive me mad.'

He stopped at the bars of the gate.

'Don't come any farther,' I said as I left.

I walked down towards Antioch. My legs had

such strength and spring, and the dust and pebbles of the road were nothing to my feet, and my eyes penetrated the night to see the full conspiracy of owls and little rodents that hovered in the trees, eyeing me, then fleeing as if their natural senses warned them against me.

Soon I came into the city proper. I think the resolution with which I moved from little street to little street was enough to frighten anyone who would have contemplated molesting me. I heard only cowardice and erotic curses from the dark, those tangled ugly curses men heap on women they desire – half threat, half dismissal.

I could sense the people in their houses fast asleep, and hear the guards on watch, talking in their barracks behind the Forum.

I did all the things the new blood drinkers always do. I touched the surfaces of walls and stared, enchanted at a common torch and the moths that gave themselves up to it. I felt against my naked arms and fragile tunic the dreams of all Antioch surrounding me.

Rats fled up and down the gutters and the streets. The river gave off its own sound, and there came a hollow echoing from the ships at anchor, even from the faintest stirring of the water.

The Forum, resplendent with its ever burning

lights, caught the moon as if it were a great human trap for it, the very reverse of an earthy crater, a man-made design that could be seen and blessed by the intransigent heavens.

When I came to my own house, I found I could climb to the very top easily, and there I sat on the tiled roof, so relaxed and secure and free, looking down into the courtyard, into the peristyle, where I had really learned – alone on those three nights – the truths that had prepared me for Akasha's blood.

In calmness and without pain, I thought it through again – as if I owed this reconsideration to the woman I had been, the initiate, the woman who had sought refuge in the Temple. Marius was right. The Queen and King were possessed of some demon which spread through the blood, feeding upon it and growing, as I could feel it doing in me now.

The King and Queen did not invent justice! The Queen, who broke the little Pharaoh into sticks, did not invent law or righteousness!

And the Roman courts, bumbling awkwardly towards each decision, weighing all sides, refusing any magical or religious device, they did even in these terrible times strive for justice. It was a system based not upon the revelation of the gods, but upon reason.

But I could not regret the moment of intoxication when I'd drunk her blood and believed in her, and seen the flowers come down upon us. I could not regret that any mind could conceive of such perfect transcendence.

She had been my Mother, my Queen, my goddess, my all. I had known it as we were meant to know it when we drink the potions in the Temple, when we sing, when we are rocking in delirious song. And in her arms I had known it. In Marius's arms I'd known it as well, and in a safer measure, and I wanted only to be with him now.

How ghastly her worship seemed. Flawed and ignorant, being elevated to such power! And how revealing suddenly that at the core of mysteries there should lie such degrading explanations. Blood spilt on her golden gown!

All images and meaningful glimpses do but teach you deeper things. I thought again, as I had in the Temple, when I had settled for the consolation of a basalt statue.

It is I, and I alone, who must make of my new life a heroic tale.

I was very happy for Marius that he had such comfort in reason. But reason was only a created thing, imposed with faith upon the world, and the stars promise nothing to no one.

I had seen something deeper in those dark nights of hiding in this house in Antioch, in mourning for my Father. I had seen that at the very heart of Creation there very well might lie something as uncontrollable and incomprehensible as a raging volcano.

Its lava would destroy trees and poets alike.

So take this gift, Pandora, I told myself. Go home, thankful that you are again wed, for you have never made a better match or seen a more tantalizing future.

When I returned, and my return was very rapid, full of new lessons in how I might pass quickly over rooftops, scarce touching them, and over walls – when I returned, I found him as I had left him, only much sadder. He sat in the garden, just as he had in the vision shown to me by Akasha.

It must have been a place he loved, behind the villa with its many doors, a bench facing a thicket and a natural stream bubbling up and over the rocks and spilling down into a current through high grass.

He rose at once.

I took him in my arms.

'Marius, forgive me,' I said.

'Don't say such a thing, I'm to blame for it all. And I didn't protect you from it.'

345

We were in each other's arms. I wanted to press my teeth into him, drink his blood, and then I did, and felt him taking the blood from me. This was a union more powerful than any I had ever known in a marriage bed, and I yielded to it as I never yielded in life to anyone.

I felt an exhaustion sweep me suddenly. I withdrew my kiss with its teeth.

'Come on, now,' he said. 'Your slave is asleep. And during the day, while we must sleep, he will bring all your possessions here, and those girls of yours, should you want to keep them.'

We walked down the stairs, we entered another room. It took all Marius's strength to pull back the door, which meant simply that no mortal man could do it.

There lay a sarcophagus, plain, of granite.

'Can you lift the lid of the sarcophagus?' Marius asked.

'I am feeling weak!'

'It's the sun rising, try to lift the lid. Slide it to one side.'

I did, and inside I found a bed of crushed lilies and rose petals, of silken pillows, and bits of dried flower kept for scent.

I stepped in, turned around, sat and stretched out in this stone prison. At once he took his place in the tomb beside me, and pushed the lid back to its place, and all the world's light in any form was shut out, as if the dead would have it so.

'I'm drowsy. I can hardly form words.'

'What a blessing,' he said.

'There is no need for such an insult,' I murmured. 'But I forgive you.'

'Pandora, I love you!' he said helplessly.

'Put it inside me,' I said, reaching between his legs. 'Fill me and hold me.'

'This is stupid and superstitious!'

'It is neither,' I said. 'It is symbolic and comforting.'

He obeyed. Our bodies were one, connected by this sterile organ which was no more to him now than his arm, but how I loved the arm he threw over me and the lips he pressed to my forehead.

'I love you, Marius, my strange, tall and beautiful Marius.'

'I don't believe you,' he said, his voice barely a whisper.

'What do you mean?'

'You'll despise me soon enough for what I've done to you.'

'Not so, oh, rational one. I am not as eager to grow old, wither and die, as you might think. I

347

should like a chance to know more, to see more . . .'

I felt his lips against my forehead.

'Did you really try to marry me when I was fifteen?'

'Oh, agonizing memories! Your Father's insults still sting my ears! He had me all but thrown out of your house!'

'I love you with my whole heart,' I whispered. 'And you have won. You have me now as your wife.'

'I have you as something, but I do not think that "wife" is the word for it. I wonder that you've already forgotten your earlier strenuous objection to the term.'

'Together,' I said, scarce able to talk on account of his kisses. I was drowsy and loved the feel of his lips, their sudden eagerness for pure affection. 'We'll think of another word more exalted than "wife".'

Suddenly I moved back. I could not see him in the dark.

'Are you kissing me so that I will not talk?'

'Yes, that's exactly what I was doing,' he said.

I turned away from him.

'Turn back, please,' he said.

'No,' I said.

I lay still, realizing dimly that his body felt quite normal to me now, because mine was as hard as his was, as strong perhaps. What a sublime advantage. Oh, but I loved him. I loved him! So let him kiss the back of the neck! He could not force me to turn towards him!

The sun must have risen.

For a silence fell on me which was as if the universe with all its volcanoes and raging tides – and all its Emperors, Kings, judges, Senators, philosophers and Priests – had been erased from existence.

Well, David, there you have it.

I could continue the Plautus-Terence style comedy for pages. I could vie with Shakespeare's *Much Ado About Nothing*.

But that is the basic story. That is what lies behind the flippant capsule version in *The Vampire Lestat,* fashioned into its final trivial form by Marius or Lestat, who knows.

Let me lead you through those points which are sacred and burn still in my heart, no matter how easily they have been dismissed by another.

And the tale of our parting is not mere dissonance but may contain some lesson.

Marius taught me to hunt, to catch the evildoer only, and to kill without pain, enwrapping the soul of my victim in sweet visions or allowing the soul to illuminate its own death with a cascade of fantasies which I must not judge, but merely devour, like the blood. All that does not require detailed documentation.

We were matched in strength. When some burnt and ruthlessly ambitious blood drinker did find his way to Antioch, which happened only a few times and then not at all, we executed the supplicant together. These were monstrous mentalities, forged in ages we could hardly understand, and they sought the Queen like jackals seek the bodies of the human dead.

There was no argument between us over any of them.

We often read aloud to each other, and we laughed together at Petronius's *Satyricon,* and we shared both tears and laughter later as we read the bitter satires of Juvenal. There was no end of new satire and history coming from Rome and from Alexandria.

But something forever divided Marius from me.

Love grew but so did constant argument, and argument became more and more the dangerous cement of the bond.

Over the years, Marius guarded his delicate rationality as a Vestal Virgin guards a sacred flame. If ever any ecstatic emotion took hold of me, he was there to grab me by the shoulders and tell me in no uncertain terms that it was irrational. Irrational, irrational, irrational!

When the terrible earthquake of the second century struck Antioch, and we were unharmed, I dared speak of it as a Divine Blessing. This set Marius into a rage, and he was quick to point that the same Divine Intervention had also protected the Roman Emperor Trajan, who was in the city at the time. What was I to make of that?

For the record, Antioch quickly rebuilt itself, the markets flourished, more slaves poured in, nothing stopped the caravans headed for the ships, and the ships headed for the caravans.

But long before that earthquake we had all but come to blows night after night.

If I lingered for hours in the room of the Mother and the Father, Marius invariably came to collect me and bring me back to my senses. He could not read in peace with me in such a state, he declared. He could not think because he knew I was downstairs deliberately inviting madness.

Why, I demanded, must his domination extend to every corner of our entire house and garden? And how was it that I was his match in strength when an old burnt blood drinker found his way to Antioch and we picked up the word of his killing and had to do away with him?

'We are not matched in minds?' I demanded.

'Only you could ask that question!' came his reply.

Of course the Mother and Father never moved or spoke again. No blood dreams, no divine directive ever reached me. Only now and then did Marius remind me of this. And after a long while, he allowed me to tend the Shrine with him, to see full well the extent of their silent and seemingly mindless compliance. They appeared utterly beyond reach; their cooperation was sluggish and frightening to witness.

When Flavius fell ill in his fortieth year, Marius and I had the first of our truly terrible battles. This came early on, well before the earthquake.

It was, by the way, a wondrous time because the wicked old Tiberius was filling Antioch with new and wonderful buildings. She was the rival of Rome. But Flavius was ill.

Marius could scarce bear it. He had become more than fond of Flavius — they talked about Aristotle all the time, and Flavius proved one of those men who can do anything for you, from managing a household to copying the most esoteric and crumbling text with complete accuracy.

Flavius had never put a single question to us

as to what we were. In his mind, I found, devotion and acceptance far superseded curiosity or fear.

We hoped Flavius had only a minor illness. But finally, as Flavius's fever grew worse, Flavius turned his head away from Marius whenever Marius came to him. But he held on to my hand always when I offered it. Frequently I lay beside him for hours, as he had once lain beside me.

Then one night Marius took me to the gate and said, 'He'll be dead by the time I come back. Can you bear this alone?'

'Do you run from it?' I asked.

'No,' he said. 'But he doesn't want me to see him die; he doesn't want me to see him groan in pain.'

I nodded.

Marius left.

Marius had long ago laid down the rule that no other blood drinker was ever to be made. I didn't bother to question him on this.

As soon as he was gone, I made Flavius into a vampire. I did it just the way the burnt one, Marius and Akasha had done it to me, for Marius and I had long discussed the methods – withdraw as much blood as you can, then give it back until you are near to fainting.

I did faint and wake to see this splendid Greek standing over me, smiling faintly, all disease gone from him. He reached down to take my hand and help me to my feet.

Marius walked in, stared at the reborn Flavius in amazement and said, 'Get out, out of this house, out of this city, out of this province, out of this Empire.'

Flavius's last words to me were:

'Thank you for this Dark Gift.' That is the first I ever heard that particular phrase, which appears so often in Lestat's writings. How well this learned Athenian understood it.

For hours I avoided Marius. I would never be forgiven! Then I went out into the garden. I discovered Marius was grieving, and when he looked up, I realized that he had been utterly convinced that I meant to go off with Flavius. When I saw this, I took him in my arms. He was full of quiet relief and love; he forgave me at once for my 'absolute rashness.'

'Don't you see,' I said, taking him in hand, 'that I adore you? But you cannot rule over me! Can you not consider in your reasonable fashion that the greatest part of our gift eludes you – it's the freedom from the confines of male, female!'

'You can't convince me,' he said, 'for one

moment that you don't feel, reason and act in the manner of a woman. We both loved Flavius. But why another blood drinker?'

'I don't know except that Flavius wanted it, Flavius knew all about our secrets, there was a . . . an understanding between me and Flavius! He had been loyal in the darkest hours of my mortal life. Oh, I can't explain it.'

'A woman's sentiments, exactly. And you have launched this creature into eternity.'

'He joins our search,' I replied.

About the middle of the century, when the city was very rich and the Empire was about as peaceful as it was ever going to be for the next two hundred years, the Christian Paul came to Antioch.

I went to hear him speak one night and came home, saying casually that the man could convert the very stones to this faith, such was his personal power.

'How can you spend your time on such things!' Marius demanded. 'Christians. They aren't even a cult! Some worship John, some worship Jesus. They fight amongst one another! Don't you see what this man Paul has done?'

'No, what?' I said. 'I didn't say I was going to join the sect. I only said I stopped to hear him. Who is hurt by that?'

'You, your mind, your equilibrium, your common sense. It's compromised by the foolish things in which you take an interest, and frankly the principle of truth is hurt!' He had only just begun.

'Let me tell you about this man Paul,' Marius said. 'He never knew either the Baptizer John or the Galilean Jesus. The Hebrews have thrown him out of the group. Jesus and John were both Hebrews! And so Paul has now turned to everyone. Jew and Christian alike, and Roman and Greek, and said, "You needn't follow the Hebrew observance. Forget the Feasts in Jerusalem. Forget Circumcision. Become a Christian."'

'Yes, that is true,' I said with a sigh.

'It's a very easy religion to take up,' he said. 'It's nothing. You have to believe that this man rose from the Dead. And by the way, I've combed the available texts which are floating all over the marketplaces. Have you?'

'No. I'm surprised you've found this search worthy of your time.'

'I don't see anywhere in the writings of those who knew John and Jesus where these two are quoted as saying either one of them will rise from the Dead, or that all who believe in them will have life after death. Paul added all that.

What an enticing promise! And you should hear your friend, Paul, on the subject of Hell! What a cruel vision – that flawed mortals could sin in this life so grievously that they would burn for all eternity.'

'He's not my friend. You make so much of my passing remarks. Why do you feel so strongly?'

'I told you, I care about what is true, what is reasonable!'

'Well, there's something you're missing about this group of Christians, some way in which when they come together they share a euphoric love and they believe in great generosity –'

'Oh, not again! And are you to tell me this is good?'

I didn't answer.

He was returning to his work when I spoke.

'You fear me,' I said to him. 'You fear that I'll be swept off my feet by somebody of belief and abandon you. No. No, that's not right. You fear that you will be swept up. That the world will somehow entice you back into it, so that you won't live here with me, the superior Roman observer recluse, anymore, but go back, seeking mortal comforts of companionship and proximity to others, friendship with mortals, their recognition of you as one of them when you are not one of them!'

'Pandora, you talk gibberish.'

'Keep your proud secrets,' I said. 'But I do fear for you, that I will admit.'

'Fear for me? And why?' he demanded.

'Because you don't realize everything perishes, everything is artifice! That even logic and mathematics and justice have no ultimate meaning!'

'That's not true,' he said.

'Oh, yes it is. Some night will come when you will see what I saw, when I first came to Antioch, before you'd found me, before this transformation which should have swept away everything in its path.

'You will see a darkness,' I went on, 'a darkness so total that Nature never knows it anywhere on Earth at any time, in any place! Only the human soul can know it. And it goes on forever. And I pray that when you finally can no longer escape from it, when you realize it is all around you, that your logic and your reason give you some strength against it.'

He gave me the most respectful look. But he didn't speak. I continued:

'Resignation will do you no good,' I said, 'when such a time comes. Resignation requires will, and will requires decision, and decision requires belief, and belief requires that there is something to believe in! And all action or acceptance requires a concept of a witness! Well, there is nothing, and there are no witnesses! You don't know that yet, but I do. I hope, when you find it out, someone can comfort you as you dress and groom those monstrous relics below the stairs! As you bring their flowers!' I was so angry, I went on:

'Look back on me when this moment comes – if not for forgiveness, look back on me as a model. For I have seen this, and I have survived. And it matters not that I stopped to listen to Paul preach of Christ, or that I weave flowers into crowns for the Queen, or that I dance like a fool under the moon in the garden before dawn, or that I . . . that I love you. It matters not. Because there is nothing. And no one to see. No one!' I sighed. It was time to finish.

'Go back to your history, this stack of lies that tries to link event to event with cause and effect, this preposterous faith that postulates that one thing follows from another. I tell you, it's not so. But it is very Roman of you to think so.'

He sat silent looking up at me. I couldn't tell what his thoughts were or what his heart felt. Then he asked:

'What would you have me do?' He had never looked more innocent.

Bitterly, I laughed. Did we not speak the same language? He heard not one word I had uttered. Yet he presented me not with a reply, but only with this simple question.

'All right,' I said. 'I'll tell you what I want. Love me, Marius, love me, but leave me alone!' I cried out. I had not even thought. The words just came. 'Leave me alone, so that I may seek my own comforts, my own means to remain alive, no matter how foolish or pointless these comforts appear to you. Leave me alone!'

He was wounded, so uncomprehending, looking so innocent still.

We had many similar arguments as the decades passed.

Sometimes he would come to me after; he would fall into long thoughtful talks about what he felt was happening with the Empire, how the Emperors were going mad and the Senate had no power, how the very progress of man was unique in Nature and something to be watched. How he would crave life, he thought, until there was no more life.

'Even if there is nothing left but desert waste,' he said, 'I should want to be there, to see dune folding upon dune,' he went on. 'If there was but one lamp left in all the world, I'd want to watch its flame. And so would you.'

But the terms of the battle, and its heat, never really changed.

At heart he thought I hated him for having been so unkind on the night I was given the Dark Blood. I told him this was childish. I could not convince him that my soul and my intelligence were infinitely too large for such a simple grudge, and that I owed him no explanation for my thoughts, words and deeds.

For two hundred years, we lived and loved together. He became ever more beautiful to me.

As more and more barbarians from the North and from the East poured into the city, he felt no necessity to dress like a Roman anymore, and frequently wore the jeweled clothes of the Easterners. His hair seemed to be growing finer, lighter. He seldom cut it, which of course he would have had to do every night had he wanted it short. It was a splendor on his shoulders.

As his face grew ever more smooth, away went the few lines that could so easily design anger in his expression. As I've told you before, he greatly resembles Lestat. Only he is more compact of build, and jaw and chin had hardened just a little more with age before the Dark

Gift. But the unwanted folds were receding from his eyes.

Sometimes for nights on end, in fear of a fight, we didn't speak. There was between us always a continuous physical affection – embraces, kisses, sometimes the mere silent lock of our hands.

But we knew we had now lived far beyond a normal human life span.

You need from me no detailed history of that remarkable time. It is too well known. Only let me place here a few reminders. Only let me describe for you my perspective on the changes happening all over the Empire.

Antioch as a thriving city proved indestructible. The Emperors began to favor it and visit it. More Temples went up to the Eastern cults. And then Christians of all kinds poured into Antioch.

Indeed, the Christians of Antioch comprised at last an immense and fascinating bunch of people arguing with one another.

Rome went to war on the Jews, crushing Jerusalem completely and destroying the sacred Hebrew Temple. Many brilliant Jewish thinkers came to Antioch as well as Alexandria.

Twice or perhaps even three times, Roman legions pushed past us, North of us, into

Parthia; once we even had a little rebellion of our own, but Rome always resecured the city of Antioch. So the market closed for a day! On went the trade, the great lust of the caravans for the ships, and of the ships for the caravans, and Antioch was the bed in which they must wed each other.

There was little new poetry. Satire. Satire seemed the only safe or honest expression of the Roman mind now, and so we had the riotously funny story *The Golden Ass,* by Apuleius, which seemed to make fun of every religion. But there was a bitterness to the poet Martial. And those letters of Pliny which reached me were full of dire judgments on the moral chaos of Rome.

I began as a vampire to feed exclusively on soldiers. I liked them, their look, their strength. I fed so much so on them, that in my carelessness, I became a legend amongst them, 'The Greek Lady Death,' this on account of my clothes which to them appeared archaic. I struck at random in the dark streets. There wasn't a chance of their ever surrounding me or stopping me, so great was my skill, my strength and my thirst.

But I saw things in their rebellious deaths, the blaze of a pitched battle in a march, a hand-to-hand struggle on a steep mountain. I took them down gently into the finish, filling myself to the brim with their blood, and sometimes, through a veil it seemed, I saw the souls of those whom they themselves had slain.

When I told Marius this, he said it was just the kind of mystical nonsense he would expect of me.

I didn't press the point.

He watched with keen interest the developments of Rome. To me they seemed merely surprising.

He pored over the histories of Dio Cassius and Plutarch and Tacitus, and pounded his fist when he heard of the endless skirmishes on the Rhine River, and the push Northward into Britannia and the building of Hadrian's wall to forever keep away the Scots, who like the Germans would yield to no one.

'They are not patrolling, preserving, containing an Empire any longer,' he said. 'Conserving a way of life! It's just war, and trade!'

I couldn't disagree.

It was really even worse than he knew. If he had gone as often as I did to listen to the philosophers he would have been appalled.

Magicians were appearing everywhere, claiming to be able to fly, to see visions, to heal

with the laying on of hands! They got into battles with the Christians and the Jews. I don't
think the Roman army paid them any attention.

Medicine as I had known it in my mortal life
had been flooded with a river of Eastern secret
formulae, amulets, rituals, and little statues to
clutch.

Well over half the Senate was no longer
Italian by birth. This meant that our Rome was
no longer our Rome. And the title of Emperor
had become a joke. There were so many assas-
sinations, plots, squabbles, false emperors and
palace coups that it soon became perfectly clear
that the Army ruled. The Army chose the
Emperor. The Army sustained him.

The Christians were divided into warring
sects. It was positively astonishing. The religion didn't burn itself out in dispute. It gained
strength in division. Occasional furious perse-
cutions – in which people were executed for not
worshiping at Roman altars – only seemed to
deepen the sympathy of the populace with this
new cult.

And the new cult was rampant with debate on
every principle with regard to the Jews, God
and Jesus.

The most amazing thing had happened to this
religion. Spreading wildly on fast ships, good

roads and well-maintained trade routes, it suddenly found itself in a peculiar position. The world had not come to an end, as Jesus and Paul had predicted.

And everybody who had ever known or seen Jesus was dead. Finally everyone who had ever known Paul was dead.

Christian philosophers arose, picking and choosing from old Greek ideas and old Hebrew traditions.

Justin of Athens wrote that Christ was the Logos; you could be an atheist and still be saved in Christ if you upheld reason.

I had to tell this to Marius.

I thought sure it would set him off, and the night was dull, but he merely countered with more outlandish talk of the Gnostics.

'A man named Saturninus popped up in the Forum today,' he said. 'Perhaps you heard talk of him. He preaches a wild variant of this Christian creed you find so amusing, in which the God of the Hebrews is actually the Devil and Jesus the new God. This was not the man's first appearance. He and his followers, thanks to the local Christian Bishop Ignatius, are headed for Alexandria.'

'There are books with those ideas already here,' I said, 'having come from Alexandria.

They are impenetrable to me. Perhaps not to you. They speak of Sophia, a female principle of Wisdom, which preceded the Creation. Jews and Christians alike want somehow to include this concept of Sophia in their faith. It so reminds me of our beloved Isis.'

'Your beloved Isis!' he said.

'It seems that there are minds who would weave it all together, every myth, or its essence, to make a glorious tapestry.'

'Pandora, you are making me ill again,' he warned. 'Let me tell you what your Christians are doing. They are tightly organizing. This Bishop Ignatius will be followed by another, and the Bishops want to lay down now that the age of private revelation had ended; they want to weed through all the mad scrolls on the market and make a canon which all Christians believe.'

'I never thought such could happen,' I said. 'I agreed with you more than you knew when you condemned them.'

'They are succeeding because they are moving away from emotional morality,' he said. 'They are organizing like Romans. This Bishop Ignatius is very strict. He delegates power. He pronounced on the accuracy of manuscripts. Notice the prophets are getting thrown out of Antioch.'

'Yes, you're right,' I said. 'What do you think? Is it good or bad?'

'I want the world to be better,' he said. 'Better for men and women. Better. Only one thing is clear: the old blood drinkers have by now died out, and there is nothing you or I, or the Queen and the King can do to interfere in the flow of human events. I believe men and women must try harder. I try to understand evil ever more deeply with any victim I take.

'Any religion that makes fanatical claims and demands on the basis of a god's will frightens me.'

'You are a true Augustan,' I said. 'I agree with you, but it is fun to read these mad Gnostics. This Marcion and this Valentinus.'

'Fun for you perhaps. I see danger everywhere. This new Christianity, it isn't merely spreading, it's changing in each place as it spreads; it's like an animal which devours the local flora and fauna and then takes on some specific power from the food.'

I didn't argue with him.

By the end of the second century, Antioch was a heavily Christian city. And it seemed to me as I read the works of new Bishops and philosophers that worse things than Christianity could come upon us.

Realize, however, David, that Antioch did not lie under a cloud of decay; there was no sense in the air of the end of the Empire. If anything there was bustling energy everywhere. Commerce gives one this feel, that false sense that there is growth and creativity, perhaps, when there is none. Things are exchanged, not necessarily improved.

Then came the dark time for us. Two forces came together which bore down on Marius, straining all his courage. Antioch was more interesting than it had ever been.

The Mother and the Father had never stirred since the first night of my coming!

Let me describe the first disaster, because for me it was not so hard to bear, and I had only sympathy for Marius.

As I've told you, the question of who was Emperor had become a joke. But it really became a howl with the events of the early 200s.

The Emperor of the moment was Caracalla, a regular murderer. On a pilgrimage to Alexandria to see the remains of Alexander the Great, he had – for reasons no one knows even now – rounded up thousands of young Alexandrians and slaughtered them. Alexandria had never seen such a massacre.

Marius was distraught. All the world was distraught.

Marius spoke of leaving Antioch, of getting far far away from the ruin of the Empire. I began to agree with him.

Then this revolting Emperor Caracalla marched in our direction, intending to make a war on the Parthians North of us and to the East of us. Nothing out of the ordinary for Antioch!

His Mother – and you need not remember these names – Julia Domna, took up residence in Antioch. She was dying from cancer of her breast. And let me add here that this woman had, with her son Caracalla, helped murder her other son, Geta, because the two brothers had been sharing Imperial power and threatening to make a Civil War.

Let me continue, and again you need not remember the names.

Troops were massed for this Eastern war against two Kings to the East, Vologases the Fifth and Artabanus the Fifth. Caracalla did make war, achieve victory and return in triumph. Then, only miles from Antioch, he was assassinated by his own soldiers while trying to relieve himself!

All this cast Marius in a hopeless frame of mind. For hours he sat in the Shrine staring at the Mother and the Father. I felt I knew what he was thinking, that we should immolate ourselves and them, but I couldn't bear the thought of it. I didn't want to die. I didn't want to lose life. I didn't want to lose Marius.

I did not care so much about the fate of Rome. Life still stretched before me, extending the promise of wonders.

Back to the Comedy. The Army promptly made an Emperor out of a man from the Provinces named Macrinus, who was a Moor and wore an earring in his ear.

He at once had a fight with the dead Emperor's Mother, Julia Domna, because he wouldn't allow her to leave Antioch to die elsewhere. She starved herself to death.

This was all too close to home! These lunatics were in our city, not far away in a capital which we mourned.

Then war broke out again, because the Eastern Kings, who were caught off guard before by Caracalla, were now ready, and Macrinus had to lead the Legions into battle.

As I told you, the Legions now controlled everything. Somebody should have told Macrinus. Instead of fighting he bought off the enemy. The troops were hardly proud of this. And then he cracked down on them, taking away some of their benefits.

He didn't seem to grasp that he had to maintain their approval to survive. Though of course what good had this done for Caracalla, whom they loved?

Whatever, the sister of Julia Domna, named Julia Maesa, who was a Syrian and of a family dedicated to the Syrian sun god, seized this dreary moment in the lift of the lusty legions to put her grandson, born of Julia Soemis, in power as Emperor! It was an outrageous plan actually, for any number of reasons. First and foremost, all three Julias were Syrian. The boy himself was fourteen years old, and also he was a hereditary Priest of the Syrian sun god.

But somehow or other Julia Maesa and her daughter's lover, Gannys, managed to convince a bunch of soldiers in a tent that this fourteen-year-old Syrian boy should become the Emperor of Rome.

The Army deserted the Imperial Macrinus, and he and his son were hunted down and murdered.

So, high on the shoulders of proud soldiers rode this fourteen-year-old boy! But he didn't want to be called by his Roman name. He wanted to be called by the name of the god he worshiped in Syria, Elagabalus. The very presence of him in Antioch shook the nerves of all citizens. At last, he and three remaining Julias – his aunt, his Mother and his grandmother, all of them Syrian Priestesses – left Antioch.

In Nicomedia, which was very near to us, Elagabalus murdered his Mother's lover. So who was left? He also picked up an enormous sacred black stone and brought it back to Rome, saying that this stone was sacred to the Syrian sun god, whom all must now worship.

He was gone, across the sea, but it took sometimes no more than eleven days for a letter to reach Antioch from Rome, and soon there were rampant rumors. Who will ever know the truth about him?

Elagabalus. He built a Temple for the stone on the Palatine Hill. He made Romans stand around in Phoenician gowns while he slaughtered cattle and sheep in sacrifice.

He begged the physicians to try to transform him into a woman by creating a proper opening between his legs. Romans were horrified by this. At night he dressed as a woman, complete with a wig, and went prowling taverns.

All over the Empire the soldiers started to riot.

Even the three Julias, grandmother Julia Maesa, his aunt Julia Domna, and his own

Mother, Julia Soemis, started to get sick of him. After four years, four years, mind you, of this maniac's rule, the soldiers killed him and threw his body in the Tiber.

It did not seem to Marius that there was anything left of the world we had once called Rome. And he was thoroughly sick of all the Christians in Antioch, their fights over doctrine. He found all mystery religions dangerous now. He served up this lunatic Emperor as a perfect example of the fanaticism gaining ground in the times.

And he was right. He was right.

It was all I could do to keep him from despair. In truth he had not yet confronted that terrible darkness I had once spoken of; he was far too agitated, far too irritated and quarrelsome. But I was very frightened for him, and hurt for him, and didn't want him to see more darkly, as I did, to be more aloof, expecting nothing and almost smiling at the collapse of our Empire.

Then the very worst thing happened, something we had both feared in one form or another. But it came upon us in the worst possible form.

One night there appeared at our eternally open doors five blood drinkers.

Neither of us had caught the sound of their approach. Lounging about with our books, we looked up to see these five, three women and a man and a boy, and to realize that all wore black garments. They were dressed like Christian hermits and ascetics who deny the flesh and starve themselves. Antioch had a whole passel of these men in the desert roundabouts.

But these were blood drinkers.

Dark of hair and eye, and dark of skin, they stood before us, their arms folded.

Dark of skin, I thought quickly. They are young. They were made after the great burning. So what if there are five?

They had in general rather attractive faces, well-shaped features and groomed eyebrows, and deep dark eyes, and all over them I saw the marks of their living bodies – tiny wrinkles next to their eyes, wrinkled around their knuckles.

They seemed as shocked to see us as we were to see them. They stared at the brightly lighted library; they stared at our finery, which was in such contrast to their ascetic robes.

'Well,' said Marius, 'who are you?'

Cloaking my thoughts, I tried to probe theirs. Their minds were locked. They were dedicated to something. It had the very scent of fanaticism. I felt a horrid foreboding.

They started timidly to enter the open door.

'No, stop, please,' said Marius in Greek.

'This is my house. Tell me who you are, and then I perhaps shall invite you over my threshold.'

'You're Christians, aren't you?' I said. 'You have the zeal.'

'We are!' said one in Greek. It was the man. 'We are the scourge of humanity in the name of God and his son, Christ. We are the Children of Darkness.'

'Who made you?' asked Marius.

'We were made in a sacred cave and in our Temple,' said another, a woman, speaking in Greek also. 'We know the truth of the Serpent, and his fangs are our fangs.'

I climbed to my feet and moved towards Marius.

'We thought you would be in Rome,' said the young man. He had short black hair, and very round innocent eyes. 'Because the Christian Bishop of Rome is now supreme among Christians and the theology of Antioch is no longer of great matter.'

'Why would we be in Rome?' asked Marius. 'What is the Roman Bishop to us?'

The woman took the fore. Her hair was severely parted in the middle but her face was very regal and regular. She had in particular beautifully defined lips.

'Why do you hide from us? We have heard of you for years! We know that you know things – about us and where the Dark Gift came from, that you know how God put it into the world, and that you saved our kind from extinction.'

Marius was plainly horrified, but gave little sign of it.

'I have nothing to tell you,' he said, perhaps too hastily. 'Except I do not believe in your God or your Christ and I do not believe God put the Dark Gift, as you call it, into the world. You have made a terrible mistake.'

They were highly skeptical and utterly dedicated.

'You have almost reached salvation,' said another, the boy at the far end of the line, whose hair was unshorn and hung to his shoulders. He had a manly voice, but his limbs were small. 'You have almost reached the point where you are so strong and white and pure that you need not drink!'

'Would that that were true, it's not,' said Marius.

'Why don't you welcome us?' asked the boy. 'Why don't you guide us and teach us that we may better spread the Dark Blood, and punish mortals for their sins! We are pure of heart. We were chosen. Each of us went into the cave bravely and there the dying devil, a crushed creature of blood and bone, cast out Heaven in a blaze of fire, passed on to us his teachings.'

'Which were what?' asked Marius.

'Make them suffer,' the woman said. 'Bring death. Eschew all things of the world, as do the Stoics and the hermits of Egypt, but bring death. Punish them.'

The woman had become hostile. 'This man won't help us,' she said under her breath. 'This man is profane. This man is a heretic.'

'But you must receive us,' said the young man who had spoken first. 'We have searched so long and so far, and we come to you in humility. If you wish to live in a palace, then perhaps that is your right, you have earned it, but we have not. We live in darkness, we enjoy no pleasure but the blood, we feast on the weak and the diseased and the innocent alike. We do the will of Christ as the Serpent did the will of God in Eden when he tempted Eve.'

'Come to our Temple,' said one of the others, 'and see the tree of life with the sacred Serpent wound around it. We have his fangs. We have his power. God made him, just as God made Judas Iscariot, or Cain, or the evil Emperors of Rome.'

'Ah,' I said, 'I see. Before you happened on the god in the cave, you were worshipers of the snake. You're Ophites, Sethians, Nassenians.'

'That was our first calling,' said the boy. 'But now we are of the Children of Darkness, committed to sacrifice and killing, dedicated to inflicting suffering.'

'Oh, Marcion and Valentinus,' Marius whispered. 'You don't know the names, do you? They're the poetic Gnostics who invented the morass of your philosophy a hundred years ago. Duality – that, in a Christian world, evil could be as powerful as good.'

'Yes, we know this.' Several spoke at once. 'We don't know those profane names. But we know the Serpent and what God wants of us.'

'Moses lifted the Serpent in the desert, up over his head,' said the boy. 'Even the Queen of Egypt knew the Serpent and wore him in her crown.'

'The story of the great Leviathan has been eradicated in Rome,' said the woman. 'They took it out of the sacred books. But we know it!'

'So you learned all this from Armenian Christians,' said Marius. 'Or was it Syrians.'

A man, short of stature, with gray eyes, had not spoken all this while, but he stepped forward now and addressed Marius with considerable authority.

'You hold ancient truths,' he said, 'and you

use them profanely. All know of you. The blond Children of Darkness in the Northern woods know of you, and that you stole some important secret out of Egypt before the Birth of Christ. Many have come here, glimpsed you and the woman, and gone away in fear.'

'Very wise,' said Marius.

'What did you find in Egypt?' asked the woman. 'Christian monks live now in those old rooms that once belonged to a race of blood drinkers. The monks don't know about us, but we know all about them and you. There was writing there, there were secrets, there was something that by Divine Will belongs now in our hands.'

'No, there was nothing,' said Marius.

The woman spoke up again, 'When the Hebrews left Egypt, when Moses parted the Red Sea, did the Hebrews leave something behind? Why did Moses raise the snake in the desert? Do you know how many we are? Nearly a hundred. We travel to the far North, to the South, and even to the East to lands you would not believe.'

I could see Marius was distraught.

'Very well,' I said, 'we understand what you want and why you have been led to believe that we can satisfy you. I ask you, please, to go out in the Garden and let us speak. Respect our house. Don't harm our slaves.'

'We wouldn't dream of it.'

'And we'll be back shortly.'

I snatched Marius's hand and pulled him down the stairs.

'Where are you going?' he whispered. 'Block all images from your mind! They must glimpse nothing.'

'They won't glimpse,' I said, 'and from where I will stand as I talk to you, they won't hear either.'

He seemed to catch my meaning. I led him into the sanctuary of the unchanged Mother and Father, closing the stone doors behind me.

I drew Marius behind the seated King and Queen.

'They can probably hear the hearts of the Pair,' I whispered in the softest manner audible. 'But maybe they won't hear us over that sound. Now, we have to kill them, destroy them completely.'

Marius was amazed.

'Look, you know we have to do this!' I said. 'You have to kill them and anybody like them who ever comes near us. Why are you so shocked? Get ready. The simplest way is cut them to pieces first, and then burn them.'

'Oh, Pandora,' he sighed.

'Marius, why do you cringe?'

'I don't cringe, Pandora,' he said. 'I see myself irrevocably changed by such an act. To kill when I thirst, to keep to myself and keep these here who must be kept by somebody, that I have done for so long. But to become an executioner? To become like the Emperors burning Christians! To commence a war against this race, this order, this cult, whatever it is, to take such a stand.'

'No choice, come on. There are many decorative swords in the room where we sleep. We should take the big curved swords. And the torch. We should go to them and tell them how sorry we are for what we must impart to them, then do it!'

He didn't answer.

'Marius, are you going to let them go so that others will come after us? The only security lies in destroying every blood drinker who ever discovers us and the King and Queen.'

He walked away from me and stood before the Mother. He looked into her eyes. I knew that he was silently talking to her. And I knew that she was not answering.

'There is one other possibility,' I said, 'and it's quite real.' I beckoned for him to come back, behind them, where I felt safest to plot.

'What is it?' he asked.

'Give the King and the Queen over to them. And you and I are free. They will care for the King and Queen with religious fervor! Maybe the King and Queen will even allow them to drink –'

'That's unspeakable!' he said.

'Exactly my feelings. We shall never know if we are safe. And they shall run rampant through the world like supernatural rodents. So do you have a third plan?'

'No, but I'm ready. We use the fire and the swords together. Can you tell the lies that will charm them as we approach, armed and carry-ing torches?'

'Oh, yes, of course,' I said.

We went into the chamber and took up the big curved swords that were keenly sharp and came from the desert world of the Arabs. We lighted another torch from that at the foot of the stairs and we went up together.

'Come to me, Children,' I said as I entered the room, loudly, 'come, for what I have to reveal requires the light of this torch, and you will soon know the sacred purpose of this sword. How devout you are.'

We stood before them.

'How young you are!' I said.

Suddenly, the panic swept them together. They made it so simple for us by clustering in this manner that we had the task done in moments, lighting their garments, hacking their limbs, ignoring their piteous cries.

Never had I used my full strength and speed, never my full will, as I did against them. It was exhilarating to slash them, to force the torch upon them, to slash them until they fell, until they lost all life. Also, I did not want them to suffer.

Because they were so young, so very young as blood drinkers, it took quite some time to burn the bones, to see that all was ashes.

But it was finally done, and we stood together – Marius and I – in the garden, our garments smeared with soot, staring down at blowing grass, making certain with our eyes that the ashes were blown in all directions.

Marius turned suddenly and walked fast away from me, and down the stairs and into the Mother's Sanctuary.

I rushed after him in panic. He stood holding the torch and the bloody sword – oh, how they had bled – and he looked into Akasha's eyes.

'Oh, loveless Mother!' he whispered. His face was soiled with blood and grime. He looked at the flaming torch and looked up at the Queen.

Akasha and Enkil showed no sign of any knowledge of the massacre above. They showed neither approval, nor gratitude, nor any form of consciousness. They showed no awareness of the torch in his hand, or his thoughts, whatever they might be.

It was a finish for Marius, a finish to the Marius I had known and loved at that time.

He chose not to leave Antioch. I was for getting away and taking them away, for wild adventures, and seeing the wonders of the world.

But he said no. He had but one obligation. And that was to lay in wait for others until he had killed every one of them.

For weeks he wouldn't speak or move, unless I shook him and then he pleaded with me to leave him alone. He rose from the grave only to sit with the sword and the torch waiting.

It became unbearable to me. Months passed. I said, 'You are going mad. We should take them away!'

Then one night, very angry and alone, I cried out foolishly, 'I would I were free of them and you!' And leaving the house, I did not return for three nights.

I slept in dark safe places I made for myself with ease. Every time I thought of him, I thought of his sitting motionless there, so very like them, and I was afraid.

If only he did know true despair; if only he had confronted what we now call 'the absurd.' If only he had faced the nothingness! Then this massacre would not have demoralized him.

Finally one morning just before sunrise, when I was safely hidden, a strange silence fell over Antioch. A rhythm I had heard there all my days was gone. I was trying to think, What could this mean? But there was time to find out.

I had made a fatal miscalculation. The villa was empty. He had arranged for the transport by day. I had no clue as to where he had gone! Everything belonging to him had been taken, and all that I possessed scrupulously left behind.

I had failed him when he most needed me. I walked in circles around the empty Shrine. I screamed and let the cry echo off the walls.

He never returned to Antioch. No letter ever came.

After six months or more, I gave up and left.

Of course you know the dedicated, religious Christian vampires never died out, not until Lestat came dressed in red velvet and fur to dazzle them and make a mockery of their beliefs. That was in the Age of Reason. That is when Marius received Lestat. Who knows what other vampire cults exist?

As for me, I had lost Marius again by then.

I had seen him for only a single precious night one hundred years earlier, and of course thousands of years after the collapse of what we call 'the ancient world.'

I saw him! It was in the fancy fragile times of Louis XIV, the Sun King. We were at a court ball in Dresden. Music played – the tentative blend of clavichord, lute, violin – making the artful dances which seemed no more than bows and circles.

Across a room, I suddenly saw Marius!

He had been looking at me for a great while, and gave me now the most tragic and loving smile. He wore a big full-bottomed curly wig, dyed to the very color of his true hair, and a flared velvet coat, and layers of lace, so favored by the French. His skin was golden. That meant fire. I knew suddenly he had suffered something terrible. A jubilant love filled his blue eyes, and without forsaking his casual posture – he was leaning his elbow on the edge of the clavichord – he blew a kiss to me with his fingers.

I truly could not trust my eyes. Was he really there? Was I, myself, sitting here, in boned and low-necked bodice, and these huge skirts, one pulled back in artful folds to reveal the other? My skin in this age seemed an artificial contrivance. My hair had been professionally gathered and lifted into an ornate shape.

I had paid no mind to the mortal hands which had so bound me. During this age I let myself be led through the world by a fierce Asian vampire, about whom I cared nothing. I had fallen into an ever existing trap for a woman: I had become the noncommittal and ostentatious ornament of a male personality who for all his tiresome verbal cruelty possessed sufficient force to carry us both through time.

The Asian was off slowly taking his carefully chosen victim in a bedroom above.

Marius came towards me and kissed me and took me in his arms. I shut my eyes. 'This is Marius!' I whispered. 'Truly Marius.'

'Pandora!' he said, drawing back to look at me. 'My Pandora!'

His skin had been burned. Faint scars. But it was almost healed.

He led me out on the dance floor! He was the perfect impersonation of a human being. He guided me in the steps of the dance. I could scarce breathe. Following his lead, shocked at each new artful turn by the rapture of his face, I could not measure centuries or even millennia. I wanted suddenly to know everything – where he had been, what had befallen him. Pride and shame in me held no sway. Could he see that I was no more than a ghost of the woman he'd known? 'You are the hope of my soul!' I whispered.

Quickly he took me away. We went in a carriage to his palace. He deluged me with kisses. I clung to him.

'You,' he said, 'my dream, a treasure so foolishly thrown away, you are here, you have persevered.'

'Because you see me, I am here,' I said bitterly. 'Because you lift the candle, I can almost see my strength in the looking glass.'

Suddenly I heard a sound, an ancient and terrible sound. It was the heartbeat of Akasha, the heartbeat of Enkil.

The carriage had come to a halt. Iron gates. Servants.

The palace was spacious, fancy, the ostentatious residence of a rich noble.

'They are in there, the Mother and the Father?' I asked.

'Oh, yes, unchanged. Utterly reliable in their eternal silence.' His voice seemed to defy the horror of it.

I couldn't bear it. I had to escape the sound of her heart. An image of the petrified King and

Queen rose before my eyes.

'No! Get me away from here. I can't go in. Marius, I cannot look on them!'

'Pandora, they are hidden below the palace. There is no need to look on them. They won't know. Pandora, they are the same.'

Ah! The same! My mind sped back, over perilous terrain, to my very first nights, alone and mortal, in Antioch, to the later victories and defeats of that time. Ah! Akasha was the same! I feared I would begin to scream and be unable to control it.

'Very well,' said Marius, 'we'll go where you want.

I gave the coachman the location of my hiding place.

I couldn't look at Marius. Valiantly, he kept the pretense of happy reunion. He talked of science and literature, Shakespeare, Dryden, the New World full of jungles and rivers. But behind his voice I heard the joy drained from him.

I buried my face against him. When the carriage stopped I leapt out and fled to the door of my little house. I looked back. He stood in the street.

He was sad and weary, and slowly he nodded and made a gesture of acceptance. 'May I wait it out?' he asked. 'Is there hope you'll change your mind? I'll wait here forever!'

'It's not my mind!' I said. 'I leave this city tonight. Forget me. Forget you ever saw me!'

'My love,' he said softly. 'My only love.'

I ran inside, shutting the door. I heard the carriage pull away. I went wild, as I had not since mortal life, beating the walls with my fists, trying to restrain my immense strength and trying not to let loose the howls and cries that wanted to break from me.

Finally I looked at the clock. Three hours left until dawn.

I sat down at the desk and wrote to him:

Marius,
At dawn we will be taken to Moscow. The very coffin in which I rest is to carry me many miles the first day. Marius, I am dazed. I can't seek shelter in your house, beneath the same roof as the ancient ones. Please, Marius, come to Moscow. Help me to free myself of this predicament. Later you can judge me and condemn me. I need you. Marius, I shall haunt the vicinity of the Czar's palace and the Great Cathedral until you come. Marius, I know I ask of you that *you* make a great journey, but

please come. I am a slave to this blood drinker's will.

I love you,
Pandora

Running back out in the street, I hurried in the direction of his house, trying to retrace the path which I had so stupidly ignored.

But what about the heartbeat? I would hear it, that ghastly sound! I had to run past it, run through it, long enough to give Marius this letter, perhaps to let him grasp me by the wrist and force me to some safe place, and drive away before dawn the Asian vampire who kept me.

Then the very carriage appeared, carrying in it my fellow blood drinker from the ball.

He stopped for me at once.

I took the driver aside. 'The man who brought me home,' I said. 'We went to his house, a huge palace.'

'Yes, Count Marius,' said the driver. 'I just took him back to his own home.'

'You must take this letter to him. Hurry! You must go to his house and put it in his hands! Tell him I had no money to give you, that he must pay you, I demand that you tell him. He will pay you. Tell him the letter is from Pandora. You must find him!'

'Who are you speaking of?' demanded my Asian companion.

I motioned to the driver to leave! 'Go!' Of course my consort was outraged. But the carriage was already on its way.

Two hundred years passed before I learned the very simple truth: Marius never received that letter!

He had gone back to his house, packed up his belongings and, the following night, left Dresden in sorrow, only finding the letter long after, as he related it to the Vampire Lestat, 'a fragile piece of writing,' as he called it, 'that had fallen to the bottom of a cluttered traveling case.'

When did I see him again?

In this modern world. When the ancient Queen rose from her throne and demonstrated the limits of her wisdom, her will and her power.

Two thousands years after, in our Twentieth Century still full of Roman columns and statues and pediments and peristyles, buzzing with computers and warmth-giving television, with Cicero and Ovid in every public library, our Queen, Akasha, was wakened by the image of Lestat on a television screen, in the most modern and secure of shrines, and sought to reign as a goddess, not only over us, but over humankind.

In the most dangerous hour, when she threatened to destroy us all if we did not follow her lead – and she had already slaughtered many – it was Marius with his reasoning, his optimism, his philosophy who talked to her, tried to calm her and divert her, who stalled her destructive intent until an ancient enemy came to fulfill an ancient curse, and struck her down with ancient simplicity.

David, what have you done to me in prodding me to write this narrative?

You have made me ashamed of the wasted years. You have made me acknowledge that no darkness has been ever deep enough to extinguish my personal knowledge of love, love from mortals who brought me into the world, love for goddesses of stone, love for Marius.

Above all, I cannot deny the resurgence of this love for Marius.

And all around me in this world I see evidence of love. Behind the image of the Blessed Virgin and her Infant Jesus, behind the image of the Crucified Christ, behind the remembered basalt image of Isis. I see love. I see it in the human struggle. I see its undeniable penetration in all that humans have accomplished in their poetry, their painting, their music, their love of one another and refusal to accept suffering as their lot.

Above all, however, I see it in the very fashioning of the world which outshines all art, and cannot by sheer randomness have accumulated such beauty.

Love. But whence comes this love? Why it is so secretive about its source, this love that makes rain and trees and has scattered the stars over us as the gods and goddesses once claimed to do?

So Lestat, the brat Prince, woke the Queen; and we survived her destruction. So Lestat, the brat Prince, had gone to Heaven and Hell and brought back disbelief, horror and the Veil of Veronica! Veronica, an invented Christian name which means *vera ikon,* or true icon. He found himself plunged into Palestine during the very years that I lived, and there saw something that has shattered the faculties in humans which we cherish so much: faith, reason.

I have to go to Lestat, look into his eyes. I have to see what he saw!

Let the young sing songs of death. They are stupid.

The finest thing under the sun and the moon is the human soul. I marvel at the small miracles of kindness that pass between humans, I marvel at the growth of conscience, at the persistence of reason in the face of all superstition or despair. I marvel at human endurance.

I have one more story to tell you. I don't know why I want to record it here. But I do. Perhaps it's because I feel you – a vampire who sees spirits – will understand this, and understand perhaps why I remained so unmoved by it.

Once in the Sixth Century – that is, five hundred years after the birth of Christ and three hundred years since I had left Marius – I went wandering in barbarian Italy. The Ostrogoths had long ago overrun the peninsula.

Then other tribes swept down on them, looting, burning, carrying off stones from old Temples.

It was like walking on burning coals for me to go there.

But Rome did struggle with some conception of itself, its principles, trying to blend the pagan with the Christian, and find some respite from the barbarian raids.

The Roman Senate still existed. Of all institutions it had survived.

And a scholar, sprung from the same stock as myself, Boethius, a very learned man who studied the ancients and the saints, had recently been put to death, but not before he had given us a great book. You can find it in any library today. It is, of course, *The Consolation of Philosophy*.

397

I had to see the ruined Forum for myself, the burnt and barren hills of Rome, the pigs and goats roaming where once Cicero had spoken to the crowds. I had to see the forsaken poor living desperately along the banks of the Tiber.

I had to see the fallen classical world. I had to see the Christian churches and shrines.

I had to see one scholar in particular. Like Boethius he had come from old Roman stock, and like Boethius he had read the classics and the saints. He was a man who wrote letters that went all over the world, even as far as to the scholar Bede in England.

And he had built a monastery there, some great flare of creativity and optimism, in spite of ruin and war.

This man was of course the scholar Cassiodorus, and his monastery lay at the very tip of the boot of Italy, in the paradisal land of green Calabria.

I came upon it in early evening, as I planned, when it looked like a great and splendid lighted little city.

Its monks were copying away ferociously in the Scriptorium.

And there in his cell, wide open to the night, sat Cassiodorus himself, at his writing, a man past ninety years of age.

He had survived the barbarian politics that doomed his friend Boethius, having served the Aryan Ostrogoth Emperor Theodoric, having lived to retire from Civil Service – he had survived to build this monastery, his dream, and to write to monks all over the world, to share what he knew with them of the ancients, to conserve the wisdom of the Greeks and the Romans.

Was he truly the last man of the ancient world, as some have said? The last man who could read both Latin and Greek? The last man who could treasure both Aristotle and the dogma of the Roman Pope? Plato and Saint Paul?

I didn't know then that he would be so well remembered. And I didn't know how soon he'd be forgotten!

Vivarium, on its mountains slopes, was an architectural triumph. It had its sparkling ponds to catch and hold fish – the characteristic which gave it its name. It had its Christian church with the inevitable cross, its dormitories, its rooms for the weary guest traveler. Its library was rich in the classics of my time, as well as gospels which have now been lost. The monastery was rich in all the fruits of the field, all crops needed for food, trees laden with fruit, fields of wheat.

The monks cared for all of this. and they dedicated themselves to copying books day and night in their long Scriptorium.

There were beehives there, on this gentle moonlighted coast, hundreds of beehives from which the monks harvested honey to eat, and wax for sacred candles, and royal jelly for an ointment. The beehives covered a hill as big as the orchard or the farmland of Vivarium.

I spied on Cassiodorus. I walked among the beehives, and marveled as I always do at the inexplicable organization of bees, for the mysteries of the bees and their dance and their hunting for pollen and their breeding was all known to my eye long before it was understood by the human world.

As I left the hives, as I moved away towards the distant beacon of Cassiodorus's lamp, I looked back. I beheld something.

Something collected itself from the hives, something immense and invisible and forceful that I could both feel and hear. I was not gripped by fear, merely sparked by a temporary hope that some New Thing had come into the world. For I am not a seer of ghosts and never was.

This force rose out of the very bees themselves, out of their intricate knowledge and their countless sublime patterns, as though they had somehow accidentally evolved it, or empowered it with consciousness through the means of their endless creativity, meticulousness and endurance.

It was like an old Roman woodland spirit of the forest.

I saw this force fly loosely over the fields. I saw it enter the body of a straw man who stood in the fields, a scarecrow which the monks had made with a fine round wooden head, painted eyes, crude nose and smiling mouth – a creature whole and entire who could be moved from time to time, intact in his monk's hood and robe.

I saw this scarecrow, this man of straw and wood hurry whirling and dancing through the fields and the vineyards until he had reached Cassiodorus's cell.

I followed!

Then I heard a silent wail rise from the being. I heard it and I saw the scarecrow in a bending, bowing dance of sorrow, its bundled straw hands over ears it didn't have. It writhed with grief.

Cassiodorus was dead. He had died quietly within his lamp-lighted cell, his door open, at his writing table. He lay, gray-haired, ancient, quiet against his manuscript. He had lived over ninety years. And he was dead.

This creature, this scarecrow, was wild with suffering and grief, rocking and moaning, though it was a sound no human could have heard.

I who have never seen spirits stared at it in wonder. Then it perceived that I was there. It turned. He – for so it seemed in this ragged attire and body of straw – reached out to me. He flung out his straw arms. The straw fell from his sleeves. His wooden head wobbled on the pole that was his spine. He – It – implored me: he begged me for the answer to the greatest questions humans and immortal have ever posed. He looked to me for answers!

Then glancing back again at the dead Cassiodorus, he ran to me, across the sloping grass, and the need came out of him, poured from him, his arms out as it beheld me. Could I not explain? Could I not contain in some Divine Design the mystery of the loss of Cassiodorus! Cassiodorus who had with his Vivarium rivaled the hive of bees in elegance and glory! It was Vivarium which had drawn this consciousness together from the hives! Could I not ease this creature's pain!

'There are horrors in this world,' I whispered. 'It is made up of mystery and dependent upon mystery. If you would have peace, go back to the hives; lose your human shape, and descend again, fragmented into the mindless life of the contented bees from which you rose.'

He was fixed, and he listened to me.

'If you would have fleshly life, human life, hard life which can move through time and space, then fight for it. If you would have human philosophy then struggle and make yourself wise, so that nothing can hurt you ever. Wisdom is strength. Collect yourself, whatever you are, into something with a purpose.

'But know this. All is speculation under the sky. All myth, all religion, all philosophy, all history – is lies.'

The thing, whether it be male or female, drew up its bundled straw hands, as if to cover its mouth. I turned my back on it.

I walked away silently through the vineyards. In a little while the monks would discover that their Father Superior, their genius, their saint, had died at his work.

I looked back in amazement to discover that the figure of straw remained, organized, assuming the posture of an upright being, watching me.

'I will not believe in you!' I shouted back to this man of straw. 'I will not search with you for any answer! But know this: if you would become an organized being as you see in me, love all mankind and womankind and all their children. Do not take your strength from blood! Do not feed on suffering. Do not rise like a god above crowds chanting in adoration. Do not lie!'

It listened. It heard. It remained still.

I ran. I ran and ran up the rocky slopes and through the forests of Calabria until I was far far away from it. Under the moon, I saw the sprawling majesty of Vivarium with its cloisters and sloped roofs as it surrounded the shores of its shimmering inlet from the sea.

I never saw the straw creature again. I don't know what it was. I don't want you to ask me any question about it.

You tell me spirits and ghosts walk. We know such beings exist. But that was the last I saw of that being.

And when next I drifted through Italy, Vivarium had been long destroyed. The earthquakes had shaken loose the last of its walls. Had it been sacked first by the next wave of ignorant tall men of Northern Europe, the Vandals? Was it an earthquake that brought about its ruin?

No one knows. What survives of it are the letters that Cassiodorus sent to others.

Soon the classics were declared profane. Pope Gregory wrote tales of magic and miracles, because it was the only way to convert thousands of superstitious uncatechized Northern tribes to Christianity in great en masse baptisms.

He conquered the warriors Rome could never conquer.

The history of Italy for one hundred years falls into absolute darkness after Cassiodorus. How do the books put it? For a century, nothing is heard from Italy.

Ah, what a silence!

Now David, as you come to these final pages, I must confess, I have left you. The smiles with which I gave you these notebooks were deceptive. Feminine wiles, Marius would call them. My promise to meet with you tomorrow night here in Paris was a lie. I will have left Paris by the time you come to these lines. I go to New Orleans.

It's your doing, David. You have transformed me. You have given me a desperate faith that in narrative there is a shadow of meaning. I now know a new strident energy. You have trained me through your demand upon my language and my memory to live again, to believe again that some good exists in this world.

I want to find Marius. Thoughts of other immortals fill the air. Cries, pleas, strange messages . . .

One who was believed gone from us is now apparently known to have survived.

I have strong reason to believe that Marius has gone to New Orleans, and I must be reunited with him. I must seek out Lestat, to see this fallen brat Prince lying on the chapel floor unable to speak or move.

Come join me, David. Don't fear Marius! I know he will come to help Lestat. I do the same.

Come back to New Orleans.

Even if Marius is not there, I want to see Lestat. I want to see the others again. What have you done, David? I now contain – with this new curiosity, with this flaming capacity to care once more, with reborn capacity to sing – I now contain the awful capacity to want and to love.

For that, if for nothing else, and there is indeed much more, I shall always thank you. No matter what suffering is to come, you have quickened me. And nothing you do or say will ever cause the death of my love for you.

THE END

Final: July 5, 1997